The Greenfield Boys

Joanna,

To a special friend and her family

Love,
Ruthanne Lyons

The Greenfield Boys

Ruthanne Lyons

authorHOUSE®

AuthorHouse™
1663 Liberty Drive
Bloomington, IN 47403
www.authorhouse.com
Phone: 1-800-839-8640

© 2011 by Ruthanne Lyons. All rights reserved.

No part of this book may be reproduced, stored in a retrieval system, or transmitted by any means without the written permission of the author.

First published by AuthorHouse   08/26/2011

ISBN: 978-1-4634-2563-0 (sc)
ISBN: 978-1-4634-2562-3 (ebk)

Library of Congress Control Number: 2011911125

Printed in the United States of America

Any people depicted in stock imagery provided by Thinkstock are models, and such images are being used for illustrative purposes only.
Certain stock imagery © Thinkstock.

This book is printed on acid-free paper.

Because of the dynamic nature of the Internet, any web addresses or links contained in this book may have changed since publication and may no longer be valid. The views expressed in this work are solely those of the author and do not necessarily reflect the views of the publisher, and the publisher hereby disclaims any responsibility for them.

Contents

Acknowledgements		vii
Chapter 1	"Billy"...	1
Chapter 2	I'm Billy	2
Chapter 3	My Best Friend	8
Chapter 4	The Hospital	22
Chapter 5	Phil's Story	35
Chapter 6	New home	50
Chapter 7	Growing up	55
Chapter 8	Senior Year	65
Chapter 9	Taking Care of Business	72
Chapter 10	Basic Training	85
Chapter 11	Pre-flight Training San Antonia, Texas	92
Chapter 12	Phase Two—Basic Training	97
Chapter 13	Graduation	99
Chapter 14	Dale Mabry Field, Florida	104
Chapter 15	Boxted Airfield, England	113
Chapter 16	Mission #1	120
Chapter 17	Mission 2	131
Chapter 18	The Game	139
Chapter 19	The Morale	142
Chapter 20	Special Mission	153
Chapter 21	Washington	174
Chapter 22	Going Home	190
Chapter 23	Foster Air Field	235
Chapter 24	Changes All Around Us	263

Chapter 25	The War is over!	268
Chapter 26	Back to Work	283
Epilogue		301
The Greenfield Boys		303

Acknowledgements

My deepest thanks go to my family and friends for taking the time to read my work and make this all possible.

To my husband Charles who became my IR man and kept on me until it was finished. To my son Thomas Lyons who was the first to read my book and excite me with his encouragement. To my daughter Theresa Bunn, who is always busy, but can always find the time for me, thank you. And to my daughter Pamela DiTomaso, an important part of me, thank you. Thank you Thomas Lyons Jr. for the great sketches you did for me. Thank you Carolyne Lyons for your time checking little things for me.

A special thanks to Donna Salamon, for her time and patience, Katrina Turner Rooney for her special prayers and friendship, and Florence Fios a dear friend. To my special Mentor, Janice, Antonia Phillips Rabb, for her words of wisdom and telling me I had a unique style of my own, thank you. Writing this book has been an exciting ride!

Chapter 1

"Billy" . . .

As I heard my name being called across the room, I wanted to yell back, 'I'm not here!' I ran for cover to another room. I could hear the heavy pounding footsteps right behind me. Not this time I whispered to myself. I crouched down in the dark corner of the room as still as I could be, and he went past me. Now was my chance. 'Run as fast as you can,' I said to myself. Back through the room and out the front door, to the pricker bushes beside the house. I had been here before. It was dusk and he couldn't see me.

He must have heard me go out the door.

He came out and looked around and yelled my name out loud.

The strangest thing happened just then. My cat Cleo came running over to me in the bushes. He must have followed behind me. I pulled him in and we sat very still huddled in the bushes.

As I looked up, there he was!

I took out the pistol from my pocket and aimed it at him. I shot my Dad. Not once but three times. The bullets came out of the gun and he went down on the stairs. The blood went everywhere.

I heard no sound from him. I just sat there still huddled up under the bushes.

Chapter 2

I'm Billy

We lived in a small town in the mid-west. There were not a lot of people where we lived. There was just me and my Dad and a few neighbors.

When my Mom died I was about seven years old. I had to go with my Dad to the funeral parlor. I was so scared. He took me in a room with someone else who did all the talking. I remember we had to look at boxes you put dead people in. I had no idea what they were talking about, but my Dad had to pick one out to put my Mom in. Dad lifted me up in his arms so I could see in the box. I felt real bad. I could see there was a lock on the outside of the big box. When Dad leaned me over to look inside I started to cry. I was terrified I would fall inside, and like my jack-in-the-box toy, I wouldn't be able to get out. I wanted to get down and run outside. I was so scared. The room smelled really awful. Not like flowers or anything nice. The heavy air stayed in my nose and I didn't want to take a deep breath.

"Please Dad, let's go home." Finally we left that room. I never wanted to go back there again.

Dad was real quiet all the way home.

Things changed for me that day. I had to do a lot of things like dishes and cleaning the house and I didn't know how to do any of that. I really missed my Mom. I don't know why she had to die. I didn't know how much Dad expected me to do. I was alone most of the time. Dad went off to work every day so we could keep the farm.

I didn't go to school right now because it was summer. I played with Cleo most of the time.

Sometimes I went with Dad to Fontanelle when he picked up some parts for the trucks he was working on. I'd walk over by the train station and wait for a train to come in. One afternoon a train came in with a lot of children on it. They got off and stood around so I went over. There was one boy standing alone who looked about my age. I asked him where he was going.

He said, "I'm going to Greenfield to be adopted."

"Hey I live in Greenfield, what's your name?"

"My name is Joey, what's yours?"

"I'm Billy. Maybe we can be friends?"

"The driver is putting us on the wagon so I have to go." Joey climbed in and sat down with the others.

"I hope I see you again Billy," I heard as the wagon rolled down the street to Greenfield.

I ran back to the store to tell Dad.

He said, "That happens a couple times a year around here." I missed Mom all the time so I put a lot of pictures all around the house. I drew most of them from memory. I was afraid I'd forget what she looked like if I waited too long. I had some old crayons that Mom and I used when we colored after supper at night. I found some paper in the waste basket that only had writing on one side. I used the ones that were not all wrinkled up in a ball. Every night Dad would go through the mail and get real angry. He would put everything in the trash and go have a drink. My

Dad got angry a lot. He rattled the dishes around in the kitchen and threw things across the room. The house got real messy. Sometimes he would yell at me and hit me for no reason. At first it was just a whack on the head or a whack on the butt. I could tell when he was real angry so I'd find a place to hide for a while. At night when I was asleep he would come into my room and put his arm around me. I could hear him crying. He slept the night with me. I think he was sorry for hitting me. This went on for months after Mom died.

A few weeks before school started Doctor Deering stopped by to visit. I was alone playing outside so we sat on the porch in the shade. The doctor stopped by every week when I was little, he liked my Mom. He asked me how I was doing and if I was getting ready for school. I hadn't talked to anyone about it; Dad was always working and too busy. I told him how much I missed Mom. We sat quiet for a few minutes.

He sat for a while smoking his brown pipe and looking over the yard. The chickens were out and the cows were leaning over the fence looking back at us. He puffed away and the aroma spread around on the porch.

Then he asked, "How about I tell you a story about the old farm and your grandparents?" His arms were crossed over his chest as he looked across the fields, as if he was looking at things a long time ago.

"Yes I would like that doctor, you always tell good stories. Did you know my grandparents a long time?"

"I did Billy, but I want to tell you about how things got started here with your grandparents, Jessie and James Stevens. They were my friends a long time ago. This was a family owned farm before your Mom and Dad lived here. They delivered milk and cheese, eggs and lots of homemade pastries. They serviced many homes in this area." He paused and took another puff on the pipe. He shifted in the chair and began again.

"There were two boys here then Billy," looking out of the corner of his eye towards me. "John was the oldest and William was younger by four years. I brought them both into this world right here on the farm." He puffed on his pipe.

"They helped their father when they got old enough just like you will with your Dad someday." He reached over and patted my leg.

"The family worked many long hours milking cows, delivering all their products and taking care of the farm. Your Dad and his brother went to school when they could but the farm came first in their life.

"Your Grandmother Jessie worked long hours baking breads and pastries. What a great cook she was Billy. The extra money came in handy for taking care of her boys. She was a good mother and helped them with their school work and kept them out of trouble. Sometimes when I'd stop by they were a little rambunctious so she would send them out to ride their horses and we'd talk for a while." He paused nodding his head. "She was a great woman and I knew her for a long time." Again silence.

"When her boys got older Billy, they got their own trucks to deliver the milk, and night deliveries became common so they came home late. They liked to race around town after they were done with their work. Their father always found out and I hear he had some strong measures of his own for keeping them in line. Your Dad was smart. He liked working on engines and kept the trucks running. He got some books and trained himself."

Doctor Deering took his pipe out of his mouth and tapped it on the side of the porch. He stared off in the fields again.

I sure liked the smell of the pipe.

"What happened to Dad's brother William," I asked curiously.

"Well Billy, as the boys got older your grandfather put more responsibility on the boys. The business kept growing but the farm started to suffer from the lack of time put into it. As the years passed the boys were in their twenties now, and it was time for them to have a life of their own. "William wanted to move to the city and be with his friends. His father was very upset and tried to show him how they were all making money and working together. But William had other ideas. I heard he packed up and left one night and no one has ever heard from him again. A part of me died that day, but that's another story." He paused and filled up his pipe and lit it again. "Yup off he went." He shifted his weight again.

"Your Dad had the farm on his shoulders now and his parents were slowing down. John told some of the towns' people he needed some help. Men showed up after work to help him but it wasn't enough. Some of the deliveries were taken over by a company in town. A local creamery took over the milking business and care of the animals on the farm. So the farm got paid and farmers planted the fields and sold crops giving John some money, while he helped out the farmers by repairing their equipment.

"Now your grandfather kept working but your Dad got a chance to work in town for a machine shop that would pay him good money. When he left for work in town that was the reason the farm went down, according to your grandfather.

"Your grandmother was sad all the time because her son William never came back home. I stopped by to see her from time to time. Her health was failing and she had very hard times breathing. Her smoking didn't help." He took his pipe out of his mouth and put it on the side of the porch. The aroma was tickling my senses.

"I don't know if it was depression or maybe a broken heart or a lung problem, but about six months went by and she passed away in her sleep."

"John tried desperately to keep things running but now his father had become despondent and depressed over the loss of your grandmother. Eventually John and his Dad reduced part of his farm down to a few chickens and cows and a small garden his father could manage. Everything else was rented out and they had enough to live on. Your grandfather settled into his rocking chair lifestyle and let the world pass him by. I knew him well and he was a hard working man Billy. We all missed Jessie."

He picked up his pipe again. Looking across the fields he was quiet for a few minutes. I just sat there and let the smoke come my way. Someday I think I'm going to smoke a pipe I thought.

"The sad part of this story is what has happened to your Dad. He never heard from his brother so he couldn't tell him his mother died. He had no help with his father and I could see he had become a lonely cold and angry man. But then he met your mother. And that's another story for another day. I've got to get back to town. Are you going to be okay son?"

"That was a very sad story. Can you tell me about my Mom sometime?"

"You've got it son. Lots of people can talk about your mother. She was loved by everyone in town." He tapped his pipe one last time and slipped it into his breast pocket. "Be a good boy and say hi to your Dad for me."

My Dad worked on farms and in a shop in town. He could fix anything and he was known to be a great mechanic. Sometimes he would be gone for long periods of time on a job. I learned to take care of myself and clean up pretty good for my age.

Chapter 3

My Best Friend

I did go off to school. All I really remember is that I had to get a few things for school that I didn't have. I wore mostly baggy pants with and old flannel plaid shirt. I kept my pants up with a brown leather belt. My two favorite things were my old worn mud boots and my old straw hat that covered my neck and forehead from the sun. I was outside all the time. These were my favorite things to wear. Dad said it cost a lot of money to get me ready for school.

I made friends at school but Dad said not to bring any of my friends home. So I played at school and that was all I saw of the other kids my age.

One day in school we were introduced to a boy who just moved to town. His name was Joey Calhoun and he was adopted by the Price family. They lived about a mile down the road from my place. It was Joey from the train in Fontanelle.

At recess he told us how he came from New York a few months ago on the Orphan Train. Joey had been put in an orphanage when his father died. He was put on a train with a lot of other children. They would be going to a better place to live and be taken care of, and adopted.

My teacher told us about the Orphan Train and what it was all about. Joey's parents gave her a paper to read about the Orphan Train and she explained the information to us as she went along.

This was like story time for us. Most of us knew nothing of this train at all. She began with the railroads.

"The railroads to Iowa began in the 1850s. The orphan trains made trips with 10 to 50 children and agents aboard twice a week. They were given clean clothes to wear for their arrival to their destination. They slept most of the way out so they arrived in good condition. When they arrived at the depots, they were taken to a place to be cleaned up before they met the people for a viewing. If they were chosen by a family the papers were signed, and they would go home with a new family. Some were put on a wagon and taken to a nearby station where they would be viewed. Joey was taken to the Opera House in Greenfield and put on a stage for people to view him.

General ads were placed in the newspapers and posted in stores and businesses. People interested were asked to write. The idea was to find farms where they could help with the farm work.

The terms were set up by a committee.

Boys under 12 were expected to remain until they were 18 and must be treated by the applicants as one of their own children in matters of schooling, clothing, and training.

Boys between 12 and 15 were expected to work for their board and clothes until they were 18, and must be sent to school part of the year. After 18 they would receive wages.

Boys 15 years old were expected to work until 18 for their board and clothes. After that time they were expected to make their own arrangements if they chose to.

"The committee asked to hear from the child twice a year. If removal was necessary the agent would step in. One of the 8 agents who brought groups to Iowa in 1910 recorded 119 trips west. Most other agents recorded about the same amount of children."

"The orphan train made stops in Ohio, Indiana, Illinois, Iowa, South Dakota, Arkansas, and ended in Missouri. The process was called "the placing out system" providing homes to orphans. There were 5 New York Hospitals and Orphanages that sent babies, small children, and young adults to Iowa and other farming states for adoption. Approximately 300,000 orphans were processed across America." The teacher stopped and we all looked at Joey. The Prices said they signed papers on Joey and he was nine years old.

The first couple of days when Joey came to school he kept to himself. I tried to talk to him but he didn't say much. Joey and I became friends. Joey liked to play ball at recess, throw rocks, and tell stories about his life in New York. He had gone to school there and he had his own bike. He didn't bring anything with him from New York. He missed his friends so we decided to become best friends. Joey had a bike the next time I saw him. The Prices took good care of him. We went back and forth to school together. We talked about a lot of things. Sometimes I would go to his farm after school and we would ride horses for a while. He was in a real good place. Joey had his own room and his own horse. He could drive the tractors around the farm and he thought that was great. The Prices helped him with his homework and bought him clothes and he had plenty to eat. Sometimes I wished I was him.

His mother Judy would make us homemade cookies with some cold milk after school, while she told us some stories. She talked about everything and made it fun. One day she asked me if I wanted to know how she came to adopt Joey. She sat at the table with us and started her story.

"Tom was a handsome football star and lived with his parents on the farm. I lived with my parents who owned an upholstery business in town. We graduated together and took night classes for two years. We fell in love and got married. For our wedding we were given a small farm about 150 acres, from Tom's parents and both families work together to help us get started. My parents helped me to start up my own upholstery and curtain business in town. I was a local girl so I was accepted and did alright. My parents came from Italy to New York City where they worked in the garment district with their make-shift sewing machine, doing odd jobs for the clothing stores. They put in long hours and saved every penny for later. They were only too happy to give us the money toward our farm and help us get started." Judy stopped for a while and went to the stove and made herself a cup of coffee.

"Tom and I had plenty to do and our lives went along just fine for a while. We wanted children but I found out I could not have any of my own. Ten years passed and I was hoping we could adopt a child somehow. One day on my way home from work I spotted a flyer in the window of the town Opera House. I grabbed it and took it home to Tom. We filled out the form and I dropped it in the post office the next day. Then we waited to hear from them. I was so excited I hardly slept at night. We were notified by mail when the train would be in our area. I was outside the Opera House on Thursday night when the wooden wagon came up the road. The children were all bundled up and looked so frightened that I could have taken all of them home with me that night. As they got out of the wagon I counted about fifteen. It looked like nine boys from six months to fifteen years old, and about six or seven little girls from a year to eight years old. I couldn't count them all as they hurried them up the stairs to the hall for viewing. I ran inside and got my seat that Tom had saved for me right up front. The girls came out first. Their hair was all braided and they had pretty dresses on as they walked across the stage. The boys came out next. As I sat on the edge of my seat, I was filled with excitement. Their hair was combed and their shoes were polished. They fidgeted across the stage not knowing what was expected of them. Tom and I looked"...

"Judy, do you mind if I jump into your story for a minute," as Tom kissed her on the forehead and continued. "We knew the minute we saw you Joey that you were ours. We looked at each other, didn't say a word, just held hands and waited for the moment. You looked strong for your age, we figured you to be about nine or so. We could tell you had been through some rough times by the way you walked across the stage. But you had just had a long ride from New York City on a train full of children. You had a nice smile and curly brown hair. Judy had tears rolling down her face and she was shaking, I have to admit I was shaking a little too. They said you were in good health and your papers were in order, and asked if anyone was interested. We held our papers high and they brought you to us. When they asked you if you had any questions for us you said, "Will I be able to ride a horse?" We all smiled at that one. We signed papers and adopted you, with only one change which was your last name. They said you would tell us about that later. You asked us to call you Joey Calhoun and that was fine with us."

Tom looked down and Judy was quiet now. He leaned over. "Did I miss anything honey?"

She smiled and hugged her new son. "No I think you completed my story and my dreams with this little miracle." She moved over and kissed his head not to embarrass him.

I knew how lucky Joey was to have great parents like the Prices and to live on one of the biggest farms in Greenfield. His room was filled with toys and games and he had a great study area. Yes I did envy him because he had a family who loved him and wanted to spend time with him. It made me miss my Mom even more. The good thing was Joey was my new best friend.

I tried to talk to my Dad about my new best friend but he did not want to listen. He said he would not listen to anything about any orphan kid in town. As he left the room he said, "Don't bring him here." So I stayed at Joey's farm sometimes when I knew my Dad would be home late. I always tried to get home before him.

Joey knew I had problems at home. He saw how badly I was bruised and black and blue in the mornings before school. Sometimes I talked about it, sometimes I didn't. I made him promise not to tell anyone. He wanted to tell his new parents what was happening to me but I said no. I had no place to go and he was my Dad. On days I couldn't go to school, Joey would find a way to get to my place and find me. He never got caught by my Dad but he saw a lot and heard a lot of the fights my Dad had with me. My Dad was drinking heavy and things at the farm were not going well. It was a bad year for crops and the help was not doing their work. I stayed out of his way as much as I could.

Joey didn't tell anyone. He promised. I just claimed I was clumsy when I was asked by my teacher where I got all my bruises. Joey was my best friend and I was glad he came to Greenfield on the Orphan Train.

When the kids at school had birthday parties I couldn't go. Dad wanted me home. I got a little upset because they were my friends and I wanted to be happy like they were. My Dad would say, "There will be time for that later." So I stopped asking.

One day Joey and the kids were going down to the lake swimming. This was after school and I knew my Dad would be working late every night this week. So I decided to go along.

When I got home my Dad was waiting and was he angry. He slapped me around until I looked like a dish rag. I had a bloody nose, my eyes were all puffy and I had red marks all over my skin. I was a mess. The more I cried the more he hit me. He was yelling at the top of his lungs. "You little brat, where's my belt, you never listen to me. I'm going to beat you silly." Finally he left me on the floor sobbing and went outside on the porch. I got up and ran to get a towel for my face and climbed under my bed for a long time. When I came out from under the bed it was dark outside. I looked in the mirror in the bathroom and I couldn't believe what I saw. My jaw had become swollen and I had a cut down the side of my face. The blood had dried but the whole side was swollen and red. My arms were bruised and black and blue. I had a puffy black eye. I learned my lesson and didn't try anything like that again.

Joey told me he didn't have it so great in New York either. Another day after school he told his parents and me about his life in New York. I sat at the table and listened. Joey sat down next to me.

"I was born in New York City a few years before the depression. My real name is Joey Somerset Wilding. I have two older sisters Mary and Anna and we lived in a big house on the west side. I went to school there and I was happy.

"One day everything went wrong. I came down stairs as I did every morning, to find my father sitting in his favorite chair. This was strange because he would always be gone to work before I had breakfast. I went over to him thinking he wasn't working today. I bent down and looked at him and I could tell there was something wrong. He wasn't breathing and he was slumped to the side of the chair. I leaned over to shake his arm and his whole body fell to the floor in a thump. I remember I let out a yell you could hear a block away and my mother came running in. She told me to go outside and get some help. Down the stairs I went yelling for help and hoping someone was around to hear me.

"I found out later that my father had taken some pills and killed himself. He had lost all the money in the stock market and now we were going to lose the house. Mother tried to explain it to me but I loved my father and I couldn't understand.

"My mother, Martha Calhoun Wilding did lose the house and whatever money and possessions we had left of any value. Times were tough and jobs were hard to find. My sisters were old enough to get jobs like cleaning buildings. My mother, who came from a wealthy family and had a good life, was reduced to scrubbing floors and cleaning houses. She needed the money to keep us all together in a small third floor apartment. I saw my first rat, and other bugs around in the apartment. It was poorly lit, dirty and cold. I was left there during the day while the rest of them worked. I had no clothes to go to school in and my mother was too proud to let me go in the rags I now had to wear. I got sick in the unheated shabby apartment and we had no money to see a doctor. She would bring home some food from the houses she worked in sometimes. We were all together and that's what mattered to her. One day while I was alone and sick, someone broke in the apartment and beat me up and left me. They took everything that was left of ours. When mother found me on the floor that night she was heartbroken. She decided to bring me to the orphanage that everyone had been telling her about. People could take their children to the orphanage and they would be sent to farms out west to work and be taken care of. The next morning she cleaned me up and walked me to the orphanage. I was crying and pulling away but she told me it was the best thing she could do for me right now. She told me she loved me very much, and asked me if I would use her maiden name so she could find me again someday when things got better. She kissed me goodbye and put me on the doorsteps and rang the bell. With tears in her eyes she left me there.

"I was on my own with no money or family, sick and confused and told to use a new name. Life had changed so fast for me and I was nine years old.

"Judy was crying and Tom had stood up and walked around the kitchen during my story telling. I looked at Billy and he just nodded."

"What was it like in the orphanage Joey?"

"From my point of view Billy, it wasn't too bad. I had a bed to sleep in, food every day and I made some new friends. The deal in the house was if you were good you would get a train ride out west. I was young so I would be adopted. My problem was that I was sick and had some bites and sores on my body that needed to be taken care of before I went anywhere.

"About three weeks later I was given a bath, dressed in new clothes and shoes, given a new blanket and put on the train. There were about fifty children starting out. We rode for days stopping here and there. One day it was my turn to get out.

They put us in a wooden wagon with our blanket and sent us to Greenfield. That's where I first saw you and you saw me. End of story. I'm hungry."

We all smiled. This was a somber moment for us all. I went home feeling happy that Joey was in a good place now. He had it tough.

Months went along and things stayed about the same. Dad never talked to me, we just managed to live around each other.

One summer, Dad took me hunting with him and tried to show me how to shoot a rifle. I had a small body frame for a kid my age. The first time I fired a shot with a rifle I flew backwards almost three feet! I hurt my shoulder and bit my lip so bad it was bleeding. He took one look at me and shook his head. "You're gonna learn how to shoot a gun you little pansy." He decided to get the small pistol he had in the barn that he used on the rats. With some practice and a lot of yelling I managed to hit something. Dad would place rocks on the wall and count to three. Always the count of three and I had better get them all. I learned how to clean the gun, load it properly, and aim my shot. My Dad was a good shot. Mom would have never let me do this. Then he took me out in the fields. We had a lot of field rats and raccoons and woodchucks out there for shooting practice. I was a little scared to actually shoot something. I couldn't feel good about killing something that never did anything to me. He told me to keep still and they would come out. I heard his rifle going off behind me, that one two three shot. I walked away a little and just took a few shots in the air. I thought he had shot enough for the day when he returned. I could hear my own heart pounding. I was hoping he would want to go home now.

"How did you do son," he asked.

I looked up and I could tell whatever I said, he would know I was lying. "Great," that's all I said. On the way back to the barn he let me know he thought he had wasted his time with me today.

He put his pistol back in the barn.

Dad started drinking a lot at night after work. At first I thought it was good. He would stay in the kitchen and read the papers a lot. I missed my Mom. When I needed help with my homework, sometimes Dad could help but most of the time he would just yell at me to "do it yourself!" Sometimes I'd ask him again and he would get real angry and hit me. I always seemed to have a bruise or a black eye.

In school the teacher would say, "What happened this time?" I was thought to be clumsy.

I was getting older and hated being knocked around all the time like I was. Why did my Dad treat me like this? I cleaned up the house, cleaned up after my cat and did the yard chores he wanted me to do after school. I did the wash sometimes and I could make a really good sandwich. Watching Dad, I learned to change the oil on some of the cars he was working on. I tried to learn some of the tools he used. I was still young. None of my friends had to do anything. Dad never talked of giving me any money because everything I did was expected. Some of my friends got paid for their chores.

I was growing two or three inches at a time now. When it came time for school Dad took me to town to get some clothes and shoes. I would hear how much it cost him all the way home. What could I do? It made him angry so I would stay out of his way for a few hours.

One morning the following week he passed by the table and said, "Clean this place up quick you're going with me today."

I mouthed back, "I can't go I've got school today." Another slam to the head and I knew it was better to do what he said. No school today. School was my salvation, my place to be for the day. I made up some sandwiches and got in the truck. I didn't ask where we were going because my head still hurt from the last whack. It turned out; Dad had some machines that needed to be fixed today. I was going to be the runner for the day. I had to bring the tools and clean up the messes and whatever else he needed to have done. He yelled at me a few times. I let it in one ear and out the other. I got a boot in the pants a few times for not getting the right tools, but I learned.

Another day while working with him, I tried to find some water to drink. I went off looking and I could hear him yelling my name. When I came back to the truck, did I get it! I tried to tell him I just wanted to get some water. He didn't listen. Another beating and I could hardly get up. He left me there on the ground in the dirt and went off somewhere. I crawled to the truck and got inside. I fell asleep. I woke up on my way home and Dad was yelling about something. My head was buzzing inside and this time my back hurt. Things were a little blurry. I fell asleep even with all his yelling, but I was in a lot of pain.

A few days later I remember some more yelling. This time it was my teacher at the front door. I guess I had missed a few days of school. Dad had called the doctor because I was acting dopey. The doctor called the teacher and they came over together to talk to Dad. The doctor checked me out and wrote down something on the paper in front of him. He put it in his pocket. He gave me some medicine and he checked out all my bruises, and then went in the other room with my Dad. I heard the doctor raising his voice. I still felt like something was wrong in my head. I remember I was dizzy a lot of the time and I had a hard time remembering what day it was. I couldn't do much of anything. All I could do was sleep.

I got through another year of school. I didn't do very well. I had a lot of problems keeping up with my homework. The teacher watched me closely and I could feel it.

I didn't grow a lot that year. That was a good thing I guess.

When school was over for the year I felt real bad. I never saw my school friends except for Joey, unless I went into town with Dad. Summer meant work for me now. I had to be with him most of the time working on jobs all day. I think he thought I'd run off with my friends and get into trouble. On days that I could stay home, he would come home angry because I didn't do enough around the place. That was always reason enough to slam me around before the night was over.

I really started to resent all the punishment I was getting. I didn't think I was doing anything wrong. I stayed away from him as much as possible.

I really wanted to be with my friend Joey and have some fun. I never had the time. I heard about all the fun my friends had because none of them worked like I did. My head hurt and I'd trip over things all the time. It was a lousy summer.

My teacher stopped by one day when I was home in the summer. It was nice to see her at my house. She asked me how I was feeling and if I was reading during the summer. I couldn't remember. She said she thought I grew a few inches taller and patted me on the shoulder. She sat and talked for a while. I guess she expected to say hello to Dad but he never returned until late that night.

The summer went by and I worked most of the time only staying home a few days. I was dizzy a lot but couldn't say anything.

When it was time for school again I dreaded the thought of clothes. Dad made his usual big deal over school clothes. I got some clothes and a new pair of boots this time. Real nice boots and I really liked them.

I had a hard time in school. I couldn't get my math right and couldn't remember what I had just read for my tests. The teacher sent home a note to Dad to have me see the doctor, and of course my failing grades were in there too. That just made things worse at home. Dad yelled at me to study harder. Another note came home next month. I didn't give it to him for three days. I knew what would happen to me and it did. Dad let me have it with both fists after supper that night. He was madder than hell. He said I wasn't trying in school. I told him I wasn't feeling good and I had headaches all the time. I told him I couldn't remember what I had studied the day before. He listened but didn't really hear what I said. He lifted me out of the chair and shook me around. I started to feel real dizzy and sick to my stomach. He yelled some more and gave me a boot in the pants that knocked me down. I stayed on the floor. He went to another room still yelling at me. I had a hard time getting up I was so dizzy. I had to think where I was this time. I got to my room and fell across the bed.

The next day when I woke up I was alone. Dad had gone out on a job. It was quiet and it was the middle of the day. I had missed school again. I felt really bad inside. I knew I couldn't take anymore of this and I had to do something. My mind was confused. I really missed my Mom. I was so alone. I took my cat and went to the barn and cried. Boys are not supposed to cry but I felt so alone and sick and I didn't want to be here anymore. Dad hated me and I knew it. I fell asleep crying.

It was dusk when I woke up. I had been thinking what to do. I put the pistol in my pocket and went inside to see what time it was. I sat and waited.

As I heard my name being called across the room I wanted to yell back, "I'm not here!" I stayed quiet in the room. I could hear the heavy pounding footsteps coming closer to me. Not this time I whispered to myself. I crouched down in the dark corner of the room as still as I could be and he went past me. Now was my chance. "Run as fast as you can," I said to myself. Back through the room and out the front door, to the pricker bushes beside the steps. I had been here before. It was dusk and he couldn't see me.

He must have heard me go out the door.

He came out and looked around and yelled my name out loud.

As I looked up, there he was! I took out the pistol from my pocket and aimed it at him. I shot my Dad! Not once but three times. The bullets came out of the gun and he went down on the stairs. The blood went everywhere. I heard no sound from him. I just sat there still huddled up under the bushes.

Chapter 4

The Hospital

In the cold early morning when Mr. Perterson our farm manager, arrived on the farm for the day, he said they found me sitting in the bushes on the ground, with the pistol by my feet. The blood on the stairs in front of me was devastating and no one knew what to do. I was moving back and forth in a daze and tears were rolling down my sad, wet little face. He said it was cold out but I didn't know it. I was quickly wrapped in a blanket and put in the truck and taken into town to get some help. They took me to the Court House Building where everyone always met when there was a problem.

I don't really remember the ride into town, or how I got there, or who brought me.

There were voices in the background. People were very upset. Some were raising their voices. Others were trying to quiet people down. I sat on a hard wooden bench and I was cold and alone. People were coming in the big wooden doors and looking at me. Then they would go in the big room with the others. No one was saying anything to me. I really wished Mom was here. I didn't know what to do. Some more people came in, stopped and looked at me, and shook their heads as they walked by. Now I remember, I killed my Dad. My head hurts really badly, and I'm nauseous. I'm so scared and how did I get here? One minute I can remember something and the next minute I can't. I think these people are going to drag me off to jail for what I did. Boy I am in trouble. I'm going to be sick. Yup! I just threw up all over the floor. The heaving is making me dizzy and I can hear myself saying, "Mom help me." I can feel myself falling off the bench to the hard floor. I can't move.

There is silence.

I woke up in a hospital bed in a room with three nurses. Where am I, I wanted to ask but the words would not come out. The room was spinning as I tried to move. The room is fading out and my head is spinning and swirling in all directions. I threw up all over the bed. I tried to call out again. One of the nurses came over to the bed and another was doing something to the tubes by my bed. I felt like I was on fire and I tried to keep my eyes open and stay awake, but I couldn't.

I can feel something happening but I can't move. Something is holding me down. This room is different from before. It's cold. I can't feel my arms or my legs and there is something over my head. I'm so tired.

Again I wake up and I can hear the nurses. Someone is talking to me. I can't really see her and I can't understand her. She is holding my hand and just put a warm blanket over me. It's Mom. I knew she would come back for me. I feel the tears rolling down my face but I still can't get any words out. I am happy now and Mom will take care of me. I fall asleep again.

Some time passed, could be hours or even half a day, and I woke up again. I could see the nurses in the room. "Where is Mom?" I asked. I could speak this time but it was raspy. "Where is my Mom?" I asked again. "I know she was here, she held my hand." My throat began to close up on me and it pained me to speak.

One of the nurses came to me and asked if I could hear her. I said, "Yes." She asked if I could see her, I said, "Yes but not clearly." She asked if my head hurt, I said, "yes." I tried to move a little but my arms were so heavy I couldn't. Then I noticed my head was wrapped in bandages. Something was on my back and it was very hard. What kind of bed is this I thought? The nurse told me to lay still and rest. I was very tired. I drifted off to sleep as I looked for my Mom. I couldn't see her in the room.

I heard the sound of people talking and someone was taking pictures. As I opened my eyes there were people all around in the room. They were looking at the chart at the bottom of my bed and some papers were being passed around. When they saw that my eyes were open, they all came around the bed. Now was my chance to find out where Mom had gone.

"Please tell me where Mom is, I want to see her."

Some of the people moaned and shook their heads. I heard, "Poor boy." I was hoping they could hear me because my throat still hurt and I couldn't raise my voice.

A nurse came through all the people and stood beside me. She held my hand. Everyone became very quiet. She bent over the bars on the bed and asked me if I could see her? Oh, not those questions again. I knew the routine. I answered yes to all the questions and slowly the people cleared out of the room. The nurse remained. She bent down again and proceeded to tell me that I had just had some serious work done on my head and back, and I had some ribs broken. I would have to remain in bed for some time to heal properly. I didn't know what she was talking about but I could tell there was something wrong. She said to get some rest. She gave me some water and rubbed some ice on my lips. It felt good. Her voice was very soft as she told me that my Mom was up in heaven, and watching over me. I could feel tears rolling down my face. Boys don't cry but I guess I did. People were still moving around outside the door. The nurse was doing something to the tubes beside me as I closed my eyes again.

It was quiet when I woke up again. No one was in the room. I could just see one nurse outside at the desk reading. As I turned my head slightly she came right over to me and asked me how I was feeling. I did not know. "Good I guess. Nothing hurts me not even my head."

She laughed and said, "Don't try to move too much or try to get up. That will come later with some help. The healing is going to take a while and everyone will be here to help you." Later, she gave me some apple sauce and I fell asleep again.

Healing went on for a few weeks. I was in and out of sleep and that's what they wanted. I think they had control of my sleeping. I don't know how long I was medicated, before I started to feel better.

I started asking questions one morning while the nurse was giving me a sponge bath. I didn't know what some of the words meant, but she tried to explain what had happened to me. The abuse that I received for a long period of time had caused some swelling on the brain. My balance was distorted, and my system was unable to communicate thought waves to the body or the spine. I had many minor fractures causing the pains I had. In the course of a few years my bones had taken on scar tissue. This was the result of the abuse I tolerated from my Dad. The staff began to ask me a lot of questions when they came in to see me.

After a while I noticed that my headaches were not so painful anymore. The dizziness was gone and I started to remember things. One night I had a dream that Mom didn't love me anymore because I had killed my Dad. I remembered that night now and I don't know why I killed my Dad. I do know that I am going to jail for the rest of my life. I woke up crying and a nurse came in and sat with me for a while.

"Mom is that you?"

"No Billy I'm your nurse, I'm Maggie. You must rest now. Would you like me to tell you a story? I knew your Mom and I grew up with her. Would you like that?"

"Yes because my Mom died when I was young and I don't know too much about her. Were you her best friend?"

"Yes I guess you would call me a best friend Billy. Her name was Sara Jean Evans when I met her and our parents were friends. Sara was very tall and she had freckles and very bushy red hair. When she was little she had to stay at the store with her parents all day. She had a good life and everyone in town knew her. Her personality was what you remembered the most. Everyone liked Sara and she was a happy person to be around. I met her in school and we went everywhere together. Your Mom and I learned how to swim and ride a bike and we even did our homework together. In high school your Mom worked at the store with her parents and I worked in the Court House. On weekends we went into the city and did some shopping with our friends, Dora and Jennie. We dated some of the guys but nothing serious. We graduated and still kept going in the city on weekends. Your Mom did meet someone very nice but who knows what happened to him. I met a young lawyer who I eventually did marry. I lost track of your Mom for a while, then I heard she married your father and moved to his farm. I went to see her. Do you want me to go on Billy, or are you sleepy?"

"Tell me some more Nurse Maggie, please."

"Okay let's see. She told me she married John Stevens and her parents did not like him. She said she had a baby boy and I went in to see you. She was so proud of you Billy. She held you like you were fragile glass. She couldn't tell me enough about you. I think you were about three months old then, and all I can remember the first time I saw you was your crystal blue eyes."

"Nurse Maggie, my doctor has crystal blue eyes just like mine."

"Is that right?" Your Mom showed me around the farm and said she was glad I came by. She didn't get out too much now. I could tell your Mom was having some problems with her parents and she did sit with me and tell me all about it. Her biggest concern was that they didn't get to know you Billy. Do you want your pillow puffed up a little?"

"No please keep telling me about Mom. What happened to my grandparents? I don't remember them."

"That's another story Billy. I'll bring by some pictures for you to look at. They both died in a dreadful fire in their store. It was a sad story. Now where were we? Your Mom started to have health problems and she became very weak. It became a lot of work taking care of you alone, and doing all the things on the farm that she had to do. She did go to the doctor and got some medication and was told to rest. She seemed to get better. One day I came by and she was teaching you to sing and dance to a tune she loved. She fussed with you all the time and you two were very close. A few years went by and I noticed that she was looking weak again. Your father hired some people to take care of things around the farm. That gave him more time to be with Sara and you. That's when she heard about her parents being killed in a fire. I went with her to town and we talked to some people that saw the whole thing. That's how I got some pictures I'll show you later. When she came back after taking care of all the responsibility of the property and land and other things her parents had put aside for her, she was exhausted. She had given them a service at their church and had a big garland placed on the entrance to the cemetery. This family had gone through so much in a short amount of time. Sara never complained. She just tried to keep up with the work around the farm. She told me you were like a little sponge. You could learn quickly, you were coloring now and saying your ABCs. She loved watching you grow up to be a little person of your own. She felt bad her parents didn't know you, that kind of wore on her and she was sad. You could see she was getting weaker. I mentioned it to John one afternoon before I left. John told me she had taken a trip to the city with you a few days ago. When she came home she wasn't the same. He thought it was too much for her. About two weeks later, your father called me and said Sara had died on the way to town to see the doctor." She stopped and wiped her eyes.

"I loved your Mom Billy, we were best friends. For some reason I couldn't get along with your father after your Mom died. He was always angry and had no time to talk to me. I hardly ever saw you. Now that I am back in your life, I plan to stay around. You have been through enough all alone. Now you should get a little more rest before you have to get up and around. This is a big day for you."

She bent over and kissed me on the forehead. I was tired but I really wanted to hear about my Mom. It was almost morning now and I was supposed to get out of bed today.

I began moving around a little bit now. The nurses put my legs over the side of the bed and helped me to my feet. Whoa! The dizziness started in again. They helped me up and I walked a few steps to the chair. I felt like I had walked ten miles. My back was being kept straight with some kind of a frame. It was from the waist up. There was a lot of changing of the bandages going on. I couldn't see it so I would sit still until they were done. After the regular nurses were done, my special Nurse Maggie would check things out.

One day my friend Joey was allowed to come in and see me. He had to be with his parents because he was young. I could tell I looked bad just by looking at Joey's face. He reached around and looked at my back and asked if it hurt. I guess I had been in here so long I didn't feel anything anymore. I shook my head and looked away. I couldn't do anything but sit there with him. His parents were quiet and just watched Joey interact with me. His mother brought in some homemade cookies that she knew I liked. We talked about school and he left me some papers to read over. He couldn't stay very long. When he left I felt sad that I couldn't go outside with him. I knew I had been in the hospital for a long time.

Later that week my teacher and the doctor came to see me together. My teacher was happy to see me sitting up. The doctor checked all my records and asked some questions among the nurses. They hugged me like I was family and they told me something I didn't know. The teacher and Doctor Deering were brother and sister. I was so surprised. I was glad they came to see me.

Joey came to visit a couple of times. He said he was lost without me around. His parents dropped him off and picked him up. We talked about what we would do when I got out. It was all pretend stuff because I didn't even have a place to go.

People kept coming and going in my room. Some asked if they could take pictures of me and some asked questions about my family. I had very little to say.

During the days I would walk around in the hospital and see some of the people that were not sleeping. One man said he was a pilot in the Army Air Force and he told me some stories about his flying. I went to see him a few times before he left for home.

My special nurse took good care of me and she never let me stay up too long. Sometimes she would bring me something special when she came on duty. Today she brought me a red plaid shirt and dark brown, corduroy pants. I really liked the clothes, and I liked her too.

Then one day a man came to my room to ask me some questions. He was very nice and wanted to know what happened at the farm the night of the shooting. I thought he was a policeman, but he didn't say so. He asked about my Mom. He wanted to know a lot about my family. I told him I didn't know much. There was no family just me and my Dad. He kept asking if there was anyone he could call. Then he asked me if the nurses had been good to me and he asked me how I was feeling.

"Everyone has been good to me in here and I'm feeling okay." I said, "Last week my friend Joey came to see me and the doctor and my teacher came too. It was good to see them again."

He told me he would be coming by again and he was going to make sure I got good care. He said he was in charge of my case and he hoped I was okay with that. Before he left he bent down and said, "By the way, I'm taking care of your cat until you go home." That was the first time I remember smiling in a long time. He patted me on the head softly and then he left.

I realized one day I had been in the hospital for a very long time. But I knew they were going to put me in jail when I got out, so I just waited to see what was going to happen. Where would I go anyways?

The man came back a few weeks later. I asked him his name. He said his name was Phil Jones and he was a lawyer. I asked if he was the one who was going to put me in jail.

The man looked real sad and came over and took my hand. "You are not going to jail. I'm here now and I'm going to take care of you if that's okay." I looked at his face and his eyes were all watery. He told me he would be back tomorrow and he had a story to tell me.

He left and the nurses came in to get me ready for the night. I asked the nurses if anyone knew the man called Phil Jones. One nurse came over by my bed and sat in the chair beside me.

"I knew his wife Laura Jordan and she was my best friend. I'm Jennie or Nurse O'Neil to you Billy. Laura and I grew up together and then we went to law school. That's where we met Phil Jones. He was very good looking with his brown silky hair and crystal blue eyes. They were piercing. You had to notice his eyes. He was tall and muscular like a football player. He had a powerful and impressive voice and commanded your attention. If Laura didn't go for him I would have. He had charisma. He was a loner at law school and was quickly taken in by Laura and her family. They became a pair and moved up in the well to do society supplied by Laura's political family. The potential for the couple was obvious and the family helped move Phil into schools that would help him later. They got engaged and after graduation they got married. It was a big family wedding with all the blessings. I was her maid of honor. The family set up and office for the both of them to start their own business. The business did real well and Phil made sure Laura had everything she wanted. They bought a nice colonial home off the main street in Des Moines. Laura showed her hidden talents decorating and painting all the rooms by herself. She had gardens all around the home outside. People going by had to stop and look at the mixed colors and designs she had put together. I thought it was the most beautiful house I had ever been in. Phil thought she did such a wonderful job on the house that she should spend more time home than in the office. They could afford to hire some help. One day I stopped by and she was feeling sad that she didn't have a child yet. She went to the Doctors and after having two miscarriages he told her she would not be able to carry again. She asked Phil if they could adopt. He was not ready for that. So she went back to work putting all her energy into the business. She was content coming home, cooking and working in her gardens. Sitting with a good book by the fireplace made her happy."

"Now Phil had a very good business going on and was out all the time with friends and business companions. He opened two more business offices and the money rolled in. His business partners loved to race fast cars and stay out late. Now that he had money he got a few cars of his own. "Laura never liked fast cars or racing around the back roads. Phil spent a lot of time out at night and Laura started drinking at night to comfort her feelings. Sitting at home alone was not what she had expected and her family was upset. The marriage started to suffer and they had some disputes. One night when Phil didn't come home, Laura got in one of his cars and went looking for him. She was not familiar with the new car and had never driven his car at night in the dark. She took a back road, it was slippery from the rain that afternoon, and before she knew it she was in a bad accident. Laura was thrown out of the car and fell to the side of the road. She was not far from home. She was found by the police and brought to the hospital. Laura was pronounced dead on arrival. Phil was nowhere to be found. We heard he was out with some girlfriend having dinner. The next day when he came home, he found out from Laura's family that she had died. The family blamed Phil for everything. Her unhappiness, her drinking, and his fast cars were all blamed on Phil. That day Phil's life came to a screeching halt. A change came over him and he stopped drinking and running around and left his friends. He stayed at home and no one saw him for a few weeks. Then he came back to work and started all over. His business became bigger and he hired more people. He opened another office and became a big part of what went on in the City. He made amends to Laura's family as best he could. He sold his fast cars but he kept the beautiful home he shared with Laura. He became a very well known criminal lawyer and had ties with all the important people and businesses in the city. I can honestly say everyone wanted to be his friend. Yes, I knew Phil Jones and I knew Laura Jordan well, she was my sister. I have no idea what Phil is doing here, but you can be assured it's something important to get him to come around here."

As she got up and went by the other nurses to leave the room, she turned and said, "You are a very lucky boy, he is good."

I fell asleep wondering about that man and what kind of a story he was going to tell me. He was nice.

Today when I woke up I thought about how long it's been since I've been outside. I stood by the window and could tell it was cold outside. The leaves were gone from the trees. From my window I could see sweeping winds clearing the sidewalks, as the leaves blew down the street. It looked like we were going to have a bad storm. I remember some of the storms when I was young. The clouds would roll in and the winds would blow and the air would change quickly. The clouds would change color and get very dark and scary looking. Sometimes I would run to the barn if I was alone, and listen to the sounds of the old wood cracking as the wind picked up. The cows would come in and the chickens would head for the coop, pecking and clucking all the way in. But the clouds always told you if something serious was coming. I felt safer in the barn with the animals then I did in the house by myself. When the storm blew over, I would go outside and see how much damage was done around the farm. Most of the help would go home and check back to see what had to be done early the next morning. It's getting dark outside now. I wonder what is happening at the farm. I have to find out what is going on there.

I can't remember how long it's been since I was taken from the farm house. My head is clear now and a lot of thoughts are passing through. I need some answers. I have no Mom now. I am never going to see her again. I loved my Mom so much I guess I believed she would come back for me. I have no Dad because I killed him. I just couldn't take another beating. I still don't think I did anything wrong that he should beat me like he did. I think I went crazy. I was confused and couldn't think straight. I will have the rest of my life to remember what I did, and feel the way I'm feeling, while I sit in jail.

I have been asked so many times by the nurses about my family. Can they call someone to come and see me? I don't know anyone who can come and see me, just bring my cat.

I called for the nurse to come to my room. Nurse Maggie has been with me since I got here. When she came in she sat beside my bed and held my hand. I told her I had some questions to ask her.

She smiled and said, "Go ahead."

I asked her how long I had been here.

She said, "Billy you have been here a long time, almost three months now. The reason we have kept you this long is complicated. There are people working on your case and for now, they thought you would be better off in the hospital receiving care. Someone is taking care of all your needs."

I asked her who that was.

She said, "Someone will be in to talk to you soon and don't worry about anything right now." Before she left, she puffed up my pillow and ruffled my hair. "You need a haircut young man. I'll see what I can do."

Out of my mouth came, "Dad always cuts my hair!" I felt bad saying that I don't know why. Sometimes things fly out of my mouth and I can't stop it. Then I asked Nurse Maggie, What happened to my Dad? Did someone bury him?"

"That's all been taken care of Billy, don't you worry about it now." Nurse Maggie went out the door, and returned a few minutes later. She had some new clothes for me to wear when I went outside for the first time.

I felt warm tears rolling down my face as I turned away so she wouldn't see me cry. I stayed on the bed for a while thinking about the farm I left behind. I wondered if I would ever see it again.

Chapter 5

Phil's Story

The next morning the nurses got me up and helped me dress in my new clothes. They even had a warm jacket for me. Everyone had a smile on their face and they were happy I was going outside. It was a surprise to me.

Around 8:30am, Phil Jones came to my room. He asked if I remembered his name and I said, "Yes. You're Phil Jones and you're a lawyer from the city."

He smiled. "For now, you can call me Phil. Billy I'm going to take you out of the hospital today. Were going for a ride and I'm going to tell you that story I promised you." He helped me put on my new jacket.

We left the hospital and went to his car. It was a beauty and something I had never seen before. He had a brand new blue and white Chevy with shiny silver hubcaps. I opened the door and moved slowly across the cold leather front seat. This cost a lot of money I thought to myself.

Phil asked if I was hungry or maybe I'd like something to drink. I said, "Sure, growing boys you know." We went to the diner and got some hot chocolate and pancakes. Phil ordered the farmers' breakfast special. While we ate he told me he lived in Des Moines. He knew where my farm was. We were going to the farm if that was okay with me. I was anxious about that but glad to get the chance to see it one more time. I nodded my approval.

After we had breakfast we drove to the farm. It looked pretty good from the road as we drove in. The fields had been cut and cleared and some of the animals were romping on the hillside. The hay had been all covered and packed away for the winter. That was my job and I wondered how that was done with nobody there. As we drove in I could feel some apprehension as I rubbed my hands over the cold leather seats. I noticed a lot of workers standing along the side of the barns. What were they doing there I asked myself. It kind of looked like they knew we were coming. When we reached the front of the house I got a chill down my back. The front steps where my Dad had died, were all painted. The bushes where I hid were gone. In my mind I could still see the blood on the steps. I must have shown some signs that I was anxious, because Phil put his arm around me as we walked up the stairs together. Someone had cleaned the place up. A man came over to Phil and started talking to him just like he knew him.

One worker asked me how I was feeling and if I was glad to be out of the hospital. I said, "Yes, I felt better and I was real glad to be out".

Phil asked me to sit down on the chair on the porch for a minute and he left to talk to the help. I sat there thinking about what had happened here, and trying to remember how much time had passed since I was here.

When Phil returned he asked me if I was alright. I told him, "I remember shooting my Dad, but my mind went blank after that."

He said, "It was because you went into shock. Some day it will come back but don't worry about it right now." We sat on the steps, and Phil asked, "How do you feel being back at the farm?"

I thought about it for a minute. Then I spelled it out to him. "I am very sad. My Mom is gone and my Dad is gone. There is no place for me anymore." With that said Phil took my hand and we got up and started walking over to the barn.

"Go look inside, there is someone waiting to see you." When I went in the barn my best friend Joey was there with my cat in his lap. What a great surprise. I was so glad to see both of them that I could hardly speak. We came out of the barn and sat with Phil on the steps.

Phil acted like he knew Joey my best friend. Phil put his arm around my shoulder and asked if I would like to go inside with Joey and get a few of my things. We went inside together to my room and it had been cleaned. I gathered some pictures of my Mom that I made. I cleaned out some of my clothes but I knew not many would fit me now. I found my pair of boots that my Dad bought me the last time we went shopping. Joey picked up a pillow case and filled it with my books, my cat dish, and some other stuff he liked. I went to the kitchen and found my favorite cup. I know Mom bought it special for me and I always had my cocoa at night with her. Phil came to see how we were doing. I told him, "I had everything I want." We sat down at the kitchen table. Phil told me he was going to have some people manage the farm until we knew what to do with it. That sounded good to me. I asked Phil, "Do you know Joey Calhoun?" They both laughed.

Phil said "yes, I've talked with him several times and I know he is your best friend. How would you and your best friend like to take a ride with me to see my place in Des Moines?" We both ran out to the car and put my stuff in the back seat. We climbed in the front together and off we went.

On the way Phil told us he was working on my case, and that is why he was away so long. He said he would be around a lot more now and we would be talking to some people together. Then he asked me, "Would you like to live with me in Des Moines, now that you are ready to leave the hospital? He said he already checked out the doctors who would take care of me, and he set something up with the school for me too." I looked at Joey and

I didn't know what to say. I would miss my best friend. "Don't worry about Joey, we have that all set up with his parents. He can stay on weekends whenever he wants too. We can visit him too. Now let's check out my house."

We pulled up the driveway of a beautiful home. It had tall trees up the sides of the driveway and winding flower gardens on both sides, all perfectly manicured. It was a real nice area just outside the city and had a big golf course nearby. As we approached the front door, the cat jumped from my lap onto the cement and disappeared from sight. Joey yelled, "He's okay."

Then Phil said, "Don't worry he's been staying with me for some time now. He knows his way around."

We opened the large wooden doors and went into the foyer and down the marble hallway to the living room. We passed by a winding staircase that must have had 35 stairs going up. There was mahogany wood everywhere. Plush rugs covered the center of the rooms that your feet would sink into. When Joey sat down on the couch beside me I just looked at him like we were someplace we didn't belong. He just smiled. Then Phil asked if I liked the house. This was the biggest house I ever saw and all I could do was shake my head yes. Then Phil began his story.

He started by telling me that when he was young he worked hard on a farm in Greenfield. He worked with his father and mother and his brother. They ran a big business and it was a lot of hours and a lot of work. When he got older he didn't want to do farming or work the business, so he packed up one night and hitch-hiked to the city. He got a job and went back to school. He never heard from his family again. He became a lawyer and opened up a business. Then he got married. He had a nice wife who also worked in the office as a lawyer. They were married several years when she had a terrible car accident and died. Now he lives alone except for a housekeeper. He said he had three other offices and was planning to open another one soon. Then he asked me and Joey," What do you want to do when you get out of school?" We looked at each other and just shrugged our shoulders. Joey thought he might like to work with chemicals on the farms, learning how to save the farmlands from all the chemical sprayings. Phil thought that was a good idea, a Chemical Engineer. I was not sure of anything yet. Maybe I could fly an airplane, or be a pilot.

Phil asked, "Would you like to be a lawyer?"

I said, "I never thought about it." I think he planted the seed in my head as he went on with his story.

"After your Dad died you were put in the county hospital. The newspapers started running pictures and a story about you. Did you know that Billy?" Billy nodded no. "The stories were about your injuries and what you had gone through for the past few years. They were looking for someone in the family to come forward to take care of you. There was no one. But what did happen was a surprise to everyone. Your Doctor Deering was the first one to appear at the newspaper office. He came in your defense putting in writing that your Dad was abusive and he had seen you a few times with serious health issues, once with a concussion. He knew you had been beaten many times. Then your teacher came in with her story to tell. She told the reporter she knew you were being beaten and she kept a record of your school work. She felt there was something seriously wrong with you. Your school work suffered and you slept in the class a lot. She kept an eye on you and reported to Doctor Deering what she saw.

"I remember her watching me all the time," I said.

Joey jumped into the conversation and said, "I told my parents about what was happening to you Billy, I'm sorry I promised you I wouldn't say anything to them. I was so scared for you."

I gave Joey a big hug.

"Some of the hired help on the farm came in to tell their stories of how your Dad treated you. The men in town that worked with your Dad came in with stories of how mean he was. Then people started coming to the newspaper to see what they could do for you. After surgery you were out of it for a long time, and no one knew if you were going to be alright or not. People started dropping off money for your hospital bills and clothes for you. You're a much loved little boy, Billy. Some even wanted to adopt you, right Joey? So one day the paper called me to come to Greenfield and find out more about this boy in the papers. This was becoming a town item and a somewhat out of control situation. I came for my own reasons." He stopped talking and got up and lit a big brown cigar. I instantly thought of Doctor Deering and the wonderful scent of his pipe that I grew up with, on my front porch. He went on.

"I went around town getting the statements and that's when I met Joey. We started to research everything about you on record. Now Billy, I have some things to tell you that are going to be a big shock. I think you can handle it so please just listen to the whole story before you do anything. Okay?"

"Okay Phil."

"Your mother Sara and your father John were your parents who brought you up. But your mother Sara was pregnant with you before she married your father. This was on your record and on the birth certificate Sara filed at the court house. But she gave another man's name as your father. Sara and John lived outside of town in an apartment house until you were born. Then they moved to the farm. Sara's parents were not happy that she married John. We talked to some people in town that said Sara had the baby only a few months after marrying John. While you were in the hospital we did some blood test on you, and John was not your father. Before your mother got married, one of her friends said, Sara used to go into the city with her friends on weekends. As the story goes she met a man and fell in love with him. Her parents knew nothing about this affair. They were set on her marrying someone with money so he could take care of her. One weekend Sara found out this man from the city was married. She also found out she was pregnant. She didn't know what to do. She had met and dated John Stevens before but her parents didn't like him. Sara was told to break up with him but she did like him. She met up with John again and told him about the baby on the way. He asked her to marry him and he would give the baby a name. Do you understand the story so far, Billy?"

"I think so. I heard some of this from Mom's friend at the hospital. I knew she went to the city."

"John raised you, but I guess when Sara died, he went to pieces. The easiest one to take out his anger on was you. I'm so sorry for that Billy, if I only knew, but we'll get to that later. Let's go look at the rest of the house, are you up to it?" We were off the couch and up the stairs before you could count to five.

We went through all the rooms one at a time. We saw Phil's big bedroom with an office on the side. Next we went across the hall and stopped in front of two large wooden doors. Joey said, "Go ahead Billy open the doors." I opened the doors and couldn't believe my eyes. It was a large bedroom with a big 4 post bed. It had big puffy blankets and pillows and hard wood floors, with a large area rug bringing out the color of the room. There were windows all around the room. It had a bookshelf full of books against the wall. It had a beautiful wooden desk with a lamp. There was a big chair and window seats in front of all the windows. There was a table and two chairs in the corner of the room, and cards and puzzles and games piled on one side. There was a large closet with two wooden doors on the other side of the room. I opened the closet to find all the clothes you could ever want. As I looked up, Phil came over to me and said, "This is your room if you want to live here with me. What do you say?" I never had anything this nice. I said yes before he changed his mind. We walked across the room to a set of doors and when we opened them, it was another bedroom almost the same as mine.

"Joey, that's your room when you come stay with us. Okay with you?" A smile came across his face. I heard he was a generous man. We looked around some more then we went downstairs to the kitchen. Phil had a cook in the kitchen cooking dinner. Waiting for us she had gingerbread cookies and hot chocolate. We sat down at the kitchen table and listened to Phil again. Phil asked me to think about what I wanted to do and he would take care of the hospital records and reports tomorrow. I could move in with him in Des Moines as soon as it was possible.

I felt happy and sad. I was glad to be well enough to get out of the hospital, but sad to be leaving Greenfield and my friend Joey. And what about going to jail was the question in the back of my mind.

We finished eating and took Joey back to his farm. This was a busy day for me and I had a lot of things to think about. Much of what I heard today, I knew nothing about. Why had Phil done so much work on checking out my Mom and Dad? Why did it matter so much about my Mom?

I sat quietly in the front seat for a while. Then I asked, "Phil who was my real father on the birth certificate?"

He was quiet for a minute and then he said, "On our next trip out of the hospital we will go to the court house and you can see for yourself. I think you have had enough to think about for one day." He reached over and patted me on the head. "Here we are, and I think you need some rest now. I will be back tomorrow and we will talk again."

I thanked Phil for a great day and taking me out for a ride. I was tired. As soon as I got in my room I went right to sleep on my bed. I could hear voices in the hallway and people standing by the door. No one bothered me the rest of the afternoon.

The next morning at first light, I was up and ready for my trip to the court house. I kept asking myself, how do I handle something like this? Phil came in around nine thirty. Again all the nurses were buzzing around trying to see if Phil needed anything. Even I could see that he was very popular with the nurses here. They couldn't do enough for him. We left the hospital and headed to the court house. I felt a strange feeling when I went to get out of the car. Phil came to my side and we walked through the big wooden doors. There it was the big hard wooden bench I sat on before. I had gone full circle. This was where I ended up after I had killed my Dad. I still don't remember how I got here the day I shot Dad. I sat down on the bench again. Phil went to the window to talk to someone. It took a few minutes but he came back with some papers for me. I went to the birth certificate first. The name was William Stevens listed on the certificate as my father. That came as a shock to me and who was William Stevens? My Dad's name was John.

Again I turned to Phil who seemed to know more than me, and I asked, "Who was William?"

"Your father had a brother and he didn't live in Greenfield when you were born. Remember I told you your mother went to the city on weekends? This is where she met your father. At the time she met him he was married. So your mother never told him she was pregnant. He never knew about you." Phil told me to look over some of the other papers in my hand. There was something about a lot of money that was left to me from my mother. There was another paper about the farm being left to me if Dad died. All these papers were three or four pages long and I looked them over but I only remember the name William Stevens. Phil gave me a folder and I put everything in it.

"Let's go outside and get some fresh air." Phil told me that the people in Greenfield had been sending money to the newspaper for the past few months, to help me out. That was a surprise. I thought I was forgotten just sitting in the hospital so long. "Did you make up your mind about moving to Des Moines with me, Phil asked?"

"Will you help me with all this paper work if I do?" I asked.

"You bet. Let's get your stuff out of the hospital and go home."

This was another surprise. I was ready for a change in my life and I knew Phil would be there to help me.

When we got to the hospital, Phil said, "Why don't you go to your room and gather up all my belongings. I am going to the office to take care of all the paper work."

When I got to my room the nurses had set up for a party. There were banners on the walls and a very large, chocolate cake on the table. There was music playing and balloons everywhere. What a great surprise. They had made a special hat out of tissue paper and ribbons and bows, for me to wear. I sat in my chair all decorated with colored paper. The nurses sang, 'For he's a jolly good fellow' and they all danced around my chair. This made me feel so happy. I just sat there eating my delicious chocolate cake.

They all took turns talking to me and wishing me good luck and telling me how lucky I was. I had to promise to come back and visit with them whenever I could. I knew I would have to come back to see the doctors, so I agreed. My favorite Nurse Maggie brought me a small box and asked me to open it. It had a blue ribbon all around it and it was a silver box, about five inches by ten inches in size. I opened it carefully. The whole room went quiet. As I lifted the cotton covering off I saw a large gold key. I picked it up and on it was some writing. It said, "From the Hearts of Greenfield." I started to choke up a little. I guess it was all the attention. Nurse Maggie said, "Read the card with it." I opened the card and all the people had signed it and put little notes along the sides and all over the insides. I didn't think that many people knew me.

Just then, the door opened, and Joey and the teacher and all my classmates came running in the room. This was great. They all came over to me with cards they had made in school. The noise and confusion made me feel anxious and my heart started beating faster. Nurse Maggie took one look at me and quickly gathered the kids up and set them all down for cake at the table. The kids were given a container of bubbles and some balloons they could take home with them. Someone had gone to a lot of work to prepare for this party. I was so happy to be here with my friends.

The doctor came in with a man carrying a camera. He looked official with his badge and all. He started taking pictures. The nurses stood behind my chair for their pictures and Joey came over by me for his. The teacher and the doctor had one taken with me in the middle. The doctor had to leave, but not before he told me he would see me soon.

Phil came back in the room. He had special tickets for the whole class to go see "The Nutcracker Performance," with the teacher at the Opera House during the Christmas Season. Now my friends were really jumping up and down, screaming and hollering. This was a big deal in our town and really special.

It was time for everyone to go. My classmates put their hats and coats on and said their goodbyes. The teacher gave me another hug and they all left.

The nurses cleaned up the room and boxed the chocolate cake, what was left of it. The chairs and tables and the banners were put away. In no time things were put back in order. I kept my paper hat and my cards, and my special gold key.

Phil asked me how I was holding up and I said fine. I asked him if he knew about the party. He just smiled and winked at me. I thought to myself, what a special man he is.

I gathered my things and had plenty of help getting to the car. Everyone loved my new friend Phil. On the way out the nurses sang again. Everyone seemed to be crying or wiping their eyes. Some were throwing me kisses. I felt good today.

In the car Phil said he had one more story to tell me, but he wanted me to settle in and rest first. On the way home I felt like I was leaving a special place in my life and going to another. I thought, what else could happen? I fell asleep and didn't wake up until we were at his house. I guess I was all excited and more tired than I thought.

When we arrived at his house some people were waiting at the door. My bags were taken to my room. Phil introduced me to a woman named Janice. I shook her hand. I guess I was a bit tired but I didn't want to admit it. When all my things were upstairs, I told Phil I thought I'd lay down for a few minutes. He thought that was a good idea. He reached down near the cabinet in the kitchen, and picked up Cleo and passed him over to me. As I held him close to me I could hear him purring. I took him with me to my room and we both fell asleep across the bed. I was asleep for over two hours. I must have been tired. When I went downstairs, I noticed that it was about five thirty and just getting dark outside.

Phil was busy working on some papers on the kitchen table. He cleared the table, as I sat down near him and I told him I slept like a baby. He laughed.

"Billy, I have one more important thing to tell you. He hesitated for a minute. Your father's name on your birth certificate was William Stevens. I told you I moved to Des Moines when I was young. I changed my name to start my new life over. You knew your father and his brother grew up on your farm. Remember William left because he was not happy there. Billy, I am John's brother William. I am the one who left the farm and my family. I was married when I met your mother and her friends in Des Moines. I'm not proud of what happened, but your mother never let me know she was pregnant. We broke off our relationship the same weekend my wife died from the car accident. I broke off all contacts with my friends and family. I was unable to cope with my life for some time. I never knew about you until I saw the story in the papers about the boy in the hospital. The name captured me; I had to check it out."

Phil sat back in his chair and looked at Billy. He could see this was a powerful story to tell a young boy but he wanted to be honest with me right from the beginning. If this friendship was going to grow, he had to tell me everything right now.

I just looked at him. "Are you trying to tell me you are my father?"

"I came to Greenfield and took responsibility for what you needed. Yes I am your biological father and I hope you will let me take care of you." He hesitated, looked out the window, then came back and looked me in the eyes and said, "I am sorry you had to go through so much pain and suffering. My brother must have been suffering too. I'm sure he loved you Billy, but he took out his pain on the one closest to him. That will never happen again I promise you that." He stopped talking and waited. "Tell me what you are thinking right now Billy."

I tried to gather my thoughts. Phil was William Stevens and my real father. He is my father's brother. He grew up on the farm when he was young, my farm. He knew my Mom. How do I know this is true? I asked Phil-William-whatever, "How do I know this is true?"

He passed the papers over to me with certain areas underlined for me.

He asked Janice to get him something from his room upstairs. She went upstairs and came down with a picture frame in her hands.

"Billy, this was your mother when I knew her." He handed the picture to me. It was the most beautiful picture I ever saw of my Mom. I stared at it and held it to my chest while tears came down from my eyes. I couldn't understand all this crying lately. I'm not a baby, but I couldn't stop crying either. I never had a real picture of Mom and I was overwhelmed at this moment. "Billy, I will have a nice picture of your Mom made for your room."

I know he kept talking to me as I kept looking at the picture. Mom was so pretty. She had lots of red hair. Now I could remember her forever. I loved her so much.

I just sat there thinking for a short time. My eyes were wet and my heart was pounding. I just kept looking at the picture and looking at Phil. Finally I said, "Today is a big day for me. I find a new friend, you. I have a new home. I find out that you are my real father. I know now why my nurses said I was a lucky boy. I guess they were right. I am going to do my very best to make you glad I am your son, and I promise to do my best at school."

Phil reached over and gave me a big warm hug. His eyes were wet too.

He told me he had a special supper waiting for me." Meatballs and spaghetti with garlic rolls, special made for the newest member of the family. Janice is a great cook." That sounded pretty good to me.

"Tomorrow we have an appointment in court. You will need some rest tonight. Let's eat!"

After we ate we talked some more in the living room. He told me what to expect in court, and assured me I would not have to be uncomfortable for one minute. This is what he did every day and he was good at it. Our court time is ten o'clock. When I left the room I realized I was very lucky to have someone caring for me like Phil.

Somewhere in the middle of the night I woke up. I wanted to know if my last few days were just a dream. Was I really in this big house in my own room? I was feeling pretty good and someone was taking care of me. My father! With my cat beside me I went to sleep ready to start a new life tomorrow.

Greenfield Court room

Chapter 6

New home

I woke up the next morning and ran to the window and pulled the shades open, in my new home in Des Moines. I felt my stomach churning over and over. I really felt nauseous inside. What was going on, I was so jumpy inside. I was going to court today.

I found my clothes all folded carefully on the chair next to my bed. I got dressed and looked around to see where I was, and what I looked like in the big mirror. I went downstairs. Something smelled real good. My stomach started churning again.

My new Dad was eating toast and having some coffee, while going through some of his papers. When he saw me he cleared off the table and made a gesture to come sit down. He looked up and smiled. "Are you ready for your big day?" he asked.

My stomach did a flip flop and I guess I looked scared because I definitely was.

"It's okay. You will be fine. There is nothing to worry about so have something to eat. Janice will be taking care of you around here, taking you to the doctors and things like that, when I'm not here. She's also your cook. Her pancakes are to die for and her hot chocolate is the best."

I sat down. After I got some food in me I asked what he wanted me to do today.

"Nothing," was his reply. "You are just going to be by my side and I will do all the talking. We have some people coming in to the court but for the most part, it will be private if we can manage it. We have a county attorney handling our case. It shouldn't take long."

I still felt jumpy but breakfast did help.

We left for the courthouse early and arrived about twenty minutes to ten. We went through those big wooden doors and past the hard wooden bench. When we started up the wooden staircase I started to shake and feel sick again. I guess it was nerves. Phil took my hand and we went upstairs to the courtroom door. I looked inside and it was a big bright room. My stomach was all jumpy again and I was clammy all over, and my throat was dry. I was so scared of what could happen in here, even though I had been told everything was alright.

I heard a noise coming from the bottom of the stairs. When I turned around I could hear Joey and his parents calling me. I was so happy to see them. They came up the stairs. Joey and I went over to the side room so we could talk. I told him how scared I was.

He said, "Don't worry Billy you have the best lawyer in the world."

For some reason, I felt a little better having my best friend here. We both went inside as the courtroom started to fill up.

The room had a large wooden desk up front, something the president would sit at. There were large wooden panels behind this desk, making it look very official. In front of the large desk, there was another smaller desk, probably for someone to be questioned. There was a witness box to the left of the Judges seat and a microphone attached to the desk. There were two big flags, one on each side of the Judges chair. To the right of the Judges chair, was a large bookshelf filled with law books. There was another panel closing off the Judges area about 4 feet high, and two brown leather chairs. In front of all the wood paneling in the center of the floor, was a 4 foot by 4 foot brown oak table, shining and clean with chairs around it. This had to be where the lawyers sat. The jury seats were wooden chairs padded. From the Judge's seat looking down the room, there was about enough seats for about forty five people. A large green chalk board was along the side of the wall. The floors were linoleum with a great shine. This was a room of power, and only a few would have control in here.

I sat next to Phil and he said I would probably see some friends coming in soon. Joey and his parents sat in the first row.

People started coming in and the clerk of courts came in and went up front to his seat. He motioned to Phil to come up to the desk with his papers.

Next thing we heard was "all rise," and Phil came back to his seat, and the wooden gavel slammed down on the desk.

The procedures started with Doctor Deering coming in the door. He went to the big bench, raised his hand and repeated after the clerk. Phil went to him and asked him some questions. The doctor looked at Phil for a moment. Then he answered the questions in order. When he was finished he left. He stood at the end of the room and looked on.

My teacher came in next and did the same thing. She had some papers she had kept from school that she presented to the clerk. This took a few minutes to go over, and then she went up back and stayed with the doctor.

A man my Dad worked with in town came in next. When he started talking, he began to raise his voice. This was quickly stopped, and we were told there would be no raised voices in this courtroom.

Nurse Maggie came in and showed some charts. The pictures that were taken of me were put up for everyone to see. My x-rays were examined and the doctor was brought back for his opinion. It went on and on. You could tell the clerk of courts was getting aggravated and the court room was buzzing with noise. The clerk started to raise his voice to Phil and that was it. Phil raised his arms up in the air like a flying eagle!

Quite a few people had gathered in the room by this time and when they saw this, the room went silent.

Suddenly very loud, Phil said "The reason I am handling all Billy's affairs," and he paused, looked around the room, and came back to Billy's face, "Is because Billy is my son!" With that remark said, he tossed a pack of papers onto the top of the flat table.

The courtroom went ecstatic! Mumbling, whistling, clapping hands, and hollering; the gavel was banging down on the table, nothing was quieting things down. People started running out the door to tell some of the people waiting outside.

Finally the clerk asked Phil if he had proof of that statement, and he handed him the papers from the table. I looked over and could see these were the birth certificate and personal papers that Mom had left in the clerk's office, when her parents died. It took a few minutes for the room to quiet down, I noticed that the camera man had found his way in and was walking around getting different shots.

After looking the papers over, the clerk asked, "Phil what do you plan to do about this situation? Does Billy know that you are his biological father?"

"Yes he knows now," Phil said. "The tests showed all the damages that had been done to him as a child. They had the x-rays and reports from the doctor and nurses. He stood there and said, "As of today, there are no signs of any problems with this child. We don't have to do anything with him as far as I'm concerned and he's done nothing wrong. He was frightened and confused and temporarily out of control. He's only twelve years old and he lost his mother at a very young age. He was fighting for his life. What would you do? If it is alright with you Sir, I'd like to start his life over and give him the proper care as his father. I will be responsible."

With that, the clerk slammed down the gavel and said, "Phil I know you are a good man and you will give this boy a better life. If that's what Billy wants, and you want Phil, I'll go with that decision."

We both nodded.

"So be it, this case is closed."

Everyone started clapping and running out the doors. It was bedlam. The clerk got up and started for the door. We left the court house for the last time and I never wanted to be in there again.

We went to see Joey and his parents who were waiting outside. This was a great day for me and I didn't have to go to jail. Joey's parents hugged me and wished me good luck. The doctor and my teacher came over and were so happy for me. Again I heard I was a lucky boy. I thought to myself, what a great man Phil was to come forward and take the responsibility of his past actions. He was there for me and he didn't even know me.

We all went over to the cemetery and I said goodbye to my Dad and Mom. This was the first time I had to think about what I had done. I prayed my Dad could forgive me.

My new life had started, and I was ready.

Chapter 7

Growing up

The first thing on the agenda came the first morning after court was over. Phil asked me to call him Dad if that was alright with me. I was pleased.

I had to go to therapy for about three months. I would go once a week after school to a doctor in Des Moines, who was now my family doctor. Once a month, Janice and I would go to Greenfield to see Doctor Deering. It was like a home coming in town. My checkup took about half an hour. Then I would spend some time with the nurses and some time seeing people I wanted to stay in touch with.

On one of my visits I ran into my favorite Nurse Maggie who had some pictures for me. We sat down for a while and she showed me the pictures of my grandparents that she had told me about.

"Billy this is a picture of Sara's parents, Louise Bowmont and Edward Evans. And this one is a picture of the store they owned before the fire, and what it looked like after the fire. These were in the papers the next day. Your grandmother's family had money and they gave Louise money to buy the store when she got married. Sara told me that. Your grandparents opened their clothing store in Greenfield. They bought the best line of clothes they could. The people started asking for other items and before they knew it, they had a quality line of shoes and work boots. The next thing they knew they were selling canning supplies and pots and pans. Next they purchased yard goods and fabrics for furniture. The last thing they got involved in was animal feed and grains. A small addition was added on for the animal supplies. They spent a lot of time at the store. Remember I told you that your Mom worked at the store until she got married? She was at the farm when this happened. It was late at night when the fire started. Most people were out of the store. Someone said Louise heard a crackling sound coming from the back room. She called her husband and they went and opened the door. Louise ran inside to find the room raging with fire. With heat and smoke everywhere she fumbled around trying to find something to put the fire out. Her husband hollered for someone to help them as he ran inside and grabbed a shovel. He started pounding on the counters to put out the flames. Louise had on a cotton dress that caught fire and started to burn. She screamed and tried to put out the fire, but the heat was overwhelming and she fell to the floor consumed by the smoke and flames. She passed out and burned to death right on the floor. Her husband tried to make his way over to her but he was taken over by the heat and heavy smoke. He fell to the floor only a few feet away from Louise. The fire and smoke was so thick nobody could enter the room to help. Someone did run for help. The only horse drawn, hand pumper fire wagon came rolling down the street but it was to no avail. The building was completely destroyed and the bodies were badly burned. Someone called your Mom the next day and we went into town to take care of all the business. I went with her to the Court House and some very important papers were put away for you for later. That's about all I know about your grandparents. I just thought you'd like to have these pictures. It's a real sad story don't you think Billy? Having her parents die like that did a job on Sara. I think she always thought she could straighten things out, and you would have her parents around as you got older."

Nurse Maggie got up and left the pictures on the table. I sat there for a few minutes.

I stopped at the newspaper office that afternoon. Together with the editor, we put a nice thank you to all the people in Greenfield that supported me. It went across the front page. I was given money, clothes, and personal gifts, while in the hospital and I wanted to thank them from my heart. I was offered a job by the editor. Living in the city I had to say no. His reply was, "You'll be back, you're one of us."

My fractures had healed and I was feeling much better as time went by.

I had gained about 15 pounds now and I was about five feet eleven inches tall. My hair was light brown and I kept it short and parted on the left. I was shaving and my skin was good. No big pimples and rashes like some of the other teens had. The biggest surprise to me was how great my teeth turned out. I attributed that to the fact I drank a lot of milk. Before school here in the city, most mornings I would work out for an hour at the gym. On weekends I did some running when the weather was good. Sometimes Joey, Dad and I would go skiing.

Joey was also putting on some weight and training and lifting weights at his school. He was less fortunate with his skin problems. He had curly brown hair and the longer it grew, the curlier it seemed to be. He was about six feet tall. His parents were surprised how tall he was. He had great teeth too. Most places we went we were referred to as the Greenfield Boys, and we were always in public view.

Living in a small town gave me very little knowledge of the life style I was about to settle into.

Schooling was first. Dad set me up in a private school in the city for young men. My grades were poor when I left Greenfield. I had been sick and unable to study. Somehow he managed to get me into this expensive school. I knew I had to study hard and he got me a tutor to help me through the changeover. I did well. After six months I was at the top of my class and bringing home the grades that were expected. I felt pretty good, my head was on straight, and things were happening.

I started to see just what Dad did for a living, and the next time we talked about what direction I might want to pursue, it just jumped out of my mouth. I came out with, 'I think I want to do what you do!' My Dad just smiled. I had a vast amount of choices to choose for my future. I wanted to get involved and follow in his footsteps.

Dad was a lawyer and county attorney in the city of Des Moines, Iowa. He provided legal counsel for the board of supervisors and acted as a legal representative for the county in court cases. He represented the county, either as a defendant or plaintiff in the civil suits, and acted as a prosecuting attorney when a crime was committed. He was also responsible for juvenile justice and collections of fines.

He had several offices spread over the county and had many people working for him. His clientele consisted of the rich country club people, and the poor people trying to keep their jobs and have a place to live.

He made good money, everyone knew him, everyone liked him, and he was sincere and honest. Most of all, he was very good looking, as I was told by many of the nurses while I was a patient. While you were his client, you would feel like he was in control of all your problems. His record spoke for itself. You went looking for him if you wanted things done right. I had these feelings when I didn't even know who he was. I thought he was a great man and now I know I was right.

Dad also worked with a group of men and women to make the city progressive. He always wanted the city to be modern and ready for change. This group knew that someday they would need a bigger airport and easy access in and out of the city. There would be a need for bigger hospitals, and a sports center with an arena. This is what was on the agenda a long time before anything was set in motion. He was always planning and setting up meetings, and people listened to him from across his office table. He knew that a lot of produce, stock, and farm equipment passed over their railroads and highways here regularly. This was certain to be one of the largest cities in the country someday, just because of the location. He also kept the smaller towns around here involved with his projects, as they would benefit when the city expanded to their area.

Politics was a second interest in the city. My Dad's relatives, on his wife's side, had been involved in politics for a long time and were very well known in the city. They had a committee that kept the schools, the fire department, and police department, updated. They made sure the businesses had money to work with and the banks were secure. The right people were put in the right places, to do what the city needed done.

To say the least, voting season was mayhem in Des Moines.

There were a lot of problems to deal with in the large city and the depression had left its toll. They had a lot of people out of work. There was stealing and family problems because no one had money. It was a challenge to keep the streets safe at night. A committee was set up and paid for by the politicians, and business organizations in the area. Loans were set up for industrial and manufacturing companies and many jobs were opened up to the local people. Eventually the committee would help support affordable housing projects when the war ended.

One afternoon while talking to Joey at my home, we started talking about what we were going to do in the future. Joey was very interested in environmental problems and the chemicals that went into the ground. This was a major interest to him and he had spent a lot of time searching through the libraries and newspapers for information. He had mentioned that he might want to go to the university extension program and maybe become an environmentalist for the county or the state. He had such interest in it when he talked about it.

We happened to be talking about this when Dad came in the room one afternoon. He listened for a short time and then asked us if we wanted to go for a ride. Since Joey was staying for the weekend, we said yes.

We found ourselves at a small airport around Council Bluffs. We didn't know it but Dad kept a few small planes there for business. He drove his car down the runway until he came to a small red and silver plane, parked along the side. Joey and I looked at each other wondering what he was going to say next. "Okay boys let take a ride." We climbed out of the car and walked up to the plane. As we lifted ourselves up into the plane, he gave us some equipment for our heads, and some notebooks he had ready for us on the seat. We looked at each other. I had never been in a plane before. It looked like he had planned this surprise for some time. He spent a few minutes talking to the air traffic controller and writing some things down, then he started the engine. We waited for it to warm up. He showed us a few dials and how to read them, and what they meant, then we were off. This was a small plane. With the three of us it was crowded.

Down the runway we went slowly to the end. As I looked out the window I saw the old man from the hospital. He was the pilot I had talked to in the hospital, and he was standing by the fence waving. I looked at Dad. "I've known him for a long time Billy," was all he said. We came to a stop at the end of the runway.

Dad asked, "Who wants to be first to fly this plane?" Joey had been flying with the crop dusters on his farm. They both looked at me. "Come on Billy, move on over here and let's go," Dad said, over the roar of the engine.

I WAS SCARED TO DEATH! I had never been in a plane before, much less fly one. Dad showed me the controls I'd be using, and asked me to write some things down. My hand was shaking but I managed to write. It was time to lift off. I could hear all the people talking in the control tower through my head gear, but I didn't know what they were talking about. All of a sudden the engine started to rumble and it was ready to go. I couldn't believe my eyes as we started down the runway. Faster and faster we went until we lifted right up in the air. Joey was cheering in the back. "Great job Billy," The plane was wobbly and I was still scared, but I tried to straighten the plane out. With the help of Dad's calm voice, I got the plane to balance off some. What a view from the front window. I was thrilled and excited to be flying.

We practiced for a few hours taking turns, taking off and landing. Dad was impressed how fast I learned how to maneuver the plane. Joey was very good and had no problem with the new control panels. It was interesting to listen to the controllers talking to the other pilots coming in. Everyone had their numbers to identify with. This was a great afternoon for both of us. We couldn't wait for another lesson. Dad told us he was going to make sure we could both fly, so we could use his planes if we needed too. I was beginning to see a pattern in his thinking. He had a plan.

He told us he had been flying for about ten years now. He used his planes for short trips in the area and for business trips. Someday we could probably make some trips for him. We both liked flying on weekends with Dad.

When we were sixteen, we went together to get our drivers license. Joey took his father's pickup and I took the pickup truck from the farm. One of the helpers had a gray pickup he said I could use. I didn't think Dad's new car was a good idea for my driving test. We had been driving farm trucks since we were ten years old. You had to have a license to get around where we lived. We had no problems.

Next was our pilot's license. With Dad's help, we were able to get that license too. By this time we had soloed, and had some lessons from a friend of Dad's, named John. He was a good teacher and helped us with the book work. When he thought we were ready, he set up the test for us. Now we were able to be king of the roads, and fly the airways. It was pretty neat.

During the summer after work, Joey and his Dad would go fishing at the lake. When I stayed overnight I would go along. Fishing was new to me. I learned how to do fly fishing and I could get the line out there. Joey's father had been fishing all his life. He said it gave him great comfort to go fishing at night by the lake, and even more now that he had "his boys" along with him. He loved to tell stories about the big ones that got away.

One night when I was home doing my studies I came down stairs to get something to eat. I heard some men talking in the study so I went over by the door. It was Dad and some of the men he worked with in the office. I happened to hear one of them ask Dad how I was doing here in Des Moines. There was a slight pause, and then Dad said, "He's a good boy. He's doing his best to adjust and it can't be easy leaving your whole life behind you and starting over with someone you don't even know. He is doing real well in school, he's very smart. Every once in a while I see myself in him. He has my spirit and loves a challenge. I had him flying my plane the other day and he loves it. He has some of his mother's traits too. He is very aware of peoples' feelings, and he is very caring. I have seen no signs of anything mentally unbalanced from his brutal unforgiving past. I can't tell you how sorry I feel about that. I just know that will never happen to him again. I made a solemn promise to Sara in my heart that I would always be there for him. I really like the boy and I feel like I have been given another chance in my life with Billy."

"Here, here, Daddy oh," The guys all cheered, "let's call this a night." They moved about getting their coats and moving towards the front door to leave.

I quickly hurried to the kitchen to get my milk and cookies and meet them out at the front door. Dad was just closing the front door. He turned to ask if I needed any help with my studies. Sometimes I would come down if I had a problem. I said, 'No thanks, I'm fine.'

We went up the stairs together. He had some work to do before turning in, and I had to get things ready for the next day. He gave me a hug and I went to my room feeling pretty good that night.

My life here was good. I thought about Mom sometimes, because I had a very beautiful picture of her over my desk in my room. Dad had come through with his promise to get me a picture of Mom. I could see the special look he had for her when he had the picture put in my room. I wanted to try hard to be the kind of person my Dad wanted me to be. He sure was doing everything for me.

One afternoon Dad and I went into town to see the doctor. He said he had to get some records he needed and he dropped me off at Joey's place for a while. Were they my records? I thought nothing else about the visit. On the way back home Dad asked, "Did you know that Doctor Deering has the same color eyes as I do Billy?"

"Yes Dad, I did."

Joey and I both worked along through school. We would get together for baseball games in town and a few parties for friends. We were still close and saw each other a few times a month.

Joey was the first to get a steady girlfriend. She lived in Greenfield a few miles from Joey's farm. Her name was Lette Mae Winston and her family owned the diner on the outskirts of town. Lette Mae was a pretty blonde, not too tall, and had a great bubbly personality. She loved to talk. Sometimes I went with them when they went to the movies. One time we saw The Virginian with Gary Cooper. It was great and we paid 25 cents. After the movie we would go to the diner for pie and ice cream. Her Mom was the best cook in town. Lette Mae and Joey went to school together and planned to go to the senior prom. Joey really liked Lette Mae, I did too.

A few months later I met a girl I liked and we started dating. Her name was Ashley Thomas and she came from a large family in Des Moines. Her father owned two banks in Des Moines, one in Greenfield, and one in Winterset. Dad knew the family and was pleased when he met her. She was very pretty. She had long blonde curly hair and she was about five feet four inches tall. She was a quiet girl, not bubbly like Lette Mae. We got along like we had known each other forever. She just started talking to me one day. I asked her out and she accepted. She was gorgeous.

Joey's girl and my girl could have passed for sisters. They looked alike, same height, weight, and blonde hair. We were surprised how close they became. We seemed to go everywhere together.

We all studied hard in school and had a pretty good idea what we wanted to do in our future.

Chapter 8

Senior Year

School was getting more involved for all of us. We were moving in different directions trying to plan our future, especially schooling after graduation.

I had planned to go to Law School if my grades were high enough and work with my Dad. I was already doing that part-time after school. My courses were set. This seemed like the right thing for me to do. I was interested in law and I had this opportunity with my Dad. I was also learning how to manage the farm whenever there was a problem that came up. I had been back a few times on my own, and I was adjusting to my feelings as I went along. I think this was another way my Dad had planned for me to get along with the help. He was a coy one. Did his ability to manage me, rub off I wondered. We did work well together.

Joey planned to work on the farm with his father. After all, he was brought out here from New York just for that reason. He was very lucky though. His parents lavished him with as much as they saw fit while enjoying their opportunity to bring up someone like Joey. His one great interest in the farm had always been the soil, and how to keep it safe for the foods that were grown in it and the animals that lived on it all year. For a young person, people couldn't understand why he took such interest. We joked about it sometimes. We came up with the fact that he was glad he wasn't a pig farmer. There were a lot of them in our town too. He thought an environmentalist for the state would be something to pursue.

Ashley wanted to help her Dad when she graduated. She was planning secretarial school so she would be able to manage one of her father's banks. She worked part-time with him after school. She had an uncanny knack with figures. It was a game to her. She helped all of us in math through high school. She also loved to study the history of our towns and city. She kept records of everything happening and she hoped that someday she would be able to put it all in a book.

Lette Mae loved working with small children. After school she would work a lot of hours at the hospital in the children's wing. She would feed them and tell them stories, or just sit by their bedside and hold their little hands. Just braiding their hair made them happy and the children loved her. She decided to become a pediatric nurse. This was her calling. Sometimes the nurses would call her to come in and help out with a child they couldn't manage. She had that motherly charm.

We still managed to spend time together, dating and talking things over, the four of us.

In the fall we spent most of our time in Greenfield at Joeys place and my farm. There was a lot to be done before the winter set in. Some schools closed for the harvest season. Mr. Price purchased 150 more acres of land and had it cleared and fertilized for his spring planting. The land had good drainage, and the hired help fenced it all in before it got too cold to work outside. The wind could be fierce this time of the year. My farm was being handled with hired help and Dad and I were overseeing the workers, which had become my new part-time job. I found out we could have done that all along if my other father had only known more about it.

Christmas season brought us all to Des Moines and the Christmas time activities of decorating the big tree in the city. Many people made hand carved wooden ornaments for this occasion. The city had sleigh rides through the farmlands, and Christmas caroling at the hospital and some shut-ins. This was something we all enjoyed helping with. The city commissioner put baskets together for the needy families in town, and asked the high school seniors to deliver them. We found time for these special activities and it kept the people together and made you feel good.

The winter was exceptionally brutal on the land during our senior year. Heavy wet snow covered us up to the roof tops. The snow drifts covered the sides of the barns and roads were closed off for days. The night winds howled way into the early mornings. We knew before we got out of bed what was ahead of us.

One really snowy night I drove to Greenfield with Ashley, to see a show at the Opera House. It was a four act play and costs twenty-five cents, and we made it to town on time. While we were there it snowed, and snowed some more. We called Joey for some help and we were able to get the car to his place for the night. We stayed at his farm until morning. Then we followed a plow back to the city, seeing drifts over the car all the way back home. We didn't try that again until the weather broke.

In the spring we had our Senior Proms. Joey and Lette Mae had the first one. Ashley and I went to theirs. Then Ashley and I had ours. Each time we had the best time.

Joey and Lette Mae, being the most popular in their class, became the King and Queen for the night. Lette Mae had a stunning blue ruffled bell bottom gown, with a strapless top and blue satin jacket. The dress had a blue satin ribbon tied around the waist running down the gown almost to the floor and a bow in the back. She had blue satin slippers to match. Around her neck she wore a pearl necklace, and had a set of pearl earrings that her mother gave her to wear. Her hair was up in a bun with curls hanging down. She looked like Cinderella. She was breathtaking. Joey wore a rented black tuxedo with a blue shirt that matched her dress.

Ashley wore a yellow floor length gown with white shoulder straps, and a white ribbon around the waist tied in the back with a long bow. The dress was tight fitting with a jacket to match. She had yellow satin slippers. Around her neck she had a chain with a silver heart on it and earrings to match, that I had given her for Christmas. Her hair was done up and topped off with a tulle hair piece, her mother had given her. She was so beautiful. I had a matching yellow shirt and tie and a black rented tuxedo.

The Prices took pictures before we left. You could tell they were so proud of all of us.

My Prom was a few weeks later. My private school did a black and white theme. Joey and I were all set, just needed to get white shirts. But the girls went all out again. Lette Mae had a straight black dress to the floor with a cinch waist and puffy sleeves. She had black slippers to match. She had the white pearl earrings and pearl necklace from her mom again. Her hair was curled up on top and held with a pearl head piece. Ashley wore a black velvet gown down to the floor with a scoop neck. It was close fitting and sleeveless, but elegant. She wore black velvet gloves all the way up her arms, studded with crystals up the center. She wore crystals on a chain around her neck with earrings to match. Her hair was partially up on the top and caught with a crystal comb to the right side. She was stunning. The girls shopped together for their dresses and head pieces. You could tell they knew how great they looked. Ashley and I got King and Queen at my Prom, and the pictures were done by the school so we all got some. These were perfect nights for us all.

When the proms were over we had our finals to prepare for. We didn't have any trouble with our exams. Now we had our directions planned for after school.

The only thing we didn't plan for was the War! It was getting very hard to not get involved somehow. The recruiters were at the schools weekly. A lot of the boys were signing up for the service before they got drafted. Some of my friends were joining the Army. Some of Joey's friends were going into the Navy. Some went because of family tradition and others just wanted to serve.

The posters were everywhere. I thought about it and I talked to Dad which was a big mistake. He was very upset. He was just getting used to me being around and didn't want me going off in the service. I tried to tell him I had some flying experience and that might be good for the Army Air Corps. He said he had some friends he wanted to talk to, and not to do anything right now. I let it go. I was only seventeen anyways. I had a few months before I could enlist.

Joey had the same reaction from his parents. They were very upset and wanted nothing to do with the service. They sat down with him and explained how they planned to leave the farm to him in the future. They had bought extra land and had hopes of handing it over to him when his schooling was over. Joey told them how much he loved them and wanted to please them. He really wanted to do some time in the service, maybe flying planes.

"You could be exempt because I need you here on the farm," Tom said. This was the topic of conversation for a few nights at the supper table. Finally Joey said they relented to his ideas of flying. He could feel the tension between them for the first time.

After exams my graduation was first in our group. Dad gave me a big house party for all my friends from school and included some teachers. He had it catered and the inside was a place to greet the guests. Outside in the yard the caterers took over. Tables of food were set up in different areas. There was a seven piece band playing over by the gazebo, and the area was all lit with tiny white lights for the occasion. There were streamers and balloons all around the yard bouncing up and down in the light breezes of the afternoon. It was delightful to be out in the yard with all my friends. Some teachers stopped by, and my doctor. I saw Dad talking to some of them. He knew most of them from when he was in school. Ashley and her parents stopped by and Joey and his parents came by later. We were the class of forty-two, and we celebrated.

Joey and Lette Mae had their party together at Joey's farm. They all chipped in and both families invited friends and family. Lette Mae's mother did a lot of the cooking and she loved every minute of it. We arrived later stopping to pick up Ashley first. Her parents and some friends stopped by later. Everyone wished Joey and Lette Mae good luck. They were happy graduates smiling from ear to ear.

Joey's past was behind him now and he tried to keep things in perspective. He planned to check his family out later when he had time to figure out what he could to do for them.

When graduation was over the girls got jobs for the summer and started making plans to get an apartment in the fall, together. Ashley was planning to move to Greenfield and work in her father's bank while going to secretarial school. Lette Mae found an apartment that was big enough for the two of them. She moved in first. She started nursing school and was on her way.

Joey planned to work on the farm for the summer and through harvesting in the fall. He was needed now that he was out of school. He turned eighteen in August and still wanted to go in the service. He didn't want to be drafted.

I was going to get the farm in order and spend time there through the harvesting, and then sign up for the service. I had turned eighteen the end of August but I didn't talk about the service. I was waiting for my Dad to say something.

Come the middle of October, Joey and I were getting anxious to get moving on.

One night our parents planned a dinner together. We knew something was up. We all had supper at Joey's farm. Judy made her famous macaroni and cheese dinner with homemade garlic bread. The kitchen smelled so good when we walked in. After dinner Joey and I cleaned up while our parents went into the parlor. We could feel the tension when we walked in the room.

The conversation was light and they were talking about how the harvesting had gone this year, and what was left to do. This went on for a few minutes and then Judy said, "Let's get to it!"

I started the subject by saying, 'I'm ready to go in the Army Air Corps and I want to fly.' Joey made a nod of the head, as they looked to him for a remark of some kind.

Dad said, "Okay here's the deal! We have talked it over, looking over at Judy and Tom, and we know we can't really stop you from signing up in the Army, if that's what you want to do. We don't like the idea but you have made up your minds. Take care of each other the best you can, and come back in one piece!"

The room went silent. We were both feeling good about what he said. Judy got up and went into the kitchen to get the coffee and dessert. When she returned we could see she had been crying. Joey and I just sat quiet and tried not to look too happy about the decision.

Chapter 9

Taking Care of Business

Now that Joey and I had the okay from our parents, to sign up in the service, that's just what we did.

The next morning, Monday October 1942, we met in Des Moines and went to the recruiting office on Main Street. We were not the only ones signing up that morning. About nine others had the same idea. Some were older than us, but we were with five just out of school like us. I knew two of the boys only by sight, from my school. I'm sure we both looked nervous and neither of us had eaten breakfast.

We filled out the usual forms and answered all the questions. Next they needed our medical history. I had papers from my two doctors stating I was fit, and what my past surgery consisted of. Joey was healthy and had been to his doctor in his senior year.

We stood in line for our shots and a service medical check-up. It was somewhat different from our own doctors. Teeth and gums, eyes, ears, and feet were important, along with other areas we were asked to expose, we won't discuss. And yes we had some shots the service was famous for.

After pledging our allegiance to our country, which is the same oath our President takes, we took our papers that were processed, and we were told to report to this office the next day at 7 a.m. That was it.

We left the building and went to my house where Janice, had a nice breakfast waiting for us. As we walked in the kitchen I think we both had the same idea. This might be our last great breakfast for a while.

We had to get everything done today. We were on our way tomorrow.

As we sat on the front steps outside after eating, Joey asked me if I would go shopping with him for a ring for Lette Mae. He wanted to get engaged today right after she got out of work. I was surprised at his timing but of course I said, 'Sure let's go!'

We took his pick-up truck and rode around until we found a real nice jewelry shop. As we walked in the door a bell rang, and an elderly man came out from behind the door in the office. The display cases were full of shiny jewelry. The rings were all sparkling with the special lighting he had over each glass case.

We looked at each other. Where do we start was written all over our faces. Just then a younger woman came out and asked if we needed any help.

I stepped back. This was Joey's idea!

He proceeded to tell her, he was leaving tomorrow for the Army and he wanted to get engaged tonight. She was very nice and explained all about a diamond, the color, cut and clarity, and then she asked him if he knew her size. He looked at a few sizes and was sure it was a 6. She told him if it didn't fit she could bring it in for an adjustment. He picked a full caret tiffany style setting, on a gold band that had the brightest color and clarity. The woman was impressed with his decision.

As she did up the paper work involved in the sale, I just happened to see something I liked right in front of me under the lights. I walked away trying not to look excited, and not to look interested. For some reason I found myself slowly moving back to this little beauty. I told myself I didn't feel ready to buy a ring for Ashley, but then I didn't think Joey was ready either. He looked over at me and looked so happy. Was I ready or was this just being here that made me feel like this ring in front of me was the one. I could see Ashley's face in my mind. I looked at Joey again. I still procrastinated. I tried to tell myself that we were just good friends. We didn't seem to need more than that right now. But then, I stopped thinking and said to myself, that's it. I was not going to leave this beauty here. Joey was finished. The ring was put into a small blue velvet box, and then put into a lovely small, silver bag with the store card in it. Happiness was all over his face.

Slowly the woman made her way over to me, standing by the counter. Again she asked, "Do you need any help?" Joey had a surprised look on his face.

"Billy, what do you see?"

As she reached down to the one I had pointed to, and picked up the ring that had captured my heart, holding it in my hand made my heart skip a beat. Would she like it, was running through my head. Joey looked at it with me and he had a smile as he looked me right in the eyes. He gave a nod. This ring was a flawless, full caret, triple stone diamond on a gold band. I never saw anything so pretty in my life.

"Well what are you going to do Billy," asked Joey.

The woman remained quiet.

"I really want to leave without it. Is this crazy or what? I don't think we are ready yet."

From the corner of the room the old man said, "No one ever is, son. No one ever is."

At that moment I made the decision to buy that little beauty that was tugging at my heart. I was hooked. As this beautiful ring was placed in the little blue velvet box and sent across the counter for one last look, I knew in my heart I did the right thing. I just hoped we were ready to take this next step.

We left together, a bit poorer but delighted at what we had just accomplished.

Joey dropped me off at home and went about with the things he had to do.

I jumped in one of my Dad's cars and went to the office. I had to show him my ring for Ashley and tell him about tomorrow. When I walked in the office he looked up from his wooden desk, and he knew something was up. I was spouting out about the Army as I raced across the room, and placed the blue box down on the desk. "What do you think Dad?" As he reached across his desk and opened the velvet box his eyebrows lifted and his eyes got bigger. "What's this son?"

"I have decided to propose to Ashley, what do you think Dad?"

"This is beautiful, son. I think it's a good idea. I'd like to help you with your plans if that's okay." He just looked at the ring, and his hands were shaking a little.

I knew he'd be happy for me.

Next I went to the farm to look around one more time. In my heart, I still had strong feeling here and I would still see my Mom in different areas were we spent time.

I went into the barn to look around. I spent a lot of time in here watching my father work on the farm equipment and fix parts and machinery for others. I talked to some of the help working here now, and they had problems to work out but I couldn't help. When I was little I could, but now I had been away from the new equipment for the farm, and didn't have a clue. I found myself looking over all my father's tools, and felt the need to handle all the washers and nuts and bolts, in the tool box.

I left the farm telling all the help I would be back someday for good.

I went to town to buy some flowers at the square. I stopped at the bank to see Ashley and ask her if she would meet me for supper at the hotel dining room after work.

My next stop was up the hill to the Greenfield Cemetery to visit with my parents and grand-parents. I put flowers on the graves and told them I was going off in the service, and I felt they would have wanted me to. I bent down and cried as I looked at my Dad's spot in the ground. What a terrible thing I did. I prayed for his forgiveness.

I caught up with Joey and he was packing up some things in his room. I could tell he had told his mother about leaving tomorrow; she met me at the door with tears in her eyes. He was meeting Lette Mae at the hospital after work and going to supper at the diner. I went back home to get dressed and get ready to meet Ashley at five at the Old Hotel dining room. I had some flowers for her.

I sat by my desk for a while, trying to write a note to Dad about how much he meant to me and how glad I was that he found me. I thanked him again for the beautiful portrait he had made of my Mom that he put in my room. This had really kept me focused through the last few years. I also wrote a special thanks to Janice for always being there to listen to my meanderings from time to time. She was a silent blessing. I left the notes on the desk. I was sure Dad would find them. I finished packing a few of my things and went on my way to dinner. On the way down stairs I asked Janice if she would take care of my cat while I was away. She laughed. She knew who the cat really favored.

Janice had been there for me from the first time Dad brought me to his house. He told me that she would be there to do anything for me that I needed, and she was.

She made my meals, cleaned my room and washed and ironed my clothes. This was all new to me. At first I thought she was family. So one day just after I moved in, I asked her how she came to working here for Dad.

We sat down at the kitchen table and she began to tell me her story.

Janice was the mother of a troubled son. His name was Jeffrey. They lived in the city in a small apartment on the west side. Their life had been bad there for a long time. She tried very hard to keep her only son from joining any gangs on the streets or getting into any trouble. Not much was done to help the area. It was a poor, black section that had slipped through the cracks as far as keeping the young people in school. This was a big city and during the depression and war going on, nothing was done to clean up the school grounds or parks for the young to play. To clean up the problems would cost the city a lot of money and there was none. Janice kept a close eye on Jeffrey. When he started school she got a job at the school cafeteria, and worked cleaning houses during the summers.

Her husband, an alcoholic, had left her before Jeffery started school so he was no help. She managed alone, saving every penny she could for his college someday. He was a good student and the teachers all spoke highly of him. He wanted to be a teacher.

But eventually he dropped out of school to be with his friends and got into some trouble.

Janice shifted her weight in the chair, leaned over, picked up Cleo, and began rubbing his ears.

"I did everything I could to keep him in school. I went to the priest at the church for some help, thinking maybe one of them would talk to him. I went to the police and asked them to watch the school yard more carefully. There were a lot of older boys hanging around enticing the younger ones to drop out of school. I did everything I could think of."

"But Jeffery dropped out of school at fifteen years old, left home, and I hardly saw him after that. He lived on the streets and worked for the labor forces once in a while, when he needed money. I couldn't help him. He did not want to see me. I felt heartbroken and I had nowhere to turn."

"One day I saw a sign in the window in town that said, *'Give me a chance, I'll do my best!'* I went in the door. It was your Dad's new law office, his second office right here in front of me. I told him about my boy and how I was running out of things to do to get him back in line and home again. I was so afraid of losing him, or something bad happening to him. I couldn't sleep at night worrying about him."

"Your Dad took down all the information he could from me, and he went out to see what he could do."

"Jeffrey had been picked up and put in jail the very day I had gone into the office for help. He had been put in jail for being drunk along with his friends, and he had no money to call for help. While kept in the jail overnight for court in the morning, he was stabbed by another inmate, seven times. Since he had no identification on him, it took a while to find out who he was. Your Dad was told by someone out on the streets that someone had died at the jail last night. I had given your Dad a picture of Jeffery. He went to the jail and made the identification."

"He came to my apartment and told me what had happened and that he was too late to help him, he was already dead. He stayed with me all afternoon and helped me make some plans to have him buried. He never left me alone and he sent someone from the church to look after me for a few days. Now my heart was really broken. I quit my job and I got very despondent. I stayed in the apartment by myself all the time."

"One day your Dad came by and sat down with me. He offered me a job taking care of his house. He was alone and could use some company. He gave me time to think about it. Your Dad was very good to me. Later I found out he paid for the funeral that he told me the city had paid for through social services."

"About a week later I showed up at his door. When he opened the door, I said, 'Janice reporting, Give me a chance, I will do my best!' We hugged and I have been here ever since. He is a good man, kind, and generous. He gives to a lot of people. No one knows about it. He took me in and gave me a place for as long as I want it, and a reason to go on. You have been a special blessing to your Dad and this house, and to me, Billy. God bless you."

I stayed with Janice for a while and told her of my plans for the rest of the day.

Ashley was at the Old Hotel when I got back in town. I went in and handed her some beautiful flowers and she had the perfect smile to match. I was going to miss her warm presence. I enjoyed her company and we had an easy comfortable relationship. I had told her about going into the Army Air Corps, Sunday night after dinner at Joey's house.

So we had dinner and we promised to write as often as we could while I was away. Our conversation was slow and easy until dinner was over. When the table was cleared I reached across and held her hands in mine.

"Ashley I want you to marry me." Just like that it popped out of my mouth. "I know I'm going away for a while. I think we are ready to get engaged, don't you? I want you here for me when I get back. Will you marry me?"

Her eyes widened and she smiled. She was not the type to jump up and down over anything. She looked surprised. She hesitated. She looked down at our hands now clenched together on the table.

I waited.

"Yes Billy, I will marry you." That's all she said. My head was spinning. Did I really ask her and did she really say yes? I reached in my pocket and slipped the ring out of the velvet box, and pulled it out and put it on her finger.

She looked down to see it was a ¾ inch washer from my Dad's tool box that I had put on her finger. "What's this Billy," she asked and smiled.

When I looked down I couldn't believe what I did. I had changed my clothes at home and must have thought the washer was a coin, and put it in my pocket. I reached in my pocket again and pulled out the little beauty that started all this excitement for me. I took off the washer, set it on the table, and replaced it with her diamond. Tears came down her face. You could tell she really loved it. We both sat there looking at it for some time. She said it was the most beautiful ring she had ever seen. Then we started laughing at the whole thing about the washer. She said someday she would find a way to write about it. We left the hotel dining room but not before I saw her slip the washer, into her pocket.

In the car we kissed and promised to tell the story to our children some day. This was a night to remember. She left in her own car and we met at her apartment, to wait for Joey and Lette Mae to come home. I told Ashley what he was planning. She was as surprised as I was, when she found out that he asked me to go shopping with him this morning.

After Joey got his room in order, he came downstairs and left a letter he had written to his parents on the table. He let them both know just how much he appreciated what they had done for him, and what they were planning for him in the future. He could only hope that some of the other children on the Orphan Trains had been so lucky. He thanked them for his schooling, and the confidence they had given him, along the way. Then he told them of his plans to get engaged to Lette Mae. He had discussed it with his Dad a few weeks ago, but tonight was the night he had planned to ask her. He promised to write often. He loved them both very much and was going to make them proud. He signed it; all my love, Joey. Then he left to pick up Lette Mae at the hospital.

She was standing outside the hospital when he arrived. It was a cool night and she had a tan jacket over her white hospital pants and white shoes. She was carrying papers and a note book under her arm. Her long blonde hair was blowing in the breeze as she ran to get into the pickup. A quick kiss and they were off to her parent's diner.

Her Mom and Dad were busy as usual, this time of the night. They managed to find a table where the lattice work separated them from the kitchen. Every table and soda counter stool was taken. They wrote their order on a napkin, and Lette Mae took it in the kitchen. Her Mom hollered out, "Hi Joey, love you both." When their meal was ready her Mom brought it out and gave both of them a kiss. Although she was busy, she sat down with her only daughter and wanted to know how her day went. After some conversation, she went back to work leaving Joey and Lette Mae to have their meal together.

Lette Mae talked all the way through the meal. When the table was cleared, they sat there for a minute just looking at each other. She could tell Joey was acting funny so she asked, "Joey what's up?"

Joey reached across the table and held her hands. "I want to ask you something, think about it, and then let me know what you think. Lette Mae will you marry me?"

Lette Mae let out a scream the whole room could hear. Silence came over the room. She jumped out of her chair and came over to Joey hugging and kissing him all over. "Yes, yes, yes she cried out."

Joey sat her down and then reached into his pocket and took out the little silver bag, and handed it over to her.

Everyone in the diner was waiting with excitement for her. This was a big deal in our town to be part of an engagement. She opened the little silver bag and took out the box. Tears were rolling down her face as she took out the little blue velvet box and opened it. She was so happy and everyone was clapping and cheering for them.

Her parents came out just as Joey was placing the beautiful diamond on her finger. Now her Mom was crying. The newly engaged couple got a round of applause from everyone in the diner. Her father went and got a few bottles of his best wine for a very special toast. Everyone enjoyed the wine and the special toast to his beautiful daughter and her future husband to be. They paraded around the tables and showed off the beautiful diamond that made the night so special. Everyone had a great time that night.

A little while later, they returned to the apartment. They came in all smiles and holding hands.

We all sat down together at the kitchen table and told our funny stories of the night. Joey told his story over and over. He loved to tell a good story. These were probably our last stories together for a while and we savored every word, not wanting the evening to end.

IN THE ARMY-AIR FORCE NOW . . .

Chapter 10

Basic Training

The next morning, Joey and I met at the Greyhound bus station with eight others, and we were put on the bus heading for Texas.

We had a drill instructor Sergeant Jones. He was tall, grey-haired, and in a military uniform. He spoke loud and looked old enough to be retired.

Our bus driver's name was Watson. He was in his sixties and probably a retired Army Veteran. He dressed in Army pants, and had on a Greyhound shirt and cap and shiny black shoes. He seemed pleasant.

We left Des Moines, Iowa and headed for Kansas City, Missouri. It didn't take long to realize this was going to be a long haul. The driver talked constantly to Jones, and the bus never seemed to get out of second gear. It was a bumpy ride. The weather was a bit windy. The bus swayed from side to side on the empty road and we got pulled along with the trucks that passed us.

Some of the guys told jokes and kidded about how they got in the Army just to pass the time. Joey exaggerated a little with his story but it was funny.

We rode all day only stopping for gas and stretching our legs a little, or getting a cold drink at the station. It was a cold day and the past few miles it was misty. Not much to see on the sides of the road, everything had been harvested. The land was barren and ready for the winter.

We pulled into Kansas City around supper time and we had a hot meal. "On the house, Uncle Sam's paying," came out loud and clear from Sergeant Jones.

The bus driver Watson signed off but stayed and ate with us, still talking a mile a minute to Jones.

A new driver was waiting to take over. She was an older heavy set woman, grey haired and very staunch looking. She had a blouse and skirt uniform with black shoes, and her hair was up in a bun. She carried a big shopping bag. It looked like her time was spent knitting things. We were all introduced to Martha, no last name, just Martha. She had few words to say and just wanted us to finish eating and get back on the bus. Officer Jones waited for the new recruits and did the paper work, and seven more recruits came on board. He called all the names as we climbed on board and two guys were missing. Someone named Brian, and another one named Lester. Martha started calling them with no answer. She called them several more times and no answer. Her voice got louder. This probably happened before. Martha, Jones, and Watson took off looking for them.

Joey and I just sat in the bus wondering what happened. One of the guys in the back of the bus joked about maybe they were having a cigarette or something. We heard a lot of yelling but couldn't see anything. Coming around the corner of the building was Martha with our two run-a-ways being held by the nape of their necks marching back to the bus. She took no mercy on them. When she got them back to the bus she let them have it. "Don't ever try that again on my watch, you won't live to tell about it. Be glad I found you. You could be on your way to Leavenworth. That was not a smart move. Now sit down." They ran to their seats.

Watson took off for the diner and Sergeant Jones and Martha stood outside the bus. "So Martha does this remind you of anyone, these two runaways?"

"Yes Sergeant, my own two boys some years ago. They didn't want to go in the Service either. We managed to get them to Texas. Today they are both officers in the Army. One is here in the States and the other one is in Europe. My husband and I can't wait for them to both be back with us again."

They climbed back on the bus and no one made a peep for a long while. I heard a voice from the back, "Don't mess with Martha."

It was dark now so most of us slept. We were going to Wichita, Kansas this time. There was a sign up over the driver that would change destinations when the drivers changed. You could hear the wind outside. It was cold and the bus was swaying side to side. Martha had a heavy foot and she wasted no time getting us to our destination. We made a few stops for gas and something to eat. Some got out and some slept all the way.

The next day we arrived in Wichita around noon. There were eight more recruits and a new driver waiting. Sergeant Jones did the paper work on the new guys and introduced us to the new driver. This was beginning to be the highlight of the trip. His name was Joe. He looked to be in his late fifties. Maybe he was a retired truck driver but he was in uniform, and glad to see Officer Jones. He was a happy man and loved to tell us stories about his driving experiences. He drove slower than Martha and he loved to blow the horn. He knew all the drivers on the roads and I'm sure they all knew him.

Our next stop was going to be Oklahoma City, Oklahoma.

This bus was not comfortable and bouncing around all day got old fast. When we stopped for gas everyone got out just to stretch. At one stop Joe got us all a candy bar. He must have been related to the owner. He continued his stories as he drove, and that seemed to pass the time and it gave us a few laughs. One of the guys on the bus got sick a few times. Joe brought him up front and told him to look out the window. That seemed to help him. I think he just couldn't hear Joe's stories down back.

We came into Oklahoma City late at night. When we arrived at the station there were six more recruits waiting with a new driver. His name was Matt and he was from Texas. He was a military man, driving busses after retiring early. His family lived here with him. He was in uniform and about five feet eleven. I thought that was quite tall for a bus driver. He just put the seat back like a rocking chair and settled in. Jones did the paper work and we were off, after saying goodbye to Joe.

Matt told us we were on our final destination to Wichita Falls, Sheppard Field, Texas. We were all sore and tired. Again we drove all night and half way through the next day. It was sunny and cold when we finally got out of the bus to stretch and have something to eat. Sheppard Field was about two miles from where we were. After getting some gas we climbed on the bus for the last time. There was some cheering and clapping going on as we moved things around on the bus. We had about twenty-nine recruits now. Everyone had clothes and food wrappers and bottles all around inside the bus. Orders came from Sergeant Jones, "Clean up," just the thought of getting out of this bus was enough incentive for me.

We pulled into the base and unloaded. Basic training would begin at Sheppard's Field, Texas.

Boot Camp . . .

The young men going off to the war were often an accident of birth, with the opportunity to serve their country or not. The government was calling.

Some believed their country needed them and some just answered the call of their country in need.

Some just wanted to prove their manhood, carry a gun or fly a plane.

They fought for their cause and their destiny.

Brainwashing was part of the Army, Air Corps., and Marines. New ideas were set in place to be followed, and you were built up to be a solid soldier.

This was a learning process with one important fact: There is no 'I' in the word team.

Basic Training gets started . . .

Not having been around an Army Base, Basic Training was all new to me. We soon found out our Sergeant was our lord and master.

We were sent for haircuts along with the other guys. We got "real baldies," they made your ears cold and winter was on its way.

They issued us our clothes consisting of underwear, socks, pants and shirts, jackets and hats, and two new pair of boots.

We were sent to the barracks to find our bunks. The pillow and sheets were piled on the bed. We had a foot locker at the bottom of the bed, and a closet off to the side with locks.

We started putting our things away and making our beds when we heard a loud whistle. There was a lot of yelling going on outside. Joey and I wasted no time getting out the door. Our Staff Sergeant in charge was yelling at one of the new recruits about something. I missed the reason for all the yelling and excitement.

We all lined up as he called off our names checking us out and making some comments along the way. He had a mean way about him. He proceeded to tell us what was expected of us. Soon some of us found out he wasn't just talking. Before they knew it, some were doing fifty push-ups. They had never done push-ups so five would have been enough. If you laughed you were next.

Basic training did intentionally break you down to get your full attention. Then they would build you back up the way they wanted you to be. Some of the men had some baggage that needed to be left at the door. The first couple of weeks of Basic Training were very hard for some men to go through. From the first day we had drills, exercises, and commands, day and night. No time for us to think, that was the Sergeant's job. We were never alone. There were drills and duty, day and night until we couldn't stay awake. Rainy and cold weather was what we had most of the time. No liberty for at least a month. We had twenty mile runs, exercises, marching, drills, running up and down stairs, running hills in the mud and this was pretty much our routine. At night if you didn't have duty, most of us just hit the showers and hit the bunks wiped out. Now if you thought you could buck the system, you learned the consequences. More guard duty nights, kitchen patrol, and your name was on a list to be called for anything needed. One of the recruits named Eric seemed to fall into that category early on.

We learned to take care of our uniforms, polish our boots, keep the barracks spotless and ready for inspection at any time, and make the perfect bed. "Bounce that quarter" was the word.

My boots were killers. It took me two weeks of walking, running in the mud, climbing hills, marching and guard duty, to finally get my feet to feel some relief. I still don't know if I broke the boots in, or my feet just gave in. Maybe I just stopped complaining about the pain.

We were learning to become a group. We were set up to be team mates. All kinds of personalities came out. Some guys found it hard to get along with others. Racial problems occurred and some wanted to fight about everything. I did notice the Army enforced rigid racial segregation; the black soldiers were all trained by white officers.

Schooling was hard and every minute we could find, we hit the books. We were so physically tired that a lot of us fell asleep reading at night.

Time passed quickly because there was a war going on. Some of the basic training was geared to specialized skills. You learned the basics, morale, educational programs, maintaining your health, and learning why you were in the war. Most of this was done with films. Loyalty was a very important part of training.

By the end of the eight weeks you had a pretty good idea who was in charge. When someone told you to do something, you did it. That was the foundation of the Army and it worked.

When we finally got our first leave it was straight to a local bar and restaurant for something to eat. We played cards and danced with the locals. We had some time to think.

This was probably our first time to think about our girls back home. Our letters were coming in faithfully but we had very little time to write back. They probably wondered what happened to us. We had promised to write every day.

I had become a group leader mostly because I took control. I had my own way of doing things and I saved time by planning ahead. The group quickly learned that Joey and I were a team not to be reckoned with, we were teased about being the Greenfield Boys. Yes we were farmers, but we survived the basic training. It was physically and mentally exhausting but we made it through without any trouble.

Chapter 11

Pre-flight Training San Antonia, Texas

Our next stop was off to Pre-Flight training at San Antonia, Texas. This was Air Cadet Training school.

We thought the weather would be better but it wasn't. It was still rainy and cold most of the time, just miserable.

This training was all about learning the rules and regulations of being a pilot. You were tested for your eyesight and your hearing. You were checked for vertigo and your level of control under stress. They were looking for any type of problem you might have under stress and how you would handle it. We used a T-6 trainer plane. Joey told me later that he didn't like sounds he couldn't figure out. This happened to him in Greenfield one day while flying. He heard a strange noise on the right side of the plane and when he looked over he couldn't see anything. He knew it wasn't a normal sound but everything looked okay at the time. When he got back on the ground he went outside and looked to see what had made that noise. Someone had left a tie-down rope hanging off the side of the wing and it was flapping in the wind. He wanted no more surprises.

For myself the more they tested me the happier I was. I loved being in the air and being challenged. These planes could sing like a bird. They floated through the air and there was no challenge getting them up or down. I couldn't wait for practice time, especially when I had a pilot that let me run things from the front. Joey and I sat in the trainer plane and took charge of the planes right away.

I don't know about the rest of the guys, but I couldn't wait to get up in the air and fly this plane. I felt power and I know I was good. I hit the targets head on every time. I could dive and catch the wind like an eagle.

I wasn't that dumb little kid I was when I was young. I was smart, Mom was right, and people followed me and wanted me in charge. I liked that feeling. I realized that I really liked flying up here in the sky. I had control and I loved the feeling of power and I knew this plane inside and out. I don't think I'm as sure of anything else in my life as I am, of flying a plane. It's me and my plane.

In my life I have had a hard time committing. I know I do love my Dad, but I don't know if I show him enough. I try to be the person he wants me to be. I know I have strong feelings for Ashley, but I have held back trying to not promise something I can't give her right now. I watch Joey and his girl and I can't let anyone hang all over me like she does. It doesn't feel right to me. When I was young my Mom loved me and my Dad loved me before Mom died. Then my life changed. Bringing myself to care and feel for another person has taken me a while and my reactions are slowly changing, I hope.

In the air I am free and I'm alone to think and try to figure things out. I feel like that giant eagle I would see flying over the barn when I was little, catching the wind and sailing off across the sky. What a beautiful sight. Wow I think I better have the oxygen level checked in this plane when I get down. I seem to be daydreaming more than usual, today.

We kept our grades up. School was getting harder and some cadets needed help. I found myself teaching some of the book work at night while I studied. We lost a few guys we started with because they just couldn't keep up. It was a lot of hours. It seemed like they were rushing us to get through this phase. We were always aware that they needed pilots as soon as possible. That was our real challenge.

They still made sure you knew your place. No one came to class late, you could be grounded. Failing grades were tolerated for only so long. There was no fighting with any member of your squad, for any reason. Always show respect to your Officer and that was a big one. If you were grounded for that fault it was pretty much good-bye to you.

We were sectioned off into smaller units for training purposes after a few weeks as a result of the war. There were shortages with the weapons and equipment. We had a lot of educational programs shown on films the government supplied us with. We all studied hard and it was difficult for some to keep up. Joey and I plugged along and helped as many guys as we could. Our barracks were very quiet at night. We all had put some time into this endeavor and now we wanted to get our wings.

Primary Flying School . . . Ballinger, Texas

Our next stop was off to Ballinger, Texas for Primary flying school. This would be 'in the air' training at the Air Training Command at South West. We were now Air Corps Cadets.

We got new uniforms and more pay, and a chance to fly in some of the newer trainer planes we had been studying. Our daily sessions were split up between studying in class and flying. This was a five day routine. The studying was grueling. A lot to learn in a short amount of time and we had to be the best.

Flying was different. A few of us had some experience flying but not this kind of flying. We were into rolls, loops, spins, and flying in rotation with others. I loved being up in a plane, flying and rolling, dipping and diving, show me more. But I quickly learned to stick to business. The fun part was over and you were training for the war. You had a responsibility to learn how to protect the plane and yourself in any emergency. You better know what and where everything was and what it was there for. Some had a hard time with oxygen levels, power-off training, and forced landings. Joey and I had no trouble with that. We learned all kinds of stuff with my Dad's friend in Greenfield. Many times when we were young we got out of the plane a little green.

We did get some time off on weekends. Joey and I, along with a few other guys, would go to the local bar for a few drinks. To my surprise Joey had become a great little story teller for the guys we hung out with. Joey could be found in the corner at a table telling stories about his life in New York, his family, and his farm life. He could really tell a tale and he was funny and believable. I figured out he also loved the attention. I would play some pool for a while leaving him to his tales, and then I would work my way over to listen for a while. He would always start telling the story of how we met when I showed up. I was more a private person with my life. I had some things I would rather keep to myself. I guess I planned to deal with things in my life by myself.

Our squadron came from different parts of the country, but Joey and I were the only 'farm boys' as they called us.

But to our credit we ranked the highest in the class, on the ground and in the air. No one had any doubt that the best pilots were in this squad.

We always left the bars together and had some good laughs on the way back to the barracks.

Our family life back home was almost non-existent. Sundays we wrote home trying to remember what was going on there. My housekeeper Janice sent some cookies to us a few times. They went fast. My Dad opened up a new office but didn't say where. He sent some pictures of him and the girls, Ashley and Lette Mae, having dinner with him and his new friend. Joey's mom and dad sent a picture of a new colt that Joey's horse had delivered. They named it 'Fly-Boy' hoping he would be pleased. Our girlfriends wrote often. Both of them were working and going to school. Weekends they volunteered at the community center sending out packages to the soldiers overseas. Joey told me that one day he was going to write Lette Mae and tell her how many times he threw up in the plane last week, but he didn't. We couldn't write about what we were really doing. Between swimming, diving, dropping from high places, some of us afraid of water, some were afraid of heights, we had a lot of mental and physical conquests going on inside of us. We knew some of us would not make it through, but we were determined to make it to Pilots School. We were a team trying to help each other as much as possible. Promotions came in, we were now 2nd Lieutenant.

Chapter 12

Phase Two—Basic Training

Our next training program was phase two—air basic training. This was very different. This was about how to handle your plane. A lot of landings and take-offs, mixed with moves we never even thought about before. Sometimes I wondered if the plane could do these things but it always did. We were teamed up the first few times up in the air, with other pilots. Not many of our squad needed help for long.

The tests were harder. The maneuvers were very difficult for some of the guys and they began to drop out. Flying was always on my mind, and you always had a book in your hands. The conversation was always about the last flight you had, or something your squad leader was trying to explain you didn't get. Not much time was spent in the bar. Joey and I and several others just sat and studied our books.

Final Phase Air Training . . .

We went into our final phase of training with a ten week concentrated flying course. It was mental and physical strain every day.

Some of the maneuverings were scary the first time you did it by yourself. You did it. This is what you were all about now. How you performed under pressure was important. What you remembered, and how fast you could react was tested every day.

I was learning how to react and think about it later. I guess I had a good handle on things. I was still in charge of the squad and it was their choosing.

Some of the runways were bumpy. Take offs and landings were difficult and the rain didn't help, or the wind. We had our share of bad landings with a few burned out tires and some wing damage. We had a crew that worked day and night to keep the planes flying. We were not issued any new planes, they were needed overseas. So we made do with what we had to practice with.

Schooling was hard. We spent all our time in our books for the next test or in our plane, being tested. There was no free time. We did get letters regularly, but had no time to write.

The course got harder and we lost some of the guys we tried so hard to keep with us.

Ten weeks later Joey and I made it through phase two, the final phase of flying school. We were the two top pilots of the squad. Promotions came through, we were now 1st Lieutenants.

Chapter 13

Graduation

Our graduation was in Victoria, Texas, where we got our wings and it was a great day. Phil and Tom and Judy, Lette Mae and Ashley were all there for the graduation. There was another person with them I didn't know.

It was held outside in a large field with bleaches on both sides of the field. They had a big Army Band playing all the way through the ceremony that made things go so smooth. This is what we were working for since we started.

As our names were called out we passed by the officers and received our salute and our wings. I was so happy to see so many of our group had made it to the end. Back in our seats we were like kids with a new toy. We couldn't look at the wings enough that day. And the bonus was the family was here to enjoy it with us.

We only had a few hours to spend with our families. We were going to be shipped out the next morning for combat flight training. The scuttle butt was we were going to Florida.

After graduation Dad gave me a real nice watch and a picture for my wallet. It was him and my Mom. These two gifts meant a lot to me and my Dad knew it.

Marion . . .

Joey and I were introduced to a woman named Marion Ludlow. We took her to be a friend of my Dad's.

We took pictures and headed for the car. Dad asked me to ride with him and Marion. The others went together to the small restaurant my Dad had reserved for dinner.

Dad proceeded to tell me all about Marion and how they met.

While I was away in the Army, Dad was very busy with his life. He had set up projects for organizations to work on, such as building some new schools and a bigger hospital in the city. It seemed like he was always working late into the night and had no home life. He said he missed me more than he thought he could.

"So one night after a meeting with some of the men from city hall I stopped by a small bar I once visited a long time ago. I went in and had a beer. There were a few people at the bar but one very pretty woman stood out near the end of the counter. She slowly made her way over to the seat next to me."

Marion smiled as he went on.

"She asked if the seat was taken and that started a relaxing conversation between us. She said her name was Marion Ludlow and she worked on the finance committee at Mercy Hospital. We talked about our lives and what we were doing out this time of night. We moved to a small table and had another drink. After exchanging numbers we agreed to see each other again. Maybe it was time to have a new interest and someone to spend some time with."

"The following weekend I called Marion and we had dinner and went to see *'White Christmas'* at the theatre. This was the new movie of the year that everyone wanted to see. It was a perfect movie for the first date. We had a glass of wine at my home and that was the beginning of a great relationship."

Marion jumped in, "As always, he was the perfect gentleman, picking me up in his newly polished car, with shiny hubcaps. I thought he was the nicest man I had met in a long time. I took him for mid forties, very good looking, tall, still worked out, wore the best clothes, and was aging well with his slightly graying side burns. I thought he had a smile that could melt butter. He was a great talker and I love being around him."

Dad jumped back into the conversation. They were like two kids fighting for their own time.

"She was slim, medium height, wore a business suits, high heels, and carried a large pocketbook. She had light skin, crystal blue eyes, a wonderful smile, and sometimes a slight giggle. She's well educated, knows about life in the city and has her own apartment. She said she was married before and it didn't work out. She didn't want to talk about it and she had no children. All she did say was she was too young and was not ready for marriage. I think our relationship was mostly out of loneliness, but now we're an 'item' showing up at fund raisers and meetings together. We go flying together. We went to California with some friends to see the Golden Gate Bridge. We both wanted to see it. We spent the weekend, took some pictures, and enjoyed the ocean and the sea breezes. Janice likes her very much. They get along well."

This was a lot to take in. I was happy that my Dad was doing so well and he seemed very happy.

It was good to be with Dad again. I realized what he meant to me now and how lucky I was. I really liked him and when he put his arms around me I knew he missed me too.

I had some time to talk to Marion before we left for the base. She seemed to really like Dad. I told her I was happy she was there for him. She hugged me and said she was glad to meet me, and she loved Ashley. I guess my Dad had made the rounds with her. She knew about everyone.

Joey's parents had a lot to say to him about how much they missed him.

Ashley hung to my side not saying too much, only talking about what she was doing at home and in school. I think she just wanted to listen to me talk. Lette Mae talked all through the dinner until we had to get ready to leave. Then the tears started for both girls.

We took two cars back from the restaurant. Joey and his parent's along with Lette Mae went in one car, we all went in another. As we sat in the back seat alone for the first time, I realized just how much I missed Ashley. She had become someone of comfort to me, I felt good with her, and I was glad she came to the graduation. I had missed her during training but we had little time to write. I talked to her about how hard it was to not be able to write her about everything that was going on, but we were so limited for time, and so tired with all the studying.

Her question to me was, "do you still love me?"

I remembered how some of the guys said they got letters from their girls, who said they thought the guys were going out with other girls. I assured Ashley, I loved her very much, and I planned to marry her just as soon as the war ended. We hugged and kissed the rest of the way back to the base.

We were fortunate to have this time together to renew our feelings that had been kept intact by our officers. They really did try to get us to write home.

Back at the base we said our goodbyes to our family and girls. We were told by the officers to go and wait for the roster to come out. When our names came up we were scheduled to go to Dale Mabry Field in Tallahassee, Florida. We were both First Lieutenants now, fighter pilots in the United States Army Air Corps. We did it together.

This was one of the best days in my new life with my new family and friends.

Chapter 14

Dale Mabry Field, Florida

The next morning, we were put on a plane to Tallahassee, Florida, Dale Mabry Field, for Combat Training School.

This was a 200 acre air field that had once been a municipal airport. It was named after an Army Captain Dale Mabry, commanding the Army semi-rigid airship, Roma. This small grassy runway was built by the Public Works Administration (PWA) funds, all local people looking for work during the depression.

Dale Mabry Field was an after-thought put together for the needs of the Army. It was quickly paved making two runways with a single hangar over on the North West corner. The runways were 4000 feet and 2,500 feet, running north and south but looking from the air, they could be easily missed.

In 1938, Eastern Airlines began services to local cities and states.

As the airport developed during WWII, courses were offered in flight training, aerial photography, and charter services.

In 1940, military personal began constructing improvements to overcome the poor drainage conditions at the airport.

In 1940, the United States Army Air Force took over the control of the air field.

The U.S. Senator and State Governor influenced the Army to make Dale Mabry Field a United States Army Air Force airfield. Military personal started arriving in 1941. From this base, five of the largest fighting squadrons trained and were sent overseas for their missions.

We were told that the aircraft used for training at the base were all famous in their own right. They were the P-47 Thunderbolts, P-40 War hawks, P-39 Air cobra, and later the P-51 Mustangs. Also the B-26 Marauder and the Hellcats were seen there.

On the base the Chinese and the French cadets trained there too.

From Dale Mabry a gunnery base at Alligator Point and the bombing range at Sopchoppy on the Gulf of Mexico were used for training purposes.

This base compliment increased to 1,300 officers and 3,000 enlisted men and women. The base also had 800 civilian employees.

The base had a PX and a Prisoner of War compound that held 150 POWs. These people worked on the base.

For us the training was mostly air and ground targets, aerial gunnery, and formation flying, day and night. There were planes here we had only seen in pictures. There were planes everywhere. Not all were flying but the ground crews worked day and night to get them in the air.

On some of our flights we would go up as high as 14,000 feet. This was serious stuff to us. They were separating the men from the boys. We were using the AT-6 trainers.

Some flights early in the mornings were brutal. The fog was so deep you couldn't see the runways. You felt like you were flying blind.

We had become a commodity now. We were very much needed overseas as the war was sending home many wounded pilots. The amount of planes was dwindling. We learned about identifying targets, dropping color coded flares to get familiar with what could happen in turbulent weather and storms and heavy rain. We learned how to use special devices for bombings, how to use the radar, and learned how to distinguish rivers, coastlines, and commercial structures, from the air. Joey and I managed to work out a plan for the fog. It was an old farmer's trick. We showed our squad how to keep the windows clear. Some of our ideas went over big, some were a disaster.

Student pilots got debriefings. We spent most of our time training with the squadron. We were First Lieutenants and the pressure was on. And pressure we got. Flying brought on pressure in your muscles exerted by negative 'Gs'. When you flew at 14,000 feet, it could cause failure to your oxygen supply. This would make you goofy, disoriented, and a few other feelings. Some of the guys liked that feeling, but it had its consequences. We practiced spinning, flying in formations, lining up the target, and gun practice. We knew the Gulf of Mexico like the back of our hand. Over and over we practiced.

As the days and weeks went by some of our squad was sent to other fields for specific training.

Brian and Lester our goof offs, who tried to get off the bus their first day, got sent to Page Field, on the west coast in Fort Myers. This was another small base taken over by the United States Army Air Force for anti-submarine patrols and conventional bomber training in the B-24 Liberators. Brian and Lester trained there for some time before they were sent overseas on a mission. We heard from one of their friends that they were making 428 B-24s a month. The pilots slept on cots in the building, waiting for their plane to come off the assembly line. Then they flew them to England.

Another one from our squad Eric, we called him our KP man, was sent to Hendricks Field in Sebring, Florida. Hendricks Field started up in 1941, as a basic corps training center. They trained for engine pilot and crew training programs. This base was known for its good weather all year and the fact that it was named after a Florida native. Eric was from Florida so he felt at home.

John Martin one of the guys I helped out with his studies, was sent to Maxwell Air Force Base 42nd Air Base Wing. Maxwell in Alabama mostly trained pilots in combat support, and air educational and training command.

Joe Konnah, one of the guys Joey helped out went to Taylor Field, Ocala. These were all small bases but they were very busy shuffling the pilots around and getting them overseas as soon as they could. Some of the guys we lost track of but most of our squad stayed right here in Dale Mabry.

Joey and I were kept in a special squad with our own crew working on our planes. There were about nine of us.

In the mornings we were called into our make shift office and asked to be seated. We got our assignments for the day from our squad commander.

Today was a little different. We were going to be shipped overseas tomorrow and that was our assignment. We would be going to Boxted Airfield near Colchester, England. It was also known as Langham Airfield.

As I collected my mail before we left I found a small card with a picture inside. The card was a letter from Marion and a picture she had taken of me and my Dad at my graduation in Texas. Her note was personal and I could understand why my Dad felt so good around her. She made sure I had this picture to take with me to England.

That night I caught a glimpse of the ferrying pilot that had just come onto our base. She was a woman. She was going to take us overseas tomorrow. I went over and introduced myself and asked her how she became a pilot.

She said her name was Officer Theresa Walsh. She was twenty five years old and had attended college and was a teacher. She said, "Then I decided to go to Fort De Moines Officer's Candidate Training School. I read about women pilots. The Women's Auxiliary Army Corp (WAAC) started in 1942 and by September 12,000 enlistees for 150,000 positions were assigned to women. Some women trained at Lockbourne Ohio and became part of the Women's Air Force Service Pilots (WASP). Some of us became Ferry Pilots for the B-17s and the B-24s here and overseas. I have been ferrying for about twenty three months now, and couldn't think of anything more rewarding to do. I travel all over the states and sometimes overseas. Just the fact that I have an opportunity to fly during the War is amazing. This wouldn't have happened during peace time. Some of my friends were able to get jobs in map reading, customs and protocol, supplies, translation, radio operators and some folded parachutes. Women serve on land, in the air and on our hospital ships."

She said there were about 1,100 fliers in the WASP, and they had put about 60 million air miles testing bombers and transporting troops.

To look at her, she was small framed. She was dressed in her Santiago Blue dress uniform. A short skirt, white shirt and tie, belted blazer, beret and a black leather shoulder bag. She wore her WASP Wings, patches and lapel with pride. When she entered the area everyone looked in her direction.

When I commented on her uniform she said, "This is a far cry from what I wear flying. I have the Eisenhower jacket and general pants, or the zoot suit, and a baseball cap most of the time in the plane."

She was talkative and delightful to listen too. We had to cut our time short as she had to change and get some sleep. I gave her my address back home. I told her to look me up after the War was over.

"I'll take you up on that offer Lieutenant Stevens. I live close by. See you back home."

Early the next morning we were loaded on a B-24 Liberator, piloted by Officer Theresa Walsh, who ferried us up to Ft. Bragg, North Carolina. From there we went to Newfoundland, over to Ireland. From Ireland, we went to Lewiston England and on to Boxted, England. Stopping for gas and picking up more pilots we made it over in four days.

BOXTED AIR FIELD, ENGLAND...

Boxted Air Field, England

Chapter 15

Boxted Airfield, England

Boxted was located just outside Colchester England, in Essex County. Boxted was also known as Langham Airfield and was given USAAF designation Station 150[BX]. It was located three miles north of Colchester, and was built almost entirely in the village of Langham in Essex. It became an adjoining village and had been known to house the two most successful USAAF fighter groups in the air to air combat fighting; the Eighth Air Force and the Ninth Air Force, along with the RAF Fighter Command.

Colchester England had a lot of History behind it. It had old churches and a famous "Norman Keep", a great castle in Europe.

The English Channel was always an opening for the German air borne raiders, with their Luftwaffe.

The air base had its own Emergency Rescue Squadron with a code of '5F.' They used the P-47 Thunderbolts and they were modified to carry inflatable rafts, marker buoys and flares on their bomb racks. Their job was to locate pilots that had bailed out, drop a life raft, and inform the sea based rescue units (the pby-5s), where to pick up the fallen pilots.

The P-51s were sent to England to take down the Luftwaffe; they had the power.

Boxted Airfield was a Military airfield not fully useable until 1943. Some 350,000 Americans served on over 55 airbases in England.

The base was built for heavy bombers. The main runway was 2,000 yards long, and the two intersecting runways were 1,400 yards long. Lighting was installed, hangers were constructed and an old farmhouse was used as the administrative and headquarters building. Twenty nine hundred people could be accommodated, with temporary buildings around the field. The Eighth and Ninth Air Force, and the RAF Fighter Command were all based here from the beginning. The base stayed in use from 1943 until it closed in 1947 when the fighting was over.

Special training programs were set up, due to the increase in pilots and planes in use. The UAAF Training Command set up eighty courses lasting four weeks to forty-four weeks. These consisted of repairs, maintenance, engineering, equipment, weather and photography, to name a few.

The P-51 was the backbone to the 8th Air Force and did independent fighter sweeps and ground attack missions.

In 1943 the USAAF 8th Air Force arrived in England and started the massive daylight 'precision' bombing campaign that lasted until the war ended. The base was flying P-51 Mustangs that had a sufficient range to escort the B-17s and B-24s, all the way to the target and return. There were B-25 Mitchells, a medium bomber widely used, twin engine, 275 miles per hour; it had a range of 1350 miles. The planes we saw the most were the A-26s, 24s, and the 17s. They were used every day here.

One day out on the runway I saw something different. It was a Junker Ju 88G-1 plane that was taken by the British when it made an emergency landing. This plane was taken apart to learn how their SN-2 radar system worked. The Germans carried wing mounted antennae that could hone in on the British bombers.

Another time I saw a P-40 that was on its way back to the States. It belonged to one of the Flying Tigers and the plane had been used in training operations. This plane was used for intercepting raids on airfields, river crafts, and railroads. The P-40s were later replaced with the P-51-Ds. The crew loved talking about the 'nose art' designs on these planes. Some became famous.

WWII was a war of air power. Air power affected the tactics, strategy and logistics of the war. The war began and ended in the skies.

When WWII began the USAAC had 23,455 men, a few hundred planes and were the 6th in size, among the Air Force in the world.

Five years later the USAAF would have 2,372,292 men, nearly 80 thousand planes, and be the largest Air Force in the world.

So here we were . . .

We were assigned to our Officer's Quarters. That turned out to be a Quonset hut with a tin roof. I think you could see through the seams if you looked hard enough. A bunch of bunk beds, a few closets, and an old pot belly stove in the corner with a few chairs. That was it. At this point we settled in and slept.

I'd like to say we had some fun, me and Joey, but now it was all business.

The first thing you noticed coming out of your four star hotel quarters in the early morning was the weather. It was lousy, rainy, cold and balmy; we were told to get use to it. This was normal.

Meeting the men took all of five minutes. No ceremony, no uniforms or special salutes, just a bunch of guys with notebooks, talking over business and smoking up a storm. The room was another small building, with a few tables and fold up chairs, a pot belly stove for heat, and a large blackboard with plenty of chalk pieces. We were introduced as the new guys. We were Billy and Joey to the rest of the crew.

The rest of the day we spent getting our equipment, learning about the briefings, hearing about the missions going on as we spoke, and meeting our crew and some pilots. We got some warm jackets that Eisenhower sent over, that was the joke of the day, and warm uniforms and pilot calf-length boots. At least we were warm.

We met with the base crew and introduced our crew that came with us.

Our first flight was set for the next morning. We were taken to the airfield to look over our planes. We had P-51 Mustangs and they were beauties. By that I mean they had seen some missions, and been put back together on a wing and a prayer. There were about eight of us going up for the first time this morning. We got in and proceeded down the runway very carefully. The first run was called the 'milk run' to see how you reacted. The hardstand and parking lot for the planes were close to the sides; this must have been murder in the rain or fog. We moved slowly down the rather bumpy narrow runway. Other pilots went up with us newbies and they got a big kick out of this. The idea was to go around the base and try some of the different changes this plane had, that the Mustangs in Florida didn't have.

Missions were in groups of six. For every six trips you got a medal. You received one air medal for the first six; then you received an oak cluster on the ribbon, for each additional six.

The hardest promotions for an officer to receive were Captain, Colonel and Brigadier General. A promotion was put in for me and Joey to become Captains. This was happening along with other guys moving up in the ranks.

A combat mission was four squadrons of nine planes, totaling thirty-six aircraft. Missions were a specific target area, timing and weather was important for the delivery.

The lead pilot was always the best.

You went up about 10,000 feet and checked all your equipment, then the oxygen was put on. The heat in the uniforms came from an outlet tube in the plane, created by the engines. At 20,000 feet it was real cold at twenty degrees below zero sometimes. The uniform was heavy underwear, heavy socks, and wool pants and shirts. Leather jackets and over pants, heavy lined boots and lined gloves, and lined helmets covering the ears, were very important. You couldn't move very well, but you were warm. It was also important to carry a gun, usually a colt .45 holstered over your shoulder.

The fighter pilot was different. Most of their time was spent in the air, on the ground, or going over their next moves. There was little time for anything else until they had some time off. To these men it was all about planes and its mechanics. The Merlin engine was always the topic of conversation. When the mission was scrubbed, the conversation was always about techniques and what could happen, and what almost happened. The pilots were always concerned about inverted spins and bailouts.

The pilot's crew was all specialists in their own field. Bombs, machine guns, radio communicators (for combat and weather), parachute riggers, fuel service, oxygen system and mechanics were all important to the welfare of the plane. The pilot and crew were like family.

General Arnold set plans for two crews for each bomber. This made the men feel confident they might make their twenty five missions. Getting good pilots was not happening and operational losses were high.

So we lifted off the ground and got into a solid formation about a thousand feet up. We had leaders, but we had a very bad radio system directing us. To me this plane was running fine. It was real noisy, but because the radio was so bad, I couldn't put anything in my ears to stop the noise. The one big complaint with the pilots was the loss of hearing from the loud engines and the guns.

We circled the base a few times, taking off and landing for about ten minutes and then we got to fire our guns. We used a special bullet for target practice. It had paint that would leave a mark on the target so you could tell if you hit it. Ammunition was scarce for practice. We spent about an hour flying and landing, and some target practice. Then we came down and gathered at the make-shift hanger headquarters.

The squadron leader Colonel Jamerson had some questions for us and we spent about an hour acquainting ourselves with the way things were done here at Boxted, under the 8th Air Force. We read maps and had missions explained to us that were going on right now.

Colonel Jamerson had the missions for tomorrow already posted on the board. We were given a chance to ask any questions concerning anything. The weather for the next day was important and the formation order was talked over. We were part of a well organized squadron and these planes got the work done.

Our job was to escort the bombers to their destination, and return them back to the base when their work was done.

Our P-51 Mustangs were considered the best. We had Rolls Royce Merlin engines cooled by air intake from under the nose. Some had the aerodynamic bubble canopy for more visibility. We had a Browning machine gun and an 85 gallon fuel tank in the rear. We could go 441 mph and had 1,695 hp. Planes had only been invented for a short period of time and these planes were being pumped out in mass production as fast as possible.

We were released and sent back to our 'four star hotel' to prepare for our first mission tomorrow. We were ready, willing and oh so able, we all thought.

I sat with Joey for a while and we both felt a little anxiety. We talked about our home life and wondered what everyone was doing at home tonight. We didn't say a lot, but we did talk about how we became 'best friends' at school, and how we ended up here tonight. We made a toast to *The Greenfield Boys* and went to bed.

My head was full of ideas for tomorrow. I knew some were just dreams of what might happen. I was going on twenty-one very soon. My life seemed planned out for the next few years.

Chapter 16

Mission #1

We awoke to the sound of the radio. It was that crazy station that could drive you nuts if you believed anything they said. The radio broadcasts were an attempt to discourage the American and British troops. Lord Haw Haw was a term used to describe several of the English speaking German broadcasters. They reported shootings of the allied aircraft, and the sinking of ships; trying to discourage the Americans with reports of losses and causalities among the troops. It was known as Nazi propaganda, but the men listened to hear what might have happened to their friends and relatives, who did not return from the bombing raids. It was considered infuriating, inaccurate, and very much exaggerated, but the men still listened. At our location, Lord Haw Haw came in the best.

[These broadcasts started in 1939 and continued thru 1945, when Hamburg was overrun by the British Army.]

We all got dressed and took our gear and headed out to our planes.

The first thing we noticed was the heavy fog. You couldn't see 50 feet in front of you. I looked at Joey; he looked back at me and laughed. "I guess we'll have to use our 'farmer's secret' to get off the ground today," Joey commented. The rest of the guys just laughed and made some remarks.

We checked out our planes. Nine planes geared up for takeoff but one had a bad blow out just making the end of the runway. This was unusually bad because it was so foggy. We all shifted around him and managed to get up speed for liftoff. I was third up and Joey was fifth. Between us was Frank Johnson from Ft. Topola, Alabama. He was older than most of us by about ten years. He had three kills painted on his plane. He was a very experienced pilot.

The runway was almost impossible to see. Takeoff was slow and like driving blind. It was bumpy and wet all the way down. We started climbing; slowly at first about nine feet a minute with air speed about 210 mph. We leveled off about ten thousand feet feeling some bad headwinds. Our formation was set and we knew more than likely the wind was going to double our flying time.

The idea was to get this group to their destination with the least amount of flak hitting our planes. It involved going north toward the North Sea; make a half circle route after crossing out of Germany, over the North Sea, along the Friesen Islands, across the channel to England, and back to the home base.

The higher up we ascended, the clearer it became. I could see my lead pilot and some of the others following behind.

The oxygen was on and the lights were flashing on the board in front of me.

The radio was squawking and not even understandable, just a raspy noise.

In my mind I knew what was about to happen, but I got all sweaty and anxious anticipating the next move. Out of control was not my forte. Waiting in the quiet sky could do a number on you.

About half an hour into our flight things started happening. Out of nowhere the blasting started coming up before us. Loud, black billowy clouds, with a thunder like the fourth of July started going off all around us. I grabbed the stick and leaned forward. Looking to my left side I saw one of our fighters get hit near the side of the wing with a big ball of fire. That's just what it looked like to me. The plane was jolted out of position and started to decline. I was so taken by the sight of the fireball hitting the plane, I didn't realize how close I was, and more large explosions were going off all around me. I felt my plane shaking and heard some metal cracking and making noises. The glass cracked on the side window but it didn't fall in. As I looked forward, the thick black, heavy smoke was clearing. We made our way through the pounding noise and it got quiet again, too quiet.

I strained to see what was in front of me.

About a minute or two passed then I saw my first image of war.

Five planes were heading right for us. My stomach did a flip flop. We lined up as we were trained. Our guns started firing in all directions. Some of us were getting hits, and some were getting hit on. No time to look around, I got my sites on my target. I circled the plane and I could actually see the pilot inside. I took aim and fired my guns.

That plane exploded right in front of me. Pieces were flying everywhere. I must have hit the gas tank. Flames were shooting out and falling. It went down like a million pieces of trash and flaming splinters.

All I could do was think, what the hell have I got here? Then I realized I was still shooting. I quickly stopped and flew through what was left of my target, and circled around to see what else needed to be done.

I knew I only saw five coming at us so I did a right turn to see how our squadron was doing. There was one battle going on to the left, two of our planes had that one. The other guys were okay. We formed up and I could see one plane under us.

I signaled I was going after this one and I was off. I chased him and was about three hundred feet above him, and then I dropped with my guns shooting. I could see him and he could see me. I shot the right side of his plane, and I could see the flames starting, just as he did a quick turn and got my left wing about a foot and a half down the side.

A quick look and I knew he was done, he was going down trailing. I must have hit the gas tank.

I had my own problems now. I was away from the squadron. I saw more damage to the left side and my gas was running low. I know I was hit, I was losing altitude. I looked to see where I could land safely.

Just then I heard more shots. It was over me. Someone was firing at a plane that had me in their sites.

Still losing altitude I was not in real control. It was one of our guys shooting at the enemy who had lodged himself between me and the other plane above. He shot him and the enemy went down right in front of me, just missing me by inches. I think that was his plan to take me down with him.

All I could think was thank you Jesus and whoever you are in that plane.

I tried to use my radio hoping the element leader would hear my May Day call coming in, but these things rarely worked when you needed them. I was dropping fast.

I headed for the base. I knew I wouldn't make it but I wanted to get the plane out of harm's way. I was really losing altitude and I was losing control and feeling dizzy. Coming down I could see a field, it was not by choice and I landed hard. I slid in and rolled into a muddy patch of a flooded field, upside down. I had no time for a parachute or anything else. My thoughts were, did anyone see me, did that dumb radio work and was this the end?

After the plane flipped over it started filling up with muddy grass and sludge. I took out my knife and started cutting my way out of the seat and climbed out of the upside down plane. My boots got caught up in the weeds getting out. I let them slide off and I continued to get out and away from the plane. I hated those boots anyways. I rested on a small clump of rocks and sticks about twenty feet from the plane. I must have fallen asleep.

When I opened my eyes my boots were hanging together by their shoelaces, over my head.

"You might need these," as he threw me my boots. "Are you going to sleep all day Farm Boy?"

It was Joey. I was so glad to see him. He had come back for me and landed right next to my plane, except not in the mud. He tried to lift me. That's when I noticed I had blood on my jacket. I was bleeding through all my clothes. Joey pulled off the jacket and the shirts, and reached down to see where the blood was coming from. I had a bullet wound on my left shoulder. I got so excited I didn't even know that it happened until now.

He lifted me up and helped me to his plane. He was determined to get me in that plane, or he was going to tie me to his wing.

We managed to lift off. It was a pretty bad field with wet mud and all. We trained in fields back home like this so no problem. We flew high above any problem areas on our way back to the base.

I was still dizzy and I had lost some blood. I was so grateful Joey came back for me. He said he saw the firing going on but he thought my plane was alright. When the guys formed up after the fighting, he could see I was missing. He signaled to the crew and off he went to find me. He said he retrieved my papers and stuff in my plane, before he woke me.

This was our first mission. We would probably get the 'you know what' kicked out of us when we got back.

I felt very disappointed making my way back stuffed in Joey's plane, covered in mud and wounded. What a bummer!

Back at the base, our ground crew was waiting to see how many planes came back and in what condition. All eyes were in the sky as they waited.

Five came in. Still waiting, one of the guys said Joey was going back for me.

Ten minutes later number six came in.

We landed and the crew came running over to see what happened. To their surprise, I was wedged half in the front and half, who knows where my body was stuffed. I couldn't move.

"It's the Greenfield Boys," came through loud and clear, as the guys cheering and hollering came running to get me out of the plane. Helping me out was difficult. They tried to get me to my feet, as I passed out on the ground in front of them.

The next morning I woke up in the make-shift hospital all bandaged up, groggy, and still a little muddy. I slowly got up. This time there were no pretty nurses to take care of me. I got dressed and found my way outside. It was quiet. I headed for the hanger headquarters not knowing what to expect.

As I walked in the door, the crew started clapping and cheering.

I stepped back a little looking bewildered, what did I do?

Our squad leader Colonel Jamerson came down to me and brought me up front to the head table. He proceeded to go on about my superb flying maneuvers. He told me I displayed determination and good flying techniques, on my first mission. I had downed two Me-109s.

I thought my hearing was going bad. I thought I had broken the line, got shot, and downed my own plane. How could that be good? When he got done with me, he started on Joey. He got accolades for bringing me home safely. What was going on?

We found out later that the first mission with new guys is usually a disaster. They run scared. They panic and then they go into shock when they're hit.

We were applauded for taking control of the situation, using our own judgment, and getting the job done safely. With only one casualty, the bombers got through, did their job and came back home.

Joey told me some of our guys came back not in such good shape. Some threw up when they got out of their planes. Some had the jitters real bad. Some went for a drink and some ran like they were never going to come back to their plane again. Combat fighting was work, always looking out for the enemy behind you, to the side, or coming straight at you. Worrying about the guns jamming up when you needed them the most, running out of fuel, or facing the enemy during combat was stressful. You had to watch the plunge to death of the planes around you; some were enemies, and some your own. They looked like a shooting star going straight to their death.

No pilot talked of this when they got back but it was on everyone's mind after a mission. We all found our own way of dealing with it.

I had missed the de-briefings of the next few days. They took me off the roster for ten days so my shoulder could heal. I had to take some pills for infection and I ran a fever a few days.

Most of the time, I sat around and wrote some much delayed letters home. I told them about Joey and his famous rescue.

A few days later I got another plane. I got a beauty, a P-51D. I couldn't wait to get back in the air again. This time I got some 'nose-art' done on it. I picked the name "FARM BOY" and Joey picked "THE STORY TELLER". We also asked them to put a big red circle under our window, so we could tell our two planes from the others up in the air.

Nose Art was practiced during WWII and all the guys who flew at this time enjoyed painting the sides of their planes. It was to ward off the evil; some protected you from death, and the bullets. They were used for good luck charms, talisman, some were girlfriends back home, and some were pin-ups from Hollywood. It was their plane. The best nose art according to the magazines from home, was painted on the USAAF, at least that's what they claimed. We had some pretty good stuff on our planes right here.

I found some time, while the planes were out on a mission, to talk to Colonel Jamerson about what happened to me. He listened, and then he told me about his first mission. Our stories were much alike. He started telling me about himself as I sat back and listened.

He said he had been in the service since 1940. He was considered a seasoned fighter pilot. He had all the qualifications of a good leader. Physically and mentally determined, ambitious and a good planner, I thought he made a fearless and very competent leader. He did have a slight hearing problem due to the noise in the planes while flying. He said he had come from the RCAF in May 1942, and had been in Boxted the longest of any of the pilots here. He had destroyed a Me-109, damaged two Fw 190s and downed four other enemy fighters. He had been wounded, decorated with the Distinguished Medal of Honor and was sent home. When things got rough over here in England he asked to come back. He was a man we all admired and we found ourselves lucky to have him as our Colonel.

Grounded . . .

The next few days I made myself comfortable at the air base while I healed.

Many of the crew that came over with us had things to do while we were flying. Not all of our crew were pilots.

Some days the runways were so bad, the guys had to go out and fill in the holes and ruts for the planes landing later that day.

I got acquainted with my friend first Lieutenant Marty Riley again. He had been busy since we got here and was now about to become a Captain. Marty ran the maintenance department and he owned the planes. Each one had a name and number. He had a crew of four very good mechanics we asked to have come over with us. After each flight his crew would go over every inch of our plane. It was procedure here.

Marty had heard the story Joey was telling at the club last night. By the time I got up and out of the hospital I was a hero. I had taken two Messerschmitt planes down and helped two guys set up a kill. I just flew by the seat of my pants and targeted the enemy.

Joey's fly down and pick me up wounded and all was nothing short of spectacular. I vaguely remember most of it. The adrenalin was raging in my blood. When I sat up to rest after climbing out of my badly damaged plane, I didn't even know I had been hit.

I missed his glorious fly-by, spotting me on the ground, a few feet from my plane. I missed his better than my landing on a muddy field, and his quick scurrying around to get the important papers and personal stuff of mine out of the plane. According to him I was just sleeping in the grass, slowly bleeding to death.

Joey could tell a good story. I loved him dearly and he knew I would have done the same for him if the tables were turned.

I spent some time in the Officers' Quarters. The walls and ceiling were covered with old newspapers of the events the guys wanted to remember. It had all the different types of planes and some famous pilots that flew here at this base. Of course we had the Hollywood Beauties on the walls too.

One wall had a quote in red letters reading:

> **Lord, hold them in thy mighty hand**
>
> **Above the ocean and the land**
>
> **Like wings of Eagles mounting high**
>
> **Along the pathways of the sky.**
>
> *Anonymous*

Most pilots would reach over as they passed this wall and give it the high-five as they passed by.

The guys would come here after spending hours in the skies, dog-fighting, having close calls, and seeing things they never talked about. It was a resting place with its semi-soft arm chairs you could put your head back and rest in. The black boards were full of clippings of the recent missions. There was always a card game or two going on, and a lottery running on the closest guess of the day the war would end.

Our group Commander John Nelson was introduced to me one morning. He was a tall strong man, with a chiseled out face, and deep black eyes. He had a sincere tight handshake and there was no question he was in charge. I heard from the guys that he had downed twelve aircraft, spent more than several hundred hours in the air, been wounded twice and now controlled the air base with an iron hand.

My story had reached Commander Nelsons' ears and he smiled when he met me.

One morning Marty and I went for a walk to look for one of the German Bombers that was downed behind one of our buildings. It had been checked over with a fine tooth comb. The plane was a Junkers 88. We had seen the stats on it. It had maximum speed of 280 mph and a range of 1,426 miles and it carried three machine guns and could carry approximately 5,000 lbs. of bombs. This was a plane we encountered often in our air space and if we could shoot them down on their base, we were golden. Marty had some stories about this plane and how it was captured. He took about an hour to tell me all about it. Later he took pictures of it for his album, and we went to dinner.

Chapter 17

Mission 2

My second mission you could say, I went up as a boy, and came down as a man.

My first mission was such a washout in my mind. I lost my plane, came home as baggage, and got wounded. I felt I had to do a lot better this time.

I started to realize that it was an ongoing struggle to kill or be killed. No other choices. It was my job now, to kill the enemy, protect our bombers, under extreme situations and unbelievable stress of the moment. This was what I was here to do. Then we were expected to come back to the base and pretend everything was okay in your head. I would do my job. Our squadron would get the bombers through to their target areas, and protected them all the way back to the base. Then wait for them to land. The bombers landed first. Sometimes they were so badly beaten up with parts hanging off the planes; they could barely make it down the runways. We would wait for the runways to clear then the fighter planes would come in.

My second flight started off fine. We got the planes over to the target area, but on the way back the enemy was waiting for us. At one point we faced the enemy head on. We were in a tight formation and we flew straight through them. In shock because they couldn't shoot at us, they would hit themselves if they tried, we went through them like a flash, and dove with our leader as fast as we could. Then the dog fights began. They were all over us like angry ants, when you stepped on their pile. Every plane was in combat. Our planes were faster than theirs. We were fighting Fw 190s and Me-109s. I brought down two Me-109s and helped fight off two other planes. I had been tailed for a few seconds but it felt like forever. I was scared. I did everything I was trained to do. I was able to dive out of the line of fire. As he followed me, he was picked off by one of my squad, who had seen me diving. My life flashed before me as I dove into the clouds, and down I went. I could hear the machine guns firing, my heart was pounding in my chest and doing flip-flops. I leveled off to find the formation, which had been splintering across the sky. Our flight leader began forming us up to see if there was any damage to our group. This was a rough one. I could count three planes missing from formation. We circled around and led the bombers back to the base.

Joey was on my left side sending me the okay signal. He told me later he was singing loud and clear. I told him I was glad I couldn't hear him, he is always off key. Besides, he only knows the words to two songs, Happy Birthday and Jingle Bells.

When I got out of the plane this time, I realized how close I had come to not returning. I felt so confident the first time. I only felt scared and alone out here on this cold desolate airfield. I started thinking about what I had back home and I wanted to return in one piece if I could.

I went to find my buddy. We talked through the night and he had a lot of the same feelings going on.

When we set off on a mission in formation, Joey was always on my right. That's the way we wanted it, we made a pact. I knew he was there and he knew I was on his left. With our planes painted with a spot on the side we could see each other in flight.

When Joey said lets go, I followed him down. I just figured he had better eyes than me, and when I said dive, he was with me. We made it through many of our flights that way. Sure we picked up flak and had holes in our planes but we always flew together. Mutt and Jeff, Frick and Frack, and even Laurel and Hardy, we took all the nicknames but we returned together. Sometimes the guys would follow us down and sometimes they didn't. We always got what we were after. We would use our whole nine yards of ammo. We racked up many German planes being hot dog pilots, and as a two-some.

We didn't kid ourselves because we knew at any given moment we could be shot down like anyone else. Each flight was a fifty-fifty deal of coming back or being shot down. That's why some of our crew started drinking. It was a way of managing to stay alive from month to month. We did begin to show the wear and tear on our body and mind. Nothing was real, you didn't even think too much anymore.

Our card games became more important to win. Letters were read over and over. We didn't always write back. After all, what could we write about that we did here? Sometimes a cigarette and cold beer over in the corner of a dark room, flopped in a stuffed chair was enough to get you through the night.

Joey was feeling the depression as much as I was. His story telling was the height of some nights with the guys in the rec hall. Other nights he would talk about marrying Lette Mae and having lots of kids when he got home. I would start thinking of Ashley and start to write a letter again. I hardly ever finished. I found myself wondering how she was doing. Her letters came in weekly and I would read them over and over. I could tell she was busy at home. She talked about everyone I knew and what they were all doing. She had about three part-time jobs going on; I guess that's how she wanted it. I just felt I had nothing to say to her that she would want to hear. Kill or be killed, smoke too much or not able to sleep at night, these were not things I wanted to put on paper to my girl.

Winter was definitely here . . .

Another particular mission we all had some rough times getting off the runway. We had heavy wet snow the day before, causing several accidents throughout the day. Early this morning we had another light dusting over freezing snow. The missions were not cancelled. Once in the air, the field was kept as best they could, and most days it snowed all day long.

Up in the air we set up for the target. This was a regular run so we knew where the flak would start. We also knew about where the fighters would pick us up. The fighting started and we had a clearing to work with. Head on they came. Twists and turns, rolls and dives, we plastered them full force. Right and left they were falling and smoke trailing their way through the sky. This went on for a long time and then the squadron leader made his dive. We all followed making our formation tight again in front of our bombers. We knew the flak was coming. We did our best to get through the noise and smoke and rattling of the plane as we lead the way.

We were out for almost six hours this day. Coming home with our bombers was a great relief to us all.

Landing was still hectic but we managed to all come in safe. The planes needed a lot of work. I'm sure the mechanics, working under Marty, were going to work all night long.

We had days when our leader's radio was not working. We had to fly in real bad weather, and we had heavy clouds and contrails at our bombing altitudes of 25 to 28,000 feet. This made formation almost impossible. Sometimes the flak bursts took out half the oxygen and sometimes electrical problems ruined our day. Drama at every turn gave the guys something to talk about when we landed safely late at night.

We had another special mission we were called in on. A special meeting was called early in the morning. We were all called in on this one. We were setting up for a combat mission with other squadrons to take out a place called Merseburg. Merseburg was one of the locations that had the most anti-aircraft defense and it had the largest synthetic oil plant in Germany. This was their principal source of oil for their war machinery. It was the roughest target in Europe and had to be taken out. We were called in on the raid. Most of the air bases knew this name and reputation. If taken out, this would put Hitler out of business. This target had been hit many times. Many pilots were shot down, killed in action, wounded and held prisoners when taken from the planes. There were about 400 anti-aircraft guns, much more than protecting Berlin. These were guarding the Merseburg refinery corridor and protecting the petroleum supply.

This was going to be a night hit. We were going to meet other groups at our designated spot. We were prepared and ready to hit the skies. Fully loaded, our planes took off for what could be a flight into history.

We met up with other planes and we had high formation and low. Then the fight was on. Some were in aerial combat and taking some hits. Already our P-51s were encountering head to head combat. It went like this off and on for over an hour. The German FW-190s were everywhere. The Fortresses took massive hits. Five or six fighters would slam our formation. We flew tight and tip to tip.

We were signaled to spread out. One German fighter passed inches from my left wing, then flashed down as four 20 mm tracers ripped past my windshield.

One B-17 in front of us coming out of the clouds had been hit by the second wave of Focke-Wulfs. It looked like three engines had been taken out. I could see at least six crewmen bailing out. It wasn't long before the plane caught fire and exploded, sending at least three men to a fiery death plunge. Pilots could see the iron crosses on the FWs cockpits, and see the faces of the Luftwaffe pilots, as they shot them down. Our planes, along with many others, were being plastered. As we got closer to the target, we were signaled to let the bomber planes go in together from here on in. I caught up with Joey. He looked fine. I gave him the sign I was okay and we lifted up to make our turn. I think about three other guys from our group followed us up. We leveled off and two more came in line with us. We had our route mapped out. We were out of the line of fire now. We dropped down to see if there were any unexpected surprises waiting. It was quiet.

Joey came on the line. "Billy, do you see the planes lined up down there, over there close to the oil tanks?"

I looked and didn't see anything. I answered back, "What are you seeing things?"

"No, can't you see them, just below us?"

Now I wondered. He said, "What do you have left for ammo?"

"I've got enough to get me home. Why?"

"Good," he said, "Follow me in and you'll see them when we get closer."

"Joey are you crazy, I see nothing!"

"Billy believe me, there's at least a dozen planes down there. Come on, follow me down."

"Are you sure Joey?"

"Yeah, follow me in. I called in the rest of the guys."

"But I don't see anything yet; take one more look Joey before we dive."

"Okay, okay. There just sitting there nice and pretty."

I heard the call from the other guys and they didn't see anything either. We circled around and made the plunge. Tip to tip, down we went. I felt like we were chasing moonbeams, but Joey saw something. Down we went. Oh my God! We came right in the middle of an air field, well camouflaged, and there they were. A loaded runway tucked away in covering, you would never see it from the air. Two large oil tanks, equipment and oil barrels, all lined up. This was too good to be true. We spread out, now that we could see them, and we spent every last bullet we had wiping out this place. One or two of the men still had some small bombs attached, everything else was used. We made two runs. The first run was unexpected. The second run they tried to shoot back, but once we hit the oil tanks and barrels, the place looked like Hell was burning. Flames and black smoke made it almost impossible to see what was left but it was wiped out. There were no sirens blowing and no lights on. Just flames reaching heights I'd never seen, and such thick, black smoke, in the now early morning light.

We left to go back and pick up with the bombers. Joey was on the speaker, "Well, what about what I saw, now?"

"Joey, I'm having you checked out when we get back. Are you okay, any damage?"

"Nope, I'm good, you?"

"I'm okay, let's get our bombers home. I hope they had a successful mission, I know we did."

One look at what was left of the bombers and we knew we had our work cut out for us. What a mess of rubble flying. This landing was going to be difficult. We could see tires blown off the planes, windows smashed, wires hanging, rudders shattered, and some guys faces were bleeding. My only thought was to get them home. Some of the guys left to go in first. Joey and I tried to keep talking to the ones that had been hit the hardest. We flew close to talk them in.

It was almost morning when we reached our base. With some exploding tires, a belly landing, many flak holes and twisted parts, we carefully landed the crew of beat up bombers. To some of them, Boxted probably never looked so good.

Later we learned about 153 B-17s were shot down or damaged so bad they would never fly again. November 1944 would definitely go down in history.

How Joey found this heavily concealed base was still the question.

A few days later we found out Joey was color blind! That's why he could see the planes and no one else could. That sparked a whole new line of stories for Joey to tell, and the guys really got on him with the nick names. "Spy Man" seemed to be the most popular. The guys even went as far as calling him when they lost something in the barracks. "Hey Spy Man, can you find my other boot?" Joey took the jokes and fooling around well. He never knew until that day in the air that he was color blind. To tell the truth, I really didn't believe there was anything below us when we made that drop. I made the choice and we all went down.

The squadron was awarded a special dinner the next night on the base. This story went all the way to the White House. When the dinner started and everyone was there, The Lieutenant came over to our table and thanked us for a job well done. News had come back to the base that the air base had been totaled. The best news was about the main target Merseburg, it was down. This was cause for a celebration, and we did celebrate.

Later that evening "Spy man" was painted on the tail of Joey's plane.

Chapter 18

The Game

Over and over we did these dangerous missions not knowing if we would return or not. I have to admit, they were starting to get to me. So many things could go wrong. I had dreams at night of planes coming directly at me and my gun jamming, or a fuel leak, there was no peace of mind. I guess that's why so many guys found solace in the bottle.

Joey had become very quiet the last few weeks. We talked about what was bothering him one night. He was having the same problems clearing his mind and sleeping at night as I was.

We began playing a game at the club house one night. Joey and I set up this awesome mission, just the two of us, and we were going to bomb all of Europe so we could go back home. Hitler was the tyrant and we would go after him with bombs and guns fully loaded on our P-51s. We had all kinds of ideas to blow up his bunker. Of course he would be in the bunker.

One night we even went as far as to set up our flight pattern and where the flak would hit us, with our route back home as successful war heroes.

We had lots of crazy ideas about painting the plane powder blue and white like the clouds, using the 'Window trick' which was bundles of tinfoil to mess up the radar, and putting a camera on the plane for our story telling later. We thought of everything. We played in our minds and relieved some tension. We got so into this game that some of the guys from the other tables came over to see what we were laughing about. Before we knew it everyone was throwing out ideas. We had a full fledge mission going on with half the guys involved. Plans were on the blackboard. Papers were being filled out as to what had to be done as far as preparing our two planes. This was going to be a special mission and we needed to empty some stuff out of our planes to make room for other stuff. How could we get some paint? That was no problem because we painted the planes all the time. What's a little more paint. How would we get the tinfoil, and how would we get it out of the plane? The Germans used a small chute in their planes; for our special mission, we could come up with something. One guy said, "Just throw it out the window, it's only a game!" Our planes could travel for eight hours at a time; we would take candy bars and drinks with us for our trip home. Nothing was going to happen to us, this was our game.

We went on like this for a few hours, this one night; everyone had a piece of the action, and some had great ideas. This night went by fast, and we all got things out of our heads, that had been eating away at us.

We parted late that night, leaving with good thoughts of blowing up Hitler and ending the war. We all slept well that night.

During the day some of the pilots would laugh and talk about the fun they had at night with their new game. A couple of nights later we tried that game again. On the blackboard we called the game Blowing up Hitler (BUH). The guys all had better ideas this time, like they really had been giving this mission some real thought. The table was full this night and the papers were flying in all directions. Some voices were getting a little loud and there was a lot of hand action, pretending to be the actual plane. Some guys thought this could really work. Why not? Every day the bunker was being bombed. Our ideas were as good as anyone's.

The next week to our surprise, there was paint and a bundle of tinfoil in the shed. These guys were going crazy. Even a route over and back to the bunker was put on paper. We played this game another night and we found this to be a lot of fun.

A few days later early in the morning, the Flight Commander called a meeting before he had breakfast. No one knew what it was all about. To our surprise, he had found the papers we had left all around the table from our war game. He wanted an explanation of what the mission was.

I stood up and told him it was a new game we invented called the BUH that we played at night. It would win the war for us. Everyone laughed and I sat down.

A day later, I was called to the office. Colonel Jamerson asked me to explain the game and all the papers he had in front of him on his desk. I proceeded to tell him how Joey and I started playing a game to get through the night. We were having a hard time dealing with the stress. This game opened up our minds and we got things off our chests. Everyone wanted to join in. We had some laughs.

He was glad to hear it was nothing serious, and asked me what time the game started?

I was dismissed.

Chapter 19

The Morale

The morale of the pilots on base was very important. Some would keep themselves busy playing cards. Some of the games could get quite loud and out of hand, depending on their feelings and the anxiety level of the day.

Many a radio was thrown across the room listening to the propaganda "Haw Haw out of Germany," when we could get it in our area.

Another morale booster was taking trips to Norwich, a small town not too far from the base. A bunch of the guys would load up a truck and drive to town on weekends for some fun. There were great bands and lots of dancing with the local girls in town. Norwich was famous for its 'Fish and Chips' wrapped in newspaper. That was the hit of the night. Having fish and chips, with a nice cold beer; that was a little piece of Heaven.

At these pubs we could also enjoy some of our own music from home that was sent over the airways, and became very popular in England. Music kept the guys going. *God Bless America* by Irving Berlin touched every American. It was easy to sing as Kate Smith's robust voice did bond rallies and a noontime radio show. Laverne, Patti and Maxine, the Andrews Sisters who sang *The Boogie Woogie Bugle Boy* and *Apple Blossom Time*, kept the men longing for their return home. The holiday spirits were kept alive by Gene Kelly singing *Long ago and Far Away*, and Irving Berlins *White Christmas*, introduced by Bing Crosby. Romantic lyrics became popular such as, '*I Don't Want to Walk Without You*', '*Always in My Heart*', *I Remember You,*' and '*You'd Be So Nice to Come Home To.*' They kept the sweethearts together, even though they were oceans apart. Music was a big part of the war effort to keep the Military morale high.

Painting the planes after a mission was a great morale booster. Keeping track of the planes you shot down was recorded each day at the de-briefing. There was a team that would mark the planes accordingly. You could decide what you wanted on the plane; a square, a circle, a dot or a bug, whatever you wanted, they did. This was your baby.

Another booster was our Chaplain. A lot of the guys would seek him out for some inner peace when things were going bad. The big problem was losing a friend in combat, and the second biggest problem was letters from home. Mail was always hard on the crew. Some guys really did get the 'Dear John' letters, and it tore them apart. The Chaplain had his work cut out for him. Some would hear of a brother or a father being killed in the war. Some had more than one member in the family, serving at the same time, maybe a different branch. It was possible to be bombing while your brother was on the ground patrolling. Your sister could be a nurse on a base that was bombed. One of your parents could pass away, or news could come in of a new baby born at home. Anything could happen while you were away. The Chaplains did their best.

I found myself talking to the Chaplain once in a while too. He gave me inner comfort. It was unexplainable but I felt like praying at times when things were rough. I never remember that feeling being so strong when I was little. I did go to church with my Mom. She always told me to pray to God when I needed help, and never ask for anything for myself, just try to help others. I tried to live by her ideals.

We had Captains and Majors and Colonels here at the base. Everyone earned their status by putting in hard work, long hours and the sheer luck, to still be here today. No one went around saluting. It was casual most of the time. First names worked. Of course if the Big Wigs came by on their way to somewhere else, we dressed the part and saluted. That happened rarely.

The medical front was also working hard to do their part in the war. They opened in tents with mud floors, and listened to the shells ringing in their ears as they worked. They worked whenever they were needed. They became the soldier's best friend. They sang to them and broke the bad news to them when they were going to lose an arm or leg. The medical staff moved when the troops moved.

The medical staff carried the supplies and transported the beds across the fields and over the rivers. They ate C-Rations. They were the doctors and nurses who walked away from the hospitals at home, and volunteered for duty in WWII. God Bless them all.

The Trip to New York City . . .

This wasn't known to us until later when we came home on leave. Our fathers were busy.

Phil and Tom took a trip to New York City one weekend hoping to find Joey's family. It didn't take too long to find a name like Joseph Somerset Wilding even in the city.

They found Joeys' mother Martha, and his two sisters, Mary and Anna, living in a rundown old apartment and just making ends meet.

Tom introduced himself and Phil, and proceeded to tell them he had adopted Joey when he came through Greenfield, Iowa on the train. He told them all about Joey and that he was in good health, and in the Air Force overseas. The sisters introduced themselves and you could tell they were all excited. They didn't even know if Joey was still alive.

Martha was in very poor health. She told Tom how she had once worked in a restaurant. There she could bring home some of the leftovers. Now she was not able to walk that far, so she took a job cleaning tables just across the street in a small café. This she could manage and she put in as many hours as her feet could handle.

Mary and Anna told Tom how they took the train to a manufacturing plant just outside the city. They worked as office cleaners and took their lunch every day. They were lucky to have this job. Mary managed to go to school at night. She wanted to get her high school diploma and get a good office job somewhere in the city. Anna did some babysitting at night across the hall. She worked very well with small children and got a lot of calls to take care of the neighbors' kids.

Mary studied, Anna babysat, and there wasn't much time or money for anything else. They took good care of their mother and you could tell they loved her very much.

Tom asked if it was at all possible they would consider coming to Greenfield and living with him and his wife, and of course Joey? He told them about his wife and her business, and that she could use some help. There were plenty of jobs and schools for the girls to look into. He would be delighted to help them. Joey would be coming home soon, and he would be so surprised to have them with him.

Martha had tears in her eyes through most of the conversation. You could tell she was very weak and unstable. Tom told her that he would put on an addition for them and set things up for the move.

The girls were all excited and fidgety, trying to control their feelings. Just the idea of seeing their younger brother again made them so happy.

The three of them looked at each other and decided to take the offer. Tom told them to give him about three months and he would come and get them. Meantime, he was going to write to Joey and tell him he had a surprise for him when he came home.

Phil said Joey would probably think you got him another horse, as he loved his horses. With that remark, the girls started laughing.

Before they left, Tom talked about Phil and how he had set up this visit and how his son Billy, was Joey's best friend. They were both fighter pilots over in England. Martha looked very pleased. You could tell she was getting tired, so they left. They planned to keep in touch until it was time to move.

Martha gave Tom some pictures she had of Joey when he was little, and a family picture she had taken before his father died. They exchanged hugs and kisses and Tom and Phil left.

Phil had some business of his own to take care of while in New York, so they both went to the Administration building and took care of the paper work involved. Phil had bought some land and wanted to set up an Aviation Training Center just outside Des Moines near Greenfield. This needed Military clearance and Phil had connections. What a great place for the boys to work and train other pilots when they came back home. Phil always had big ideas going on in his head. This would benefit the area and their boys.

Flying home they made a stop in Detroit at the Ford plant, to check out the new models for the year. Nothing was rolling off the line. War time planes were getting special preference right now, with tanks and trucks and Army jeeps. Phil took notes. He loved a new car every year. He'd have to wait.

Returning home the weary travelers had some stories to tell their mates over dinner and wine, at the Old Hotel in town. The pictures were set on the table. Everyone knew this was a great idea and it was going to be a great reunion for Joey.

Good news going back home to the families, mentioned that now Billy and Joey were Captains.

Back Home . . .

We got the papers from home when people could send them to us. We kept up with the news of our town. I did make a good friend at the newspaper office when I was young, and went to see him. He managed to somehow get us the news over here.

Back home the people were working hard to support the War in many different ways.

Greenfield was not a large city with factories and big businesses and manufacturing plants with hundreds of people. It remained a small town. The people worked together in small businesses and bonded together like a family.

The town saved rubber tires and rubber heels for the war efforts. They saved nylon stockings to make powder bags for navel guns, tin cans, bronze and steel, bacon grease for ammunition and waste paper for making packing cartons. It was like a big scavenger hunt to find things that could help out with the War.

The children got involved in school saving gum wrappers and tin foil from their candy. Shoes, baby toys and old carriages, and aluminum pots and pans could be brought into school to be used for armament. This would be picked up weekly and the children felt really important collecting whatever they could. The teacher would post their names on the blackboard. Sometimes this would cause conflicts if the neighbor took something from someone's yard.

The women had weekly gatherings at their houses and they would knit hats and gloves, warm socks and scarves for their family members away or overseas. They signed Christmas cards and sent them out to keep the spirits high.

Being a farm community most of the people bartered with their food, with small jobs and repairs to their homes or equipment. Some kids left school to work with their fathers to make ends meet.

The big Christmas tree was still put up in town and decorated with homemade tree ornaments, and Christmas Carols were sung around town. This was tradition and an important part of Greenfield and its people.

There was the constant fear of that telegram being delivered. A gold star would go in the window and all the shades would be pulled down, meaning the family had lost a family member. The War department telegrams sometimes would hit the same house more than once. No one was left alone in this small town. People came right over to rally and help the family to get back on their feet. The Preacher came in and made his visit. A decent funeral was conducted and everyone moved on.

People kept in touch through meetings and grange dinners and activities.

Greenfield interacted with the other small towns around them. The trains came through to pick up any collected items for the War, drop off staples for the towns, and take the pigs to the market.

The Newspapers and overseas reports were also delivered by train. The big story of the day was reported in the London Times and it was about Churchill's four week trip. He went 10,000 miles aboard the Liberator, with a U.S. pilot flying. He toured Casablanca, Cairo, Turkey, Cypress, Algiers, and the front line of the 8th Army in Tripoli. After the trip he returned to England

and watched the film, "Casablanca" starring Ingrid Bergman and Humphrey Bogart. This was the story of the week for quite some time with the people in town.

Times were tough but the town bonded together and helped each other to cope with the War.

Months rolling by . . .

We were receiving messages about the War almost every hour now at the base and it looked like things were starting to go in our favor. Industrial centers, air fields and chemical tanks, ball bearing factories, bridges and ship yards, were being destroyed. We were making every shot count.

One mid October, a bone chilling cold morning, I dressed warm and went out to the runway to see what was going on. Men were standing around waiting for something, and then I saw them. Down they came and there they were. Some of the fastest, loudest planes in the sky, coming down our bumpy little air field. Two Liberators and five new P-51 fighters, landed. These planes could carry two extra gas tanks, and travel 600 miles at 400 mph. Now we were something to be reckoned with. Those two things alone put us over the top with our enemy. The German Fighters, the Messerschmitt 109E, could only go 350 mph and only 400 miles. The Focke-Wolfe FW 190 did about the same. We could fly two thousand feet higher with no problems. Many of their aircraft were lying abandoned on the ground and destroyed before they took off.

We had our causalities too. Our squadron leader had perfected his early morning speech with the vast amount of pilots passing through. His speech went like this: "Take a good look around the room. A year from now, most of you will be dead."

Joey and I kept moving up in the ranks only because we were there and they needed leaders. We were now recommended by the Commander to become a Major. Papers were in the mail. Marty also moved up. He became a Captain and the Head of Mechanics on the base.

I ran over to take a look at the young looking pilots as they got out of the planes. I must have looked old to them. What a sight in the early morning sky. I noticed some changes from the planes we had now. The new planes had the bubble top giving the pilot more visibility. The guys said the hardest part of flying this plane was the taking off and landing it. It had a touchy rudder and you had to control the speed carefully so you wouldn't flip the plane over. Nine seconds and you were up and out of sight. Once in the air you ruled the sky. It was the fastest well equipped and most maneuverable plane anywhere. I couldn't wait to get this little baby in the sky.

Joey and I had been practicing our special maneuvers and playing our game, on the back side of the runway out of sight whenever we got the chance. We had perfected dropping bombs down a tube we had set up on the airfield. The guys set up some empty shells, loaded them with rocks and sand to equal the weight of real bombs, and that's what we practiced with. This was for our special mission we planned to take some day, maybe. We designed a special way to hit the target while getting accuracy even in the wind. We would drop down to about 1000 feet, level off, take our shots, and take off straight up in the air again. The first few times we tried it, the guys held their breath. We were pros with this stuff. We never gave it a thought. We had our mission all figured out.

The first time out in a new plane was a little challenging for some. The visibility was a plus and the fast speed in the air was exciting. Bigger engines and more guns made you feel more secure.

Orders were coming in now to seek out enemy aircraft before it left the ground, on our missions. Tactical fighting was instrumented and strafing was a big part of the mission now. Some guys took some pretty bad shots to their planes. Our squadron had been flying for some time so we worked well together and knew each other's moves. When our flight leader made that critical dive, we were on him like wall paper. We streamlined out of the occupied territory, like we were never there. We were lead crew on this mission. Coming in today we had not much damage to the planes.

After changing and reviewing our flight, I went to my bunk for some down time. As I sat on the bunk my wallet fell to the floor and a picture of my Mom slipped out. Weary and tired, I reached down and looked to see a picture of my Mom. How pretty my Mom was with her long red hair. I hadn't thought of her much lately, but I knew in my heart she was always with me. I wondered what it would have been like if she had married Phil instead of his brother. I wondered how old she was when she married. Funny how things work out, I could be sitting in jail today if it were not for Phil. I picked up the picture and placed it in my wallet, thinking how mentally and physically unbalanced I was, and very much alone before I met Phil. Now I have another chance in my life and people who really do love me. I know I want to spend my life with Ashley, have some children and be a good father to them.

Ashley and Lette Mae sent letters keeping us informed almost every week. Some of the mail got tied up sometimes. I didn't do such a good job at writing but Joey was very diligent.

It's funny what you think of before you fall asleep. Tonight I thought about me and Dad when I moved in with him. He had decided to take me to church every Sunday. The only thing was, he had not been to church himself in years. He knew Janice would get all dressed up in her royal blue Sunday outfit, complete with her big Sunday hat, and she carried her rather old beat up Sunday Missal, but where did she go? He asked her one day where she went every week. We all ended up going to her church and it became a ritual.

After church, she would make us a nice breakfast. We would listen to spiritual music on the radio while reading the Sunday papers. This was a comforting and quiet day for us to be together.

On the base I would go to the Chaplain when I needed that feeling of comfort. Life was so unreal here.

I rolled over in the bunk and dozed off to sleep.

Chapter 20

Special Mission

Time was passing by and Joey and I got our time at night to practice our BUH game, and have a little fun with the guys.

In reality we were adjusting to the new planes being delivered to our base regularly now. We had some changes from our old planes. In our old planes that we had modified on paper for the game mission, we decided to put in a chute for the tinfoil drop and jam up their radar. Then we put in a radio system for back and forth bantering, when we were on our mission. We decided the planes would be painted powder blue like the sky with white clouds scattered about. This would be a good camouflage for our day trip. While we were at it, we decided on two 1000 pound bombs to be hooked underneath. This would do the trick with our sharp shooting. Our maps were ready and we knew our way over and back.

At night we would talk about what could happen and after we scared ourselves to death, we would think how maybe this mission could be possible.

About the second week in December we had a real bad snow storm that left our base in a stand still. The temperature was 16 degrees and it was a heavy, wet blizzard leaving us with high drifts. It took us some time to get out of the buildings and get things shoveled and plowed out. Next came warming up the planes. It was going to be a long day and everyone was cold and cranky. The weather was a challenge here. We all worked together to get the base back in action.

Around four in the afternoon our squad was called to a meeting in the Officers' Club. As the men showed up one at a time, we knew something was up.

Colonel Jamerson was at the desk up front, and papers were all over the blackboard when I arrived. We sat down by the warm stove. That really felt good. There were coffee and sandwiches at a table to the side. We were told to help ourselves. We waited for everyone to show up, while we wondered what this was all about.

Colonel Jamerson asked how everything was going outside. The men reported what areas they had worked on all day, and it sounded like the base was up and running. He proceeded to get started.

"Alright men, I have something to lay on you. I'm sick of this war and I want it to end. There's only one way to do it. I say kill that crazy bastard in the bunker and all his men!" We all looked around. Some smiled. Some were in shock with the Colonel being so crass and redundant, and others were just shaking their heads agreeing. Cheers and applause were an afterthought pleasing the Colonel.

"Now I know all about this secret mission stuff you guys have been working on. I have my informants. We think it might be feasible!" He looked at Joey and me and asked, "Would you really take on a mission like this if we gave you some help?" The room went quiet.

I jumped up and yelled out, "yes Sir, we would." Joey nodded his head.

The Colonel proceeded to go over all the reasons why we shouldn't do this, and the fact we may not return was a sure bet.

He also told us he knew for sure Hitler was in the bunker right now, he had it from excellent sources.

What he didn't know was how sure we were that we could do this mission and return unharmed.

Then he went into detail how he would not sanction this mission but if we took this mission we would get another automatic promotion and be able to return to the States and train pilots. We were that good. He would take care of the paperwork later. Then he added, "If I were younger I might have tried this myself."

The papers around his desk were ideas he wanted to share with us, mostly safety precautions. There were routes and spots marked for gas or small airports we could land at if we needed help. There would be a squadron going over to a certain point with us in the morning and one joining up with us on the return. It looked like the Colonel had done his homework. Joey and I looked at the Colonel in disbelief. Could he really be saying this? Are we dreaming all this up because we are tired and cold from the snow, and were exhausted? No, he was serious.

"Are you guys ready for this mission and how long will it take you to be on your way?"

Joey spoke up this time answering out loud, "Tomorrow at 7 a.m." I nodded in agreement.

The men listening to all this, cheered and started out the doors. They knew what they had to do to the planes for us. Marty and his crew were ready, willing and able to set things in motion.

We sat around the table with all the new ideas and maps and listened to what the Colonel had to say. Again he asked if we were sure we wanted to do this? We were sure.

The mission was set for 7 a.m. tomorrow.

Marty was outside the door when we came out. He came to assure us that all the things we had planned were now in place. Our communication system was between our two planes only. Then he got all sentimental about seeing us off and said he would take care of everything here.

Joey and I went back to "our four star hotel" and put our things together for tomorrow. We had letters to write in case something happened to us. That was the hardest part of the night.

We needed extra clothes. We planned to fly high staying out of the line of fire. We knew the routine well and all the extras were put in place. Some things were taken out of our planes to make room for other items. The weight was cut down. We were going to be carrying bombs of heavy weight and we were ready.

Our Chaplain had been at another base when he heard of our special mission. He came right back and sat and talked with me and Joey for over an hour before administering communion to us. He was concerned for us.

We retired having all our dreams ready to become reality in just a few hours.

We knew Adolf Hitler built the Fuhrer bunker in the early forties. Then he added the Vorbunker [ante-bunker], with a circular staircase. The Vorbunker floor had a 7 foot thick foundation slab, and was 40 feet below the Reich Chancellery garden level. The ceiling thickness was estimated to be almost 13 feet. This was for Hitler's entourage, his officers, secretaries, guards, radio operators, some families and other personnel. Many, many times the bunker was the target for all types of planes and bomber conquests.

Hitler lived in the bunker and planned to die there. His greed and quest for glory were the major motives for his war. But he knew in 1941, his war was lost. Planes and man power were pretty much depleted. In approximately a 28 day span Hitler lost 900 planes. No country could keep up with that kind of loss. His occupied territory was slowly closing in on him. The British and American planes were faster. They were coming off the lines faster. Hitler's ammo storage areas were bombed and depleted. So he ran his War from 33 feet below the ground. What a hero.

Early morning as we got ready to take this special mission, we went out to look over the planes that we knew would hopefully change history. The crew had worked all night painting, shifting things around for the weight, and adding some extras we had asked for.

We got dressed in special gear designed to keep us warm and somewhat bullet proof.

Colonel Jamerson was there as we climbed up into our state of the art flying machines. We were ready. Joey gave me the high sign, our engines had been warming in the cold morning. We checked our maps and papers while we waited for takeoff. Marty was asking us to check out our phones he had installed so I called Joey to make sure it was working. Sounded clear, that was a first. There were four other fighter planes leaving with us and they left first. We had the bombs. These planes would lead and stay with us for a few hours. We lined up on the runway clearing with the tower, and then lifting up slowly into the cold, crisp morning air. The ground beneath us was covered white with drifts from yesterdays' snow. The ground crew had painted two large hearts at the end of the runway for good luck.

With all planes in the air, we headed out. Billy began singing some of the old Christmas Carols we used to sing in town when we were kids. His speaker sounded pretty good. His voice, well!

We got up about 10,000 feet and did our usual check of our gages on the dash and our oxygen levels. The heat had kicked on and all the gauges were reading normal.

A little over an hour into the flight, I got a red flash on my dash. I looked over to Joey's plane and he was pointing to the left. We had company coming straight at us. Immediately we separated to get our fighters into position for some action. There were six ME-109s coming right at us. We needed to scramble. We were carrying the bombs. The four fighters traveling with us took over. Our planes had the advantage of speed. We could fly higher with better flexibility and visibility. They went after them. It seemed like they flew into us unexpectedly. The enemy tried to pull out as the fighters came at them from all angles firing. We lifted up close behind the fighters. Then the heavy firing started and it was hot and heavy. We could see planes firing and flames spraying across the sky. The guns were rapid firing. They scrambled to dive and get back in position to fire again. I counted right at the beginning, two planes got hit. They trailed down out of power. Another plane had fire on the wing and smoke coming out the window. He was going down. One plane came right up under me. I knew he could see my bombs and he wanted me bad. He didn't get very close before he was pummeled by one of ours. His plane fell in pieces as I moved forward to get out of the way. I looked for Joey. He was lodged between two of our planes moving up to where we were forming again. The squadron had done their job well. We followed behind our fighters. I looked to the side and saw the last plane going down. Joey had hit one plane that got too close and he hit the gas line. It exploded right next to him and splintered and dropped through the clouds. Only one of our planes had a hit on them. He was sputtering but gave the high sign he was okay. We all continued on the mission.

About a half hour later we encountered some flak. We knew it was coming so we rose to 30,000 feet and looked down to see the smoke, and listened to the noise from our safe zone. Once through the radar zone we knew the fighters protecting us were turning back. We were on our own from here on in.

I tried my phone that Marty had worked on so hard. It was very clear and sounded like Joey was right in the plane with me. We visually checked each others' plane and everything looked fine. We dropped down to about 25,000 feet and headed for Berlin.

It was deathly quiet up here and still early. Once you got past the sound of the engine and your heart pounding, it wasn't too bad but we were all alone. A little prayer didn't hurt at a time like this.

About an hour later Joey called me this time. I could tell he sounded funny, maybe scared, I know I was a little. We decided to leave the phones open. Joey wondered if anyone could hear us down below. I told him, Marty said it was a special set-up for us. We put them close to us leaving them open.

We figured we were about twenty minutes away from the action.

Joey asked, "What did I put in my letter home in case I didn't make it back?"

I just said, "Stuff, I don't have any intentions of sending it anyways."

We talked about what was ahead and how we would signal some of our moves when we came into Berlin. Everything would move like lightning at that point. We knew this was very heavily protected. We planned to fly high, zero in on the target, deep dive, level off for ten seconds, shoot for the targets we had planned on, clear the area and get out as fast as we could. How many times had we done this move in our minds for weeks now?

One thing in our favor today, it was a nice sunny day in Germany. The Germans could hear us, but not really see our freshly painted sky blue planes.

According to our maps we were coming into the flak area real soon. Joey agreed and gave the sign he could see a land mark below. We came down about 10,000 feet. This was what we were waiting for. We opened up our chutes and let the tinfoil fly. We made a quick circle around and back in line. It was like Fourth of July. Fireballs and smoke bombs everywhere, but they were coming up behind where we had just been. Their radar was reading our tinfoil and they were all jammed up. Our planes were shaking and we knew what was ahead. Joey hollered to look to the left. As I did, I saw a fighter plane going right past me. The pilot thought he could see me but wasn't sure. What a feeling. When he realized what he had just seen, he had passed me by and Joey had him with a direct hit.

They always come in twos as I watched for the second one. Sure enough in he came. I hit him right next to the wing as quick as I saw him. He never had a chance. Down he went into the flak and smoke that was drifting all over the sky. The noise was all behind us now. The radar system was paralyzed and that was good for almost an hour.

We looked for our target now. We dropped down to be closer and see more. Joey spotted it from his window first. We checked our maps, we had to be sure. I gave the high sign and down we dove.

The Bunker was very easy to see coming down from that high. The observation tower we were aiming for was clear. My stomach was doing flip flops as I came down, it was overwhelming. Now it was time to level off. My heart was pounding as I shouted to Joey, 'keep close, give it your best shots.' We leveled off and now there was firing going off everywhere. It kind of reminded you of a bee hive being slammed with a stick. Gunfire and flak going off, we were right in the middle now and we could feel the power.

There was the Bunker!

Joey went in first dropping his thousand pound bombs. I came in quickly to the side for my target not wasting time now, or I'd be toast. I dropped my bombs, lifted as fast as I could and got out of the area so fast I didn't see a thing until I got way up in the air. The flames and smoke came up like mushrooms. Our planes were shaking back and forth. We were still being fired on even though we were almost out of their range. I really wanted to see the hits but it wasn't worth the chance of being hit. That's when we should have had cameras with us. What a feeling, I wanted to see how Joey felt. I hollered into the speaker. He was singing Christmas songs again. I thought to myself he must have flipped. He asked me if I could see the target burning when we left.

I had to say no.

He said he saw my bombs land and they were on target. I was sure all four bombs hit that target but good.

We went up about 30,000 feet and headed back.

Again I thought I heard Christmas carols coming through the speaker.

Our route back was changed just before we left the Colonel last night. He told us about a ball bearing factory that had been hit a few weeks ago and they were building it back up again too fast. He had the maps and it was not too far from our way coming back. That made us feel good that he thought we might return. We would have no problem getting in there, we had the best machine guns available and we were the best shots in our group of pilots.

We were near the site now so we dropped down to see what we could. A signal from Joey and we leveled off about 1,000 feet. We opened fire as we passed over the factory. We could see people scattering and flames coming up. Black smoke started lifting up and it was hard to see. We circled around and fired again as we lifted up into the air and out of sight.

I'm sure when they looked up they could hardly see us. The camouflage was working. We peaked at 30,000 feet and just looked at each other through our windows, as we leveled off inches apart.

Over the speaker I heard from Joey, "Are you ready to go home now?"

I was. I didn't want to tempt fate.

We knew we had more areas of conflict. We had made a mess of things down below and they would be waiting for us on our way back.

We had time to eat and talk about how it felt to hit the targets. We flew tight. We were ready for any surprises that lay ahead.

Just then, something caught my eye as I looked to the left. I signaled Joey we had company. Nothing could fly as high as us but they could shoot at us. We were flying about 25,000 to 28,000 feet staying out of the wind turbulence. We immediately lifted up knowing nothing could keep up with us for very long. It was two Junkers 88s, not much threat for speed but they could carry 5,000 pound bombs and they carried three machine guns. They looked like they had already fought their battle. We opened up on them and they started shooting. Maybe they saw us, maybe not. They fired anyways.

A few seconds more we would have been high enough to be safe. I took a few hits to my left side. I could tell Joey took some fire too. Although my plane rumbled and shook I was okay and out of the firing range. Joey followed but was lagging. One Junker was trailing. He had been hit and going down. The other plane had a small fire on the wing. I looked to see if he was going down or not. I needed to be sure; there was no room for chance. I dropped down and plastered the side until he started to flame out. He was done. I turned and came up along the side of Joey's plane. I could see his plane had been riddled all along the side.

"Are you hit?" I could see something was wrong! "Joey, are you alright? What are your readings? Can you land the plane?"

He just sat there, I got no response. I yelled louder, "Joey, are you alright, answer me, look over here!" This can't be happening, were so close to the base. "Joey, answer me!"

Finally he turned his head so I could make eye contact. This was not good. Something was very wrong with my Buddy.

Then he spoke, very softly at first. "I've been hit Billy, it's my right side and leg. I don't think I can go on, or land this thing. I'm a little dizzy."

"Hold on Joey."

I grabbed the maps that Colonel Jamerson had given us, and looked up the nearest small airport where we could land. I calculated it to be about seven minutes away. I called in to let them know there was an emergency coming in.

"Joey we are going to try and land. Follow me in, just seven minutes away Joey, you can do it. Start descending. Follow my tail and stay with me." I could see him right behind me but he was tilting and trying to level himself off. I could tell he was badly hurt. Joey was strong and could handle himself. I could see he was having a hard time and his head was weaving. I went on the speaker again.

"Joey just a few more miles, it's a small safe airport. We can do this. Joey I can see the tower can you hear me, look over at me." He turned his head and I could tell he was really hurting.

"Come on Joey, start dropping down slowly, I'll walk you through it. Listen to me it's like landing at my Dads airport. Come on Joey, stay with me, drop down a little lower, you can do it, follow me in." He did better and kept the plane steady. I couldn't tell how long he was going to be able to hang on.

We were down low enough to see the runway now. To my surprise a flash of lights went on as bright as could be. Joey would surely be able to see this. "Joey look at the runway, it looks like Christmas in Greenfield and it's all for us. Come on lets show them who we are. Were the Greenfield Boys and were going in!"

Joey was doing real well, I dropped back to see his face. He had a smile now and I knew he could do it.

"Go Joey, I'm right behind you. Slow and easy does it; let the plane do the work. He landed the plane like a pro coming in between the lights. When he hit the runway, the front right tire blew out causing the plane to lean back catching the left tire and tail wheel. He slowed to a dead stop. It could have been worse. He could have lunged forward and hit the propeller. I followed in behind him and came to a quick stop. My door was jammed in place and the ground crew pulled it open.

As I ran over to Joey's plane, I could see he was hurt really bad the way the guys were trying to take him out. Joey was covered in blood on the right side of his clothes. They pulled him out and we wrapped him in a blanket they had ready for him. We took him in their field house and took off his clothes to see what we were dealing with. He was hit two or three times down the right side.

He was not responding to us at this point. The medic came in and started working on him. My heart was pounding in my chest so hard; I thought I was going to need the medic next.

Sometime later, Joey came to, and wanted to know what happened. He didn't even remember landing. They gave him some pain pills, a shot, and wrapped him up again. He went out like a baby.

I talked to a guy named Tom who was checking out our planes on the runway. "How do they look Tom, Can we fly them home?"

"I couldn't find too much wrong with the planes inside. I think they can make it back to your base. I'll take this one back for you and you can put Joey in with you. I'll make the room for him. Give him some rest time for a few hours. "Billy, I never saw one of these planes up close, are they all this color?"

I broke into a belly laugh. It did look kind of funny. "Hey Tom, check out the inside, we really got some good stuff in there." I showed him our speakers, our tinfoil chute for the radar, and of course, our special window cleaner from Iowa. He was impressed. Tom left to get things out of the plane. I guess this time it was my turn to bring Joey home.

The planes were being checked out for the flight back to Boxted so I went back to see how Joey was doing. He was out cold. We had made it to a safe zone here, but I wanted to get him back to Boxted as soon as possible.

Tom came in and gave me the thumbs up on the planes. Then he said something funny to me. "So who's the big shot overseas that's been manipulating all of this stuff going on?"

I didn't know who he was talking about.

Then Tom said, "We had about five minutes to light up that runway. It's all flashlights and candles. Is your father the President?" He laughed.

"Not quite," was my answer.

We went in and wrapped Joey for his flight back. We put him in the back as gently as we could and covered him up and I got in the front. He was out of it. Tom left first. I followed and we headed back to the base. It was just a short hop from this airport. It was late afternoon as we approached the airport. I radioed into the tower of our two planes coming in.

Cheers and loud noises came over the air. "Come on down," was my reply from below.

Our Return . . .

Tom landed first pulling to the side, knowing I was right behind him with a heavy load. We landed on the beat up runway. It was still a little snowy from the night before. Tom got out and came over to my plane as I got my door open. Our crew came running over and cheered. That's when they noticed the other pilot was not Joey. They came over and helped us take Joey out of the plane. He was not aware of what was going on. Quickly he was transported to the make-shift hospital we had on the base.

Marty came running over to the plane to find out what had happened. All I could say was, "Well we made it. It was something we will never forget. I wish I had a camera so I could see what we did. I was too excited to turn and look back but you guys would have loved it."

Marty put his arm around me, leaned over and said, "We took care of that with another special set-up. I can't wait to show you. How did everything else work?"

"It was the best Marty. You are the best." I started to feel a little dizzy and thought it was time to sit down somewhere. As the Colonel came my way I knew he would be pleased to hear we got a direct hit on both targets. After he gave me a big hug, not very military like, he stepped back and asked how I felt and what happened to Joey. I walked him around to the side of Joeys' plane and we both looked at the damage. He took some straight-on hits. Both planes were able to fly but we had some big holes to fix. Marty had his crew coming out already.

We talked about the mission on the way over to the hospital to see Joey.

Joey had become conscious and was being checked out. All he could say was, "How did I get back," that's all he wanted to know.

"The planes are here and so are we," was my answer. I could tell he was in a lot of pain. I rubbed his arm and then I left with Tom who was standing beside the bed with him. The Colonel remained to talk with him for a while.

Outside I thanked Tom for taking time to come in with us. I took his name and address to contact him later. We had a plane ready to take him back to his base, it was getting late and he wanted to get back. I watched as he left the runway up into the cold night sky.

I went back to change and the guys all wanted to know how the mission went. I changed into something warm, and we sat in the office talking about the special mission and what just happened. Boy that wood stove sure felt good. It's funny, I drew a blank now that I was back and safe and trying to recall all the excitement of the day.

Marty came in and he was all smiles. He had some more guys with him and they were beaming. "Okay, I got it, let's fire it up." I looked over and he was carrying a set-up for a film he was about to run. He had such a smile I knew something was up. "I put two cameras on each plane Billy, they did not get hit. You and Joey can see what happened and so can we.

I sat there kind of stunned at his comment. Neither of us knew of these cameras. Now I found myself really excited. I felt bad that Joey couldn't be here with us.

The film started with us leaving the runway. How in the world did he film our whole mission without us knowing it? Now that I think of it, we never had flashing red lights on the dash when planes were approaching us either. The Colonel had come in late and sat in the back of the room.

I watched as I went through the whole mission over again. This time I saw everything going on in front of me. This was my film. We hit our targets head on just like we practiced. There were flames and smoke coming up. We hit the targets straight on. The guys were keeping score of what I did and how the plane reacted to the different ideas they had set in place. The camera was hooked up to the radio system Marty had placed in the plane. Talented beyond belief, that Marty was good.

When the show was over all the guys were cheering and talking about the Bunker hits. We were sure we would hear something over the radio about this hit. The Colonel came up front and applauded me and the crew for a job well done.

"You won't hear about this one on any radio boys, they want to keep this raid quiet," said the Colonel.

We waited while Marty put Joeys' film in. As we all watched again, we could see how Joey got hit. The colonel got up when the films were done. "You know we're looking at a new Colonel here men. Let's hear it for Colonel William Stevens and Colonel Joey Calhoun for a job well done."

The men hung around talking about the film. Later I went over to see Joey and tell him the news about the films and the promotions. This was a special day for us and we spent the rest of the night together. I slept in the chair next to his bed. I was so tired I didn't sleep very well. I was too excited and happy.

Joey had some pain. It turned out his wounds were not as bad as they first looked but he had lost a lot of blood. The doctor took the bullets out and the area was cleaned up. He had some pieces of metal floating around inside. They took out what they could, gave him some stitches and plenty of bandages. Joey received another shot and was resting comfortably for the night.

The next morning Joey watched the films while sitting up in bed. The Colonel and I sat with him, and of course Marty the genius, was there.

After we settled Joey down again, the Colonel told us what was going to happen now.

"The films were going to the next in command, several copies would be made, and the General of the 8th Air Force, would be coming by to address us in full honors. We would officially be notified of the time and date. Last night the General was notified, and he insists on meeting both of you. This is a great honor for this base, for me, and all of the men involved. The films will be distributed around the bases here, and then sent home to the States to the proper authorities for publications. This is big newsworthy stuff, you can be very proud. Enjoy your moment boys of Greenfield, you have earned it."

About a week went by and our planes were all repaired. I took two more missions because I couldn't just sit around. On one mission I shot two more planes down.

Joey got up and about and we knew he would be okay. He started telling some of his stories to the guys when they stopped by. He wasn't walking around yet but he was healing.

The news of our leaving was brought in by the Colonel.

"Next week you will be awarded in the Officer's Club with your medals and promotions. The General and his Officers and entourage will be here with us. They want to meet you in person. We will celebrate, take lots of pictures, and the news reporters will all be here.

"You know boys; you will probably be the youngest Colonels in WWII." He laughed and just shook his head. "I am making plans for your return to the States. Start packing your gear. You will be leaving after the celebrations are over, and you will fly back with the General. Who did you guys say you were?" He left smiling.

Joey started walking on crutches and seemed to be getting better. One night he ran a high fever and we couldn't get it down. The doctor came in and opened up one of his wounds that had become infected. Some of the metal that was lodged in his leg had to be dug out again. This time they got it all. We were hoping to get him back to the states before anything else happened. You could tell something was still wrong. I stayed with him that night to make sure he was okay. The next morning the fever was down and we got him up and around again.

The day finally came for our promotions.

Early in the morning the runway became alive with activity. A C-47 and two military decorated transport C-124s came in with the General and his entourage of people. The band began to set up. The flags and a red carpet were set in place for our guests. About two hours passed. The tent was up and the chairs were in place. We all met out on the field for a military ceremony with an Air Force Band. We brought Joey out and placed him in the seats saved for us. We had our new uniforms on and everything was official.

As the band began to pass by us the General from the 8th Air Force stood tall with everyone saluting. There was a small ceremony for us as the General pinned the Colonel wings on us. The General proceeded to speak very highly of our work and all our abilities that he knew, made us special. When he finished, he made sure to tell everyone, we were what the Air Force was all about, and how very proud he was of us. He turned and asked if we had anything we wanted to say.

Joey was still not able to stand for very long, so I took the floor. "Joey and I think alike, so I'll speak for the both of us. We just want everyone to know that we could not have taken this mission, without all the help we got from the men here at the base that were involved. We want to give a sincere thank you to all our friends and a special thanks to Marty, our ace mechanic."

When the program was finished we went into the Officer's Club. Joey and I had asked that all the enlisted men and ground crew be invited to the Officer's Club for the party. They were the reason everything worked for us and we wanted to show our appreciation before we left. Food and drinks were complements of the base Commander.

Joey and I relished this morning with all the special things that were said, and the feeling of family among our group. We would be leaving soon and a little sadness was felt throughout the room. Talk of meeting again after the war promoted sincere handshakes by all.

Marty promised to keep in touch and come out to Greenfield when he returned to visit us. Colonel Jamerson said he would look us up when he returned to the States. The band was packing up. The tent was down and the planes were warming up as our bags were being put on the plane.

We said our goodbyes for the last time as Joey was helped on the plane. I followed up the stairs turning to take one last look at our base and our special mission planes, stored over on the side of the airport. This was a small airport with a lot of special feelings for us to remember the rest of our lives. Colonel Jamerson waved goodbye as we taxied down the bumpy runway for the last time.

Our route back would be stopping at Goose Bay, Newfoundland. From there, we would be going to New York, and then on to Washington, D.C. We settled back and knew we would be in the States soon. Home was a peaceful warm thought we cherished and held on to. We talked about how we felt and what we were thinking. We rested all the way home. I was still not happy about how Joey was feeling. I just had the feeling something was still wrong.

While waiting in New York for our flight to D.C., I noticed Joey looking around the airport with some interest of his own. He was exceptionally quiet so I sat beside him and asked him what was on his mind. I knew that look. He told me he was feeling sad thinking about the way he had left New York when he was young. He was sitting by the window, and he couldn't help but think of his Mother and two sisters that were out there somewhere. I sat there with him really not knowing what to say to make it better for him. There was little time to dwell on anything. The press secretary had a schedule to keep.

Each time we landed we were greeted by the military officials because we were with the General. Pictures were taken and the press would ask us a lot of questions, now that we were Colonels. We felt like celebrities. Joey got a real nice wheel chair with an attendant to move him around where he was needed. We laughed about that one. He got special attention given to him to keep him as comfortable as possible. His pain was acting up, his meds were wearing off, but he was a trooper. Once he said to me, "These last few hours will make for a good story to tell when I get home."

Our last stop was going to be Washington D.C. to meet with the President and Vice President. Our press secretary was assigned to keep us on schedule, and prepare us for the next few days' activities. As we were getting ready to land in Washington our plans were laid out before us.

It went something like this. "We will probably be landing around 3:00 in the afternoon. You will leave the plane and be picked up with a military car for the ride to the Hotel Maddington, where you will be staying while in Washington."

"Dinner reservations are set for 7:30 in the Ballroom of the Hotel. The rest of the evening is yours."

"There is an 8:00 a.m. breakfast reserved in the hotel cafeteria, all homemade food for our new Colonels."

"The special dinner with the President and Vice President is planned for 12:30 at the White House followed by your special medals presentation. You will be picked up in full dress uniform, and taken to the White House with a full military entourage leading the way. There you will meet with the President, have a leisurely home-style dinner, and spend time talking about military issues. At this point, the pictures will be taken for the newspapers and service films they want to prepare for the troops."

"At approximately 2:00 p.m., there will be a special awards commemoration and you will be awarded your medals by the President and with several members of Congress who are in for the occasion. More pictures will be taken with the members of Congress and the President, and your Vice President from Iowa."

"Approximately 4:00 p.m. you will be taken back to the hotel and have some time to relax."

"The next morning at 8:15 a.m. you will be picked up and brought to the airport for your final destination, Iowa. You will be travelling military style with the Vice President who is also going home for the week. Are there any questions?"

Joey and I just looked at each other. I was thinking just how proud Mom would be today if she were here.

Joey said, "I was thinking of Lette Mae and how soon I will be able to see her. It sounds like we are going to have no time to do anything we want. I think it will be good to be home for a while."

We knew we were being used for the benefit of the news. It was something good for people to read and see in the movies about the war. People needed to hear something good for a change even if one hero was on crutches. We were going to have our moment of glory.

Joey fell off to sleep.

Chapter 21

Washington

At approximately 3:00 p.m. our wheels came down and we landed at the Washington Airport. We taxied to a secure area used by the military and came to a stop. When I looked out the door from the top of the steps, our luggage was being taken inside and Joey's wheelchair was set up at the bottom of the stairs.

It was a cold windy day and there was snow on the ground. It never looked better. I stood aside as they helped Joey down the stairs and into his chair.

There were people waiting at the gate with camera bulbs popping and people calling out our names. We had a group of people traveling with us. The Vice President led the way to a waiting car that we were going to use. With everyone in, wheelchair folded, we were off to the hotel.

Looking out the window all the stores and streets were covered in snow. It looked very busy as people were out cleaning up. It was good to be home. It was about 4 p.m. now.

As we approached the Hotel Maddington I leaned over and asked the press Secretary what he knew about this hotel. He read from a brochure he had in his lap.

"The Hotel Maddington is located in the heart of Washington, D.C.

It is owned and operated by the Maddington family.

The hotel was built eleven years ago. Completion of the hotel, complete with a Grand Ballroom, elevators and a magnificent lobby, totaled 400 guest rooms."

"The Hotel Maddington was the first hotel to take care of the people and their guests from the White House. It also had a full service fine dining restaurant, and a cafeteria that served home-style cooking every day. Homemade mashed potatoes, fresh baked biscuits, breads, pies and other desserts came right out of the oven. That's about all I can remember from the brochures I've seen. It's a great place, you'll like it there."

The Hotel came in view and Joey and I were in awe. It must have been seven stories high and was lit-up like a Christmas tree. So many lights, so many people all around the entrance, it was overwhelming. As they prepared Joey for his wheelchair waiting outside, I looked to see what the commotion was about. There were two bellboys at the doors. Then I saw Ashley and Lette Mae holding banners in the air and screaming our names. I followed behind Joey and we made our way to the entrance, past the bellboys, to the welcome arms of our girls. What a surprise! We hugged our girls so tightly. Dad and Marion were there and Tom and Judy. Cameras were everywhere as we made our way into the lobby. I was still in shock being pulled along with the crowd. Dad was talking to me and Ashley was hugging me and talking to me. Joey was being moved along with the crowd and his Mom was trying to check his leg, it was frantic. I looked up at the chandelier in the lobby and couldn't believe how gorgeous this place was. This place was so big.

We managed to make our way to the desk for our keys and our luggage was already on its way up the staircase.

The Vice President and his friends left to go to their rooms.

I had a minute to give Dad a real big hug and hold on to him. We all exchanged hugs again and just looked at each other for a few minutes. Ashley had not left my side one second. Lette Mae was now in charge of the wheelchair. Her hero was home. We found a table in the lobby to sit down and talk about this great surprise. The press let us alone for a while. I still could not believe we were all here together.

Our first topic of conversation was Joey's wounds and how it happened. He told his story and I could see he was having some pain. He stood up and got some hugs from his girl, while trying to pretend he was ok.

Our next conversation was about our itinerary. Everyone had one in their hands. We were a show for the public. Pictures were going to be taken and questions asked, all along the way. That's how it was put to us by the press secretary, who had handed out copies of our itinerary in the lobby. Our girls stayed close to us. Our parents talked to us about what had happened while we were away. We listened while Lette Mae was hugging and kissing Joey and Ashley was hugging me and laughing about a story she was telling me. Both parents were happy to just see us together again. This went on for over an hour.

It was around five now, time to go to our rooms, unpack and have a drink. Joey needed his meds now, he was a hurting puppy.

We agreed to meet in the lobby around 6:30 p.m. so we could have a drink before dinner in the Ballroom. The girls needed time to do their hair and get dressed for the night. All our rooms were on the same floor and adjoining. The girls asked for a room together, our parents had their rooms, and we had our own. We said our goodbyes for a while and I entered my room to unpack.

Whoa! My stuff was out and put away, uniforms and clothes were on hangers and shoes by the bed. My room had a large basket of fruit, cut flowers all around the room, and a fireplace giving off warmth that could put you to sleep. I sat down and realized my head was still spinning from the excitement of the day.

I knocked on the adjoining door to see what Joey was doing. It was very quiet in his room. I just assumed he had fallen asleep after taking his meds. We had about 35 minutes before we planned to be downstairs again.

I got dressed. This was just a dinner for the family in the Ballroom.

I went down the hall to see Ashley. As I knocked on the door Lette Mae came out on her way to see Joey. I gave her a hug and she looked gorgeous. I said I'd meet her downstairs.

As I walked in the room, Ashley stood ready and dressed in a long black gown. My heart skipped a beat, she looked so beautiful. We spent the next half hour catching up on lost time. I told her over and over just how much I missed her and what she meant to me. Having her in my arms made me feel good again. She told me how much she missed me and said she would never let me go again. We knew we would be spending our lives together. I loved her and she loved me. The girls planned this brief personal time that just happened.

We walked down to Joey's room and knocked on the door. They were giggling and chatting all the way to the lobby. We all went down to the Ballroom together. We arrived just in time to go for dinner.

The room was decorated with banners and flags all around. As we entered, the band started playing Stars and Stripes as we were shown to our table. We had a lovely table near the band. The rest of the Ballroom had people at tables and some were dancing. Soft colors and dim lights made the room seem elegant and warm. The room had high ceilings and brocade window drapes that gave the appearance of royalty and high society.

We sat down and just looked around wondering if we really belonged here.

Drinks were ordered and menus were read to us. The waiters were with us every minute trying to please us. Joey leaned over and asked me if they thought they were going to get a tip?

Dad heard us joking and just laughed. "Believe me boys, this is paid for." He looked at Tom and smiled.

People came to the table to give their words of gratitude. Word was out that we were here from overseas to see the President tomorrow. Some were asking Joey what happened. This was his opportunity to tell his story. Some people were talking to my Dad, while Lette Mae and Ashley were out dancing together and having a good time.

One older man came up to me and asked how I could become a Colonel at such a young age. I really didn't know what he wanted to hear, it was a long story. Everyone always wanted to hear about the bombs on the bunker, so I went into detail about the practicing we did to get the bombs in the targets we used on the base. He just couldn't believe we could do such a thing. How we did it overwhelmed him. He gave me a tight handshake and walked away.

As the night lingered on Ashley and I danced together holding each other close. Joey did get up and dance for a short time. He made it about two hours on the dance floor, off and on, before he had to give in and sit down. People had gathered around our table talking to us. Joey started telling his stories as more people came by. I knew he was feeling alright if he could tell his stories.

Dad and I found some time to talk near the bar. His first question was, "What do you want to do once you come home?"

I told him, "I really wanted to go to school and become a lawyer. My second passion would always be flying. I really loved flying and could be happy in that field."

"School will happen as soon as you get out, I'll see to that. I love you son, I'd be honored to have you work with me. Flying is also in the works, I'll tell you all about it tomorrow. Go back to your girl son, she really missed you."

I felt like my life was going in the right direction now and I had someone who really cared for me. I guess I'll never understand why my own Dad hated me so, and Phil could love me and it felt so real. If my Mom could have only written something down for me to read later when I grew up, my heart could rest a little easier.

I sat next to Ashley and watched Dad take Marion out on the dance floor. They were good dancers. Tom and Judy joined them on the floor. It looked like they had been taking lessons somewhere.

We left the Ballroom around 12:30 after saying our goodbyes to the many people that had gathered around enjoying our company.

Our parents went to their rooms reminding us to be at the cafeteria around 8 a.m.

The four of us stood in the hall and talked for a while. Joey and Lette Mae went to Joey's room. I brought Ashley to my room. We needed some time together.

As we sat in the moonlight at the table and talked in my room for a while, I could tell she was going to stay the night. She went in the bathroom and changed. I got ready for bed and just waited for her to return. When she did I couldn't believe my eyes. She stood by the bedside. As she slipped her pink, silk robe from off her shoulders, it fell gently to the floor. She was beautiful in the moonlight coming in the window. She let her long blonde hair fall to her shoulders as she fluffed it up a bit. She slowly opened her night gown and let it fall to the floor. She was shaking a little I could tell, but she tried not to show it. I felt nervous too. This was the first time for both of us. Her skin looked creamy white like a china doll. As she slid into the bed I reached over and kissed her beautiful soft lips, as she squealed with delight. At this moment, I knew what a lucky man I was. I loved her so much. From her soft curly blonde hair, to her painted little pink toes, she was sexy. We made love all through the night and finally fell asleep in each others' arms just before dawn. We would be late for breakfast.

The morning light came through the window. We showered and dressed and went down to breakfast. Everyone was there, what can I say.

The food was just like eating at home with Janice. Hot biscuits and gravy, fresh fruit and great coffee, pancakes, omelets, it was all there. My favorite was something called the sticky buns, covered with chopped walnuts. That was a hit.

Dad had taken the floor and asked for our attention for a few minutes. I thought he might be going to tell me he was getting married.

He started by telling us that he had bought some land outside Greenfield. He was planning to put in a military airport and cargo port for the southwestern states. After the War it would become a transport center for agriculture and freight for the west. This project would work with the train systems and major highways that would be going in. It would help ship our stock and our equipment, grains and produce. "I want it to be a delivery point for the southwestern part of the country. I want to know if you boys are interested in helping me with this project. You will have time for school because this won't happen overnight."

I just looked at my Dad and tried to take it all in. I had planned to go to college when the War was over and get married. I wanted to become a lawyer and work with Dad. Joey said he had a few things going on in his head, but he thought the air field sounded good.

I wondered if Ashley and Lette Mae knew about this. They looked puzzled at the moment. We just sat quietly and tried to understand what had just been said before us.

As we looked around the table we all seemed to be nodding a sign of approval. It was something to think about. It was time to go get some fresh air was my thought. The four of us got our warm clothes and coats and went outside. Joey left his wheelchair and hobbled along not wanting to slow us down, but I could tell he was hurting.

We got a cab and had the driver just drive us around the city so we could talk. The city was clean and all decorated for the Christmas Season. The only problem was he drove too fast and it was very uncomfortable worrying if he was going to hit someone or something. I felt safer in my plane.

Finally I spoke up. "Either slow down or bring us back." We headed back to the hotel. We got dressed for our dinner with the President.

At 11:30 a.m. we all met in the lobby of the Maddington Hotel all ready for the ride to the White House.

Our limousine pulled up in front of the hotel and we got in. This trip took about 25 minutes because we went a certain route to the White House. We had a special entrance with guards, and we were brought to the lobby.

Cameras and press people flooded around us. We were lined up for pictures against a wall covered with memorabilia, while the news reporters circled around us asking questions. Washington had a lot of newsmen.

From there the eight of us were lead to the Oval Office to meet with the President.

Entering the room, the President made his way over to us and shook our hands. He asked if we were being taken care of. To tell the truth, I don't remember much of anything else we talked about. I was so nervous. He did ask Joey about his wounds, and everything got a little confusing, with all the people coming in the room and trying to hear what was being said. Then I heard the President, "Let's go eat!" His entourage took him out first, and we followed along a long corridor lined with huge pictures and statues.

The dining room was elegant. Round tables with red table cloths, and white napkins, crystal glasses and shiny silverware, made the room seem so special. The backs of the chairs were covered in Air Force blue with emblems. The center pieces on the tables were little state flags standing in a dish with little stars sprinkled all around.

The main table was across the front of the room. We were placed right next to the President and Vice President. After more pictures and people shaking our hands, we finally settled down to a toast given by the President.

As they helped the President to his feet, he proposed a toast to us. Everyone rose. A loud roar of chairs sliding back over the hardwood floors consumed the room. He kept it simple.

A great applause followed, with more pictures and reporters scurrying about.

We all sat down to eat. People got up and down during the meal to talk.

The Vice President started with Joey. He started talking to Joey about his great interest in the soil and farm lands. He told him he was an inventor of some hybrid fruits, and he had a project going on to produce a prairie grass to help stop the dust storms in Iowa. He talked about hybrid corn, and went on and on about the animals and feed, and new uses for soy.

Joey was in his glory telling his side of things. He had an audience, his girl and his family. He was in Heaven.

As I listened to him go on, out of nowhere he started talking about the bus ride to Texas. He went on about the bus driver Martha. He told a tale of the ride that made everyone laugh out loud until his side began to hurt. Joey said she made such an impression on him that he would like to look her up again when he got home. She was the best.

The Vice President was not always a popular man to be around. He had a colorful lifestyle of his own and he was very much in the news and very controversial. Most of the people around him had a cause to pursue. Being young, Joey had heard of some of his causes and had seen him at different rallies he was involved in. He was a busy man. Joey found him very interesting and wanted to hear more. When the Vice President asked about college, Joey said he would like to go to the University of Iowa, like he did. The secretary took down some notes as requested by the Vice President.

The few minutes I had with the Vice President, he did all the talking about my Dad and what a great man he was. I listened and agreed. When he got to asking me what avenue I would like to pursue when I was out of the service, I didn't quite know how to answer him. I mentioned I would like to become a lawyer and work with Dad. I wanted to get married, live on the farm in Greenfield, and still be able to fly a plane. He seemed pleased with my answer. He smiled and put his arm around my shoulder. He looked over at my Dad, winked, and casually asked, "Do you have any interests in politics?" Laughter was heard around the room on that one.

My reply was, "I didn't have much knowledge of the political arena. I'm just getting back to the States and away from the enemy. I was a little out of date on things going on here now." I looked around and I could see everyone listening to what I had to say.

"That's alright Colonel, updating people is my specialty. We will catch up later." He moved on with a pat on the shoulder and a firm handshake.

I moved over near my Dad and watched the 'theater of politics' working the room.

The President had his own agenda going on throughout the dinner. He asked both of us many questions about our time spent overseas. He was most interested in the morale and the attitudes of the men at the base. We told him we knew we had the best planes, the men in charge of operations knew what they were doing, and we were all handling the War in our own ways. Joey told some stories and so did I. This seemed interesting to him. We both spent time talking about the men we were involved with and how we felt leaving them at the base. I talked about Marty and how he was the best mechanic we had ever seen. Joey wished we could have had him here with us where ever we were going next. He signaled his secretary to take notes. Maybe Marty would get a promotion or something. When asked if we thought we had enough training here before we left for England, we both had different types of answers.

I listened to Joey tell how he could never really be prepared for the first encounter of the enemy head on. He was confident in his plane and the men around him and everyone knew what to do.

That pleased the President.

After that all I could say was how amazed we were that we were so mind-trained. We reacted and had no doubt what we did and we got the job done. The Americans were there to end the War. Our Commander was in control and advised us every day, and we knew what was happening around us. We had meetings and our morale was high most of the time. We did lose guys every week but that was part of being a pilot. We had no second chances. They couldn't train us for that. You moved on because you could be next.

The President smiled and more notes were taken as we spoke.

All our comments would surely be on the front page of the papers tomorrow.

Our families were impressed how the two of us had kept the conversation going all through dinner. Our Dads just looked at each other and smiled. They were proud, we were happy.

When the dinner was over, the tables were cleared and set up for the Special Medal ceremony.

On one side of the room the band that had been playing softly throughout the dinner, began to change their music papers and move about.

Some of the President's men came in with papers and set up the head table. The medals were placed on a small table for display during the ceremony.

I could feel my heart pumping a little faster as I looked over to see the medals.

The band started playing and the President was placed next to the table with the other officers and members of Congress. The award citation was read and we stepped forward to receive our special medals. It came in a box, from the President of the United States.

We were again saluted, and the band played. Many pictures were taken of us with the President, and then the President was wheeled out of the room with his men by his side.

It happened that fast and he was on his way to take care of business somewhere else.

We had been given a great opportunity to have lunch with the President and receive our medals. Something we would never forget. This was a medal of special honors given by the President and Vice President to us.

It was time to move on. The President had left the room.

Our families were taken to the limousine and brought back to the Hotel Maddington. We were going to travel back to Iowa with the Vice President the next morning. As we waited to get out, the driver leaned over and asked if we would all like to tour the city before we left. He said he was available to us for the evening, and would be delighted to show us the lights at night. It would be dark around 5:30. That gave us some time to change. That's what we all agreed to do. It sounded like a fun evening.

We went to our rooms to change into something more comfortable. Joey and I were given a nice box to keep our medals in so I placed mine on the desk near my bed.

I knocked on Joey's door to his room. He unlocked it and I went in to see how he was doing. Joey looked tired and that was to be expected. He had put his medal on the desk as I did. He asked, "How do you feel about having your medal?" We sat in the chairs near the desk.

"I don't know. Everything has happened so quickly. I really haven't had much time to think about it," was my answer.

Joey said he knew his father was proud of him.

I answered, "Mine too, I saw him smiling." We just sat on the bed thinking.

Again we were just best friends sitting together wondering what was next in our lives. For a few minutes it was quiet. Then we heard a knock on the door.

I went to open it and Ashley and Lette Mae came rushing in all charged up and ready to go. They told us what a great time they were having as we laughed and told stories. This was a bonding time we all needed. The time passed quickly. We went downstairs to the lobby and waited for our parents to arrive. Phil suggested we have a drink before we go out into the cold night air. No one objected to the idea.

Ashley brought her notebook and pen, always the writer. Joey took his meds, and new baseball cap he got somewhere along the way. Marion took off her heels, and put on some sweat pants to be comfy. I never saw her dressed like that. Tom and Judy called home and had some kind of a notebook they looked at in the car. Dad and I just showed up ready for the venture.

As we went outside it was a beautiful clear night just perfect for site seeing Washington. The driver had the limo heated and ready to go. You could tell he was anxious to tour us around town. This was a great time for our families.

He drove around stopping at several of the famous stops and getting out and letting us walk around. We sat on the Lincoln steps, drove over the Memorial Bridge, saw the White House all aglow at night, saw the Monument, and the Capital Building. Everything was decorated for Christmas and each stop was exciting. He made about six stops and then suggested an Italian restaurant he favored for supper. It was a little cafe off a side street, all covered with Christmas lights.

We all enjoyed a wonderful meal, including our driver. We took silly pictures and told some funny stories. The waiter was fun and enjoyed telling us about the café. He took some nice pictures of us at the table.

The ride back to the Hotel was a quiet one. It had been a long day filled with excitement that would last us a lifetime. When we did talk we all got into the conversation at the same time. Then we'd laugh and settle down again.

We reached the Hotel about 11:00 p.m. The driver told us he would be picking us up at 7:30 a.m. for the ride to the airport. We all got out and went inside, after thanking him and tipping him for his services. It was real cold now and it felt like it was going to snow. The wind had picked up a little.

In the lounge we got a table and had some hot chocolate. It was a welcome change with some Christmas cookies added to our plates on the table.

We parted company and we all went to our rooms. We had some packing to do. When we got to our rooms, the bellboy was delivering our uniforms all cleaned and pressed and ready for home. We were getting some treatment here, we were Colonels now. Joey and I just looked at each other while standing at our doors. "This is a far cry from the days when we would sit in the fields and blow on a blade of grass, between our thumbs, to make it whistle huh Joey?" He just smiled. "Did you ever think we'd be in Washington with our families receiving a special medal?"

"Not really. I'm going to miss the guys in England especially Marty, he was like family. He did promise to come to Iowa when the war was over and I hope he does." Joey went into his room.

I heard a knock on my door and it was Dad. He came in to tell me how proud he was, and he wanted me to know it. "You have done everything you promised, I love you son."

I got that big hug that always made me feel secure, and then he left.

When I turned around and looked on my dresser I got quite a surprise. There was a picture in a frame of me in my uniform. On the dresser next to the frame, was another picture of me with Ashley in her black gown and hair done up, another picture of me and Dad, and another of me and Joey. There were about eight pictures neatly piled on the dresser. Beside the pictures was a note from the press secretary saying, "It was a privilege to assist you and your family, please come back again. PS; hope you enjoyed the tour of the city, and the cookies and hot chocolate. That gave us the time to get all the pictures back to the rooms."

Chapter 22

Going Home

We got up early and put our bags out in the hall to be brought down to the car. When I put my bags in the hall Dad called out to me.

"Look out the window son, I don't think we're going anywhere for a while. We will have breakfast downstairs in a half an hour," and he went back into his room.

I went back in my room and opened the drapes. We had at least two feet of new wet snow on the ground. Nothing was moving on the streets. Nothing was even plowed yet. I guessed the airport was in the same shape. Dad was right. We'd probably be here for a while longer.

I knocked on Joey's door. I went in and we looked out the window and had a good laugh. "Oh well Billy, we can wait a little longer, let's go eat!"

I guess Joey was feeling good this morning so we went and got the girls.

When we came downstairs, the press secretary and the Vice President were talking to Phil and Tom. Voices were raised and hands were flying up and down. We could tell things were not figured out yet and no time was set for our leaving. The girls went in the dining room and sat with Marion and Judy. We walked over to join in the conversation. They told us the streets would be cleared within the hour and the airport was being cleared right now. The plane was de-iced and ready when the runway was suitable for traffic. The estimated time for leaving the hotel was eleven o'clock and we would be boarding the plane around noon. We could do nothing to make things different so we went and had breakfast. Time with the family was precious to us and we enjoyed the moments spent catching up.

Again Judy made a call to home. I began wondering if everything was all right at the farm. When I approached her later at the table she said she wanted to let people at home know we would be coming in later than expected. I wondered what people she was talking about, but I let it slide. Judy ran a business in town. I figured she meant those people.

Dad was busy making calls too. He kept going to the lobby and returning with some updates about the conditions at the airport. Things were going as planned.

We ate together and talked about the wonderful pictures we all received last night on our dressers. I passed the note from my dresser around. It brought a smile to most faces.

The Vice President came in with several congressmen. They had their own table, but they came over and apologized for the inconvenience, and said the plane was almost ready. They were all carrying briefcases. We knew they had something to discuss. "By the way," he began, "Marty has been promoted after that special mission. He sends his regards." We all smiled. They moved over to their table.

Around 10:30 a.m. the streets were cleared and trucks and cars were moving about again. Our press agent, who thought by now we would all be on our way back to Iowa, came in the room where we were all sitting having coffee.

"Okay folks were ready for the final trip to the airport. So sorry for the delay but the plane is ready and I'm sure all your things are on board by now. If you'll follow me, I'll say my goodbyes to you as you leave by the front door. It's been a pleasure."

We took our ride to the airport and boarded the plane with no problems. Because of the storm we were the only people in the plane with the Vice President and a few press people. Joey talked to the Vice President the first hour going home.

It was a long trip back to Des Moines, Iowa. Some of us slept and some played cards or read magazines. Ashley and I just talked about what had been going on the past few days, and looked out the window just holding each other. Joey and Lette Mae snuggled up back. Joey still wasn't feeling all that well. He was running a low-grade fever that had his mother quite concerned. I think a trip to the hospital was in store for him on his return to Des Moines. Marion had connections with the hospital there.

Phil and Tom talked with the Vice President later on the way home. I heard the words "airport" and "planes" being talked over. I'm sure Dad was working on the airport he was talking to us about in the hotel. We'd be brought up to date later with Dad. There were a lot of papers being handed back and forth and it looked like a new project was in order.

Marion spent time with Judy and planned to set up something at the hospital when we got in. She worked in the hospital administration office and could get him a doctor right away.

Judy and Tom had planned to stay with Dad until Joey had seen a doctor. It would all work out somehow. Just getting him back home was the important thing right now.

We heard the ten minute warning of arrival and the Vice President came over to us all and announced if we needed a ride home, there would be cars to handle the rides. He told us he enjoyed visiting with us and being part of the very special visit to the White House, and being part of the Special Medal Ceremony. He hoped to see us again soon. He had his bags ready and went to the front of the plane. We thought the car would make things easier for us, but it really made us look important when we landed.

We loaded all the bags into the cars with the new wheelchair they gave Joey. We headed for our house. On the way home we found out Joey's fever had become worse and we knew we had to do something right away.

The city was all decorated and it looked special. It was good to be home. There was snow on the ground.

We drove up the driveway. I could see the tall trees covered with snow. What a beautiful sight. All the trees had colored lights on them; reds, blues, greens and yellows. The front door was wrapped up like a package with shiny red paper and a large gold ribbon looking like a giant bow. There were gold candles in all the windows and colored lights all around the roof and down the sides of the house. Home never looked better. Janice was standing at the door with Cleo in her arms.

We all went inside giving Janice a big hug as we passed by. I held my cat and tried to remember the last time I felt his furry body as he purred away.

We made our way to the kitchen. I passed by the living room and saw a big radio standing in the corner. The music was soft and there was a Christmas song playing. What a nice addition to the living room. I figured I'd check that out later.

We gathered around the big pine table and pulled in our chairs. The house was warm and the room smelled of apple pie and fresh coffee brewing. Janice had a plate of cookies on the table and biscuits and gravy on the stove. There was a big old pot of homemade beef stew on the back burner that smelled terrific. She made her way around the table taking care of everyone's needs. No one knew us better. She was the best cook and she had made all our favorites. We ate and laughed and talked for a while and then we turned our attention to Joey. He didn't look good. He was quiet and not too hungry. That was unusual. He loved it when Janice would cook for him.

My Dad leaned over and asked, "Do you want to see a doctor before you return home?" His answer surprised us all.

"Yes, I'm hurting quite a bit."

Marion immediately left the table and went to the phone. The appointment was made. They would be waiting at the hospital. Tom and Judy and Dad and I went with Joey to the hospital. Marion followed with the girls in her car.

A Doctor Wyess was waiting for us when we got to the hospital door. Joey had some of his papers from the doctor he saw in England, but there were no x-rays. That's the first thing the doctor started with after looking at the infection that had occurred on his way home. He figured that's what was causing the fever but wanted to be safe, so he did some extra testing and new x-rays.

We all waited in the waiting room until the doctor came out with the results. About an hour or so later, Doctor Wyess came out and gave us the news. "It turns out that Joey still has some pieces of metal lodged in his leg and side of his hip. He had to be opened up again, cleaned out of debris and infection. He will be stitched back up leaving some drainage to be taken care of while in the hospital. This time he will be monitored and remain in the hospital until the fever goes down, and the infection has cleared. He was operated on and is in the recovery room. He will stay at the hospital for about two or three days. He will be fine." Doctor Wyess turned and went right back to surgery.

We all felt better knowing this was a problem that would be better in a few days.

Most of them left to go home for the night. It had been a long day and we were all pretty tired. I stayed with Lette Mae and Ashley.

The nurses told us we could see Joey when they put him in his room for the night. Marion gave me the keys to her car and she went home with the others.

While we were sitting and waiting, I asked Lette Mae if everything was all right at Joey's farm.

She asked me why I was asking.

I told her I heard Judy call home a few times in Washington.

She said Tom and Judy had some things going on at the farm but everything was under control. Don't worry.

I saw Ashley and Lette Mae give each other a wink. I felt something was going on.

The nurse came in the waiting room and led us to his room. He was bandaged up and set up in the bed so he could be somewhat comfortable leaning more to one side. He looked a little groggy but that didn't stop him from talking. "They gave me some drugs and a shot for the pain. I'm nauseous and a little sleepy, but I'm glad you guys all came in." He fell off to sleep. Lette Mae leaned over and kissed him good night. I patted his arm just to make contact with him, and then we left. At this point he needed his sleep more than us being there.

When we arrived at the house, the house was full. Tom and Judy had taken my room and the two girls had the upstairs spare room. I went in the office next to Dad's room on the couch, and Marion left to go home to her apartment. Janice had made up the couch downstairs in the den for Joey in case he came home and couldn't climb the stairs.

Soon the house was quiet. Cleo had found my feet and was purring away.

I awoke to the smells of homemade biscuits, scrambled eggs, bacon and coffee. I pulled the blanket up over my neck and just laid there for a few minutes. In my mind I said a prayer that my best friend would be okay. Cleo was chewing on my shoe laces and jumping on my boots. I guess it was time to get up.

I dressed and came down the stairs as Dad was letting Marion in, and getting his paper off the steps. I felt the cold air come in the front door. Things were back to normal as Dad kissed Marion good morning and took the paper to the kitchen table, while Janice poured his coffee. Marion had a few more papers tucked under her arm that she laid across the table.

She announced out loud, "Headlines, The Greenfield Boys Are Home!" Big letters, big pictures, were splashed across the front page. I browsed through and it was all about the past two days in Washington. How did they get the news so fast? I looked puzzled.

Dad could read my mind. He said, "Good news travels fast son. After breakfast we will take a copy to Joey at the hospital. Tom and Judy left a few minutes ago and we will meet them later."

"That sounds good Dad."

I went over and gave Janice a big hug as she handed me a special breakfast she had waiting. She knew what I liked and boy did it smell good.

Ashley and Lette Mae came in the kitchen gabbing away, as usual. They went right for the papers on the table. After looking at the pictures, they sat down and read the stories. They looked at the pictures, looked at us, smiled, and passed pages back and forth to each other.

Dad and I just watched them carry on. Marion had her coffee and muffin and sat down beside Dad. I continued eating. Soon the girls were getting something from Janice at the stove.

The girls were both going to classes today. Ashley had to leave and get to school by 9:00 a.m. She had to hurry across town, call her parents and let them know how she was doing, and get her bags out in the driveway. She ate in a hurry, said her goodbyes, thanked Janice for breakfast, and left saying she would see everyone at the hospital around five. A quick kiss for me, and she was off. I put her bags in the car.

Lette Mae wasn't far behind her. She had school but classes didn't start until 10:00 a.m. So she stayed and helped Janice with the cleaning up. She called her parents and talked for a while. She packed her bags and I brought them out to the car for her. She left for school.

That left Marion and Dad and me sitting at the table with all the papers scattered, and a fresh cup of coffee being poured.

I had a feeling of anxiety and not knowing what I was supposed to do. I just sat there.

The phone rang. I went to answer it. It was Joey.

"Did you see the papers yet? We are all over the cover and insides. There are pictures of us everywhere. How did they get them so fast? Billy did you see them?"

I laughed. We were going to bring him the papers.

"Yeah Joey, good news travels fast. We're reading them now. We got extra copies from Marion and we will save you some."

"What are you guys doing? Are you coming in today? I'm feeling pretty good this morning."

"Calm down Joey, the girls had to get to school, they will be in later. Dad and I will be in after we drop Marion at the office. Anything we can get you Joey?"

"Yes, maybe some of Janice's biscuits and gravy for breakfast, if you can manage it. She makes the best breakfast. I'm starving!"

"Okay Joey, I'll work out something, see you soon."

Janice packed a full breakfast for him and put it on the table with a note on it. She loved Joey and always enjoyed him being around the house.

We got dressed and went out in the cold morning air. I was just glad to be home for a while. Right now I just wanted Joey to get better. I could think about everything else later. We left for the Hospital.

When we arrived in Joey's room, Judy and Tom were fussing with the pillows on the bed. Joey was sitting in the chair looking pretty good. He was all smiles when he saw us and the basket packed by Janice. We rolled the tray over to him and put the breakfast out. He dove in like he hadn't eaten in over a week! Dad and I sat down and watched. Judy had a sigh of relief when he ate almost everything in the basket. To her, eating was a good sign.

The nurse and Dr. Wyess came in and Judy had a bunch of questions for him. He came over and took Joey's temperature and it looked better. Then he asked us to sit down.

"We got all the pieces of metal out of your body this time." He looked at the parents. He looked at Joey. Joey should be fine. He will need a few days to have this area bathed and kept clean. He is going to be kept on medication for the pain which he doesn't feel right now. I can tell because he is smiling. The temperature is still higher than I want to see it. We are monitoring this and will continue to check him for any other infections that may result from this episode. Joey I think you did the right thing coming in as soon as you did. Who knows what could have happened if you let this go any longer. Try to be patient, be a good patient, and the secret to this is rest."

Doctor Wyess introduced the nurse going to handle this procedure. Her name was Nurse Maddie and she was the best. He left the room and everyone seemed happy with the results. Of course Judy had tears in her eyes, as she stood by her son. All she could say was, "Thank you Doctor Wyess."

We stayed a while longer while Joey looked over all the papers we brought. He was delighted, or maybe it was the medications acting up. All I know is I would be taking an empty basket home to Janice. That would surely make her day.

Judy and Tom left to do some errands and check out her business.

Dad said goodbye to Joey and me and left to go to work. He promised to be back later. He put his head back in the door to tell me he had Marion's car, I could use his car and he threw me the keys.

There we were the two of us again, looking at the papers and wondering what we were going to do next. I have to admit it felt a little strange.

Three days passed and Joey was ready to go home. I went with Dad and Judy to the hospital to pick him up. His things were ready, and we wheeled him out the door in his new wheelchair from Washington. We got everything in the car. I had been told on the way to the hospital that we were bringing him home to Greenfield.

Surprise!

Dad and I sat in the front seat of our car and Joey had been placed near the door in the back. He could angle his leg for comfort. Tom and Judy were there with him.

About ten minutes later Tom started the conversation. "We have made some changes at the farm Joey. We have put on an addition along the side of the house with a second floor. We have some people living there that you might enjoy meeting again."

Joey listened and tried to figure out what they were talking about.

I turned around and looked at Joey. He raised his eyebrows up and down. A jester he often gave me when he was in doubt of something.

"What's going on Dad?" he asked.

"Joey, we love you and we wanted to do something for you we thought you might like. We all worked together on this and we hope you like the surprise."

He didn't say anything. I was busting inside to ask questions. When I turned to say something, Dad gave me a nudge and a look. I knew enough to shut my mouth.

We drove for a while and I looked at the snow drifts along the road. Curiosity was killing me but I watched for the farm to appear. Nothing else was said. I was surprised Joey just sat there.

Tom and Judy had been very busy the last few months getting the addition put on their farmhouse for Joey's mother Martha and two sisters, Mary and Anna. Tom and Phil hired some help from the labor force they had in town. These were all older local men with a trade and they were now out of work due to the war and the depression. Every week they would go into town and pick up about five or six men to help with the work. They got some pay, stayed on the farm all week, and had food and a place to sleep.

While Tom built the addition, Judy was busy making braided rugs, curtains, quilting bedspreads, making table cloths, knitting slippers, gloves and hats. She had her whole sewing club helping out. All the women in town always helped each other when there was a special project going on. They looked forward to the time spent together. If you couldn't sew, you could cook. There was always something you could do to be useful. Gossip ran rampart too. Judy ran a fabric and upholstery business in town and she knew all the women, and this was her turn to ask for help. The women made clothes for the sisters, and someone donated a rocking chair for the mother. Other people offered furniture and some had job offers.

This was going to be such a surprise for their son on his return.

The farm appeared. There it was, a large addition along the side of the house, just like we were told. I just looked in awe. We drove up to the front door of the farm and got out and went in. Some of the help brought in the bags. Tom and Judy and Joey sat down at the table. Dad and I stood up across from them. I was bursting to ask a question.

Tom and Judy were excited and at this point, I could see a strange expression on Joey's face. Finally Joey smiled and asked, "What's going on Dad?"

"Are you up to going over to see the apartment Joey? If you are, go check out the bottom apartment. Someone is waiting to see you."

Joey got up and went out the door, being careful not to slip on the snow.

We all went to the door to watch.

As the door opened, three people stood before him.

"Hello son, it's me, your Mother and these are your sisters, Mary and Anna."

Joey grabbed onto the side of the door! He looked at them and tried to remember what they looked like the last time he saw them. His mind was racing back to being young in New York, and all the memories of them that he had. His mother was much older and bent over with age. She still had those caring eyes he had always remembered to this day. His sisters were older women now and quite different from what he remembered the last time he saw them. As he stood there looking at them, he started to weave a little. He didn't know what to do.

What were they doing here? How did they know where I was after all these years? How did they feel about me? He knew why his mother had to do what she did. Now he had moved on to another family and a different life, and a farm he called home. He had a strange look on his face. With his thoughts still racing around in his head he muttered, "Mom I can't believe I'm seeing you again."

She came to him and hugged him close to her. His sisters came and hugged and kissed him. They went inside and all sat down at the table, with tears rolling down their faces. They just looked each other in the eyes and tried to bring back the memories and feelings of the past.

After Joey left for the apartment, Tom asked me to come inside and sit down at the table. The kitchen had been all done over since I was here a few years ago. Tom asked if I liked what he had done to the house, as he could see me looking all around.

"It's so modern," was all I could say. "What's going on in the apartment with Joey, I can't wait another minute."

"It's a long story," Tom said. "Judy, sweetie, let's have some coffee. While you boys were away, your Dad and I went to New York to see if we could find Joey's mother and two sisters, he left behind when he was younger. With a name like Somerset Wilding and the location we were able to get from the police department, we got lucky. We met his mother and sisters at their apartment and realized they were just barely getting along. I explained who I was, and that I had adopted Joey. I told them all I could about him and showed them pictures of when he was young. I could tell they loved him very much. I asked them if they would like to come and live with us and Joey at our farm. I told them we would make them a place to live and help them find a job. They seemed very excited about the whole idea. I gave them a time period to get ready to come to Iowa and I would be back to pick them up. We just made it Billy; they have only been here a couple of weeks. The girls have jobs and your mother keeps busy here at the farm, and helping Ashley with some paper work. We can't wait to see how this goes for Joey."

I just looked at Dad with a surprised look. This was a lot to take in all at once even for me.

"Let's go see how it's going," Judy blurted out.

We went over to the apartment. When Tom and Judy, Dad and I went in, it was a sight to be seen. The mother and sisters and Joey were all around the kitchen table talking and laughing and holding hands, trying to make up for lost time. Joey was so happy he probably couldn't remember he was recuperating from a hospital stay only hours ago.

I thought one of his sisters Anna, looked a little like him, same color eyes and same color hair and definitely his smile.

I introduced myself to them. Joey proceeded to tell them I was his best friend in the world as they all came over to hug me.

Joey got up from the chair and went over to his Dad and hugged him as hard as he could. There were tears in his eyes as he tried to tell him how happy he was, and how glad he was to see his Mother and two sisters again. He was sure they had died by now.

Things were so bad when he left. Judy got an extra special hug too. All these emotions were racing through him as he looked his Dad and Mom in the eyes. A look of love and gratitude for everything they had done for him. He was shaking a little now. It was all setting in.

I came over to him and we hugged as friends do. This was a lot for him to go through and I could tell he was glad I was here with him.

Judy spoke up and suggested we all go over to her kitchen and have something to eat while we figured out what to do next. She had a nice roast prepared with lots of vegetables. She had some of the help put it together, with Joey's mother assisting.

"That's what some of the phone calls were all about Billy. We just didn't know how long Joey would be at the hospital," said Judy. "I know you were curious."

They all walked back to Tom and Judy's kitchen and sat down at the table.

His sisters were eager to tell him about their new jobs. Mary was working as a hair dresser in a shop in the square. She thought it was funny because they also sold fresh eggs there too. She laughed and that really seemed funny to her. Anna was working at the hospital taking care of the elderly people. She just fell right into a great job, good pay, close to the farm, and she liked working with older people. She met Lette Mae there on her first day. Tom introduced them and they became good friends. Lette Mae also met Anna and the three of them got along like sisters.

They only met Ashley before she left for Washington, so they didn't know her very well yet. They said she was busy taking care of her very sick mother most of the time, which I knew nothing about.

"Well I guess we all have some catching up to do," I said, as I sat back and thought about what I had just heard.

We ate and talked and made some plans for the next few days. We would all go in and see the Christmas tree in town. We'd plan a night we could all go together.

Soon we would be hearing from the Army Air Force as to when and where to return. We would become fighter pilot trainers when we were recalled to duty.

I excused myself and went to call Ashley so I could meet with her later.

Joey needed some rest now. He had plenty of people to fuss with him so Dad and I said our goodbyes and we left for home.

This was an exhausting few hours. I was going to enjoy the ride back talking to my Dad. As we started back, he asked if I had some energy left for one more stop.

"For you, I have all the time in the world."

"How about the farm, I have something I want you to see son."

"Fine, let's go."

Phil and Marion were busy getting permits for the new airport they were designing for the future of the Southwest. The trains and highways were in place, but the planes had to be set in place to make this Military-Cargo airport base work. Phil knew what he wanted to achieve. Marion checked the legality and possibility of the ideas. They were a good team. Phil now had five offices of lawyers working for him. His small airport at the Bluffs was very busy with traffic from his business. He now owned four planes and had two other pilots working for him. His business traveled coast to coast.

In his spare time he had some work done on the farm house adding some new bedrooms and baths to the old house. He put another apartment building of two apartments next to the house. He planned the right side to be used for me and Ashley, if we wanted it. Maybe later he would use the other apartment for him and Marion. I had mentioned that I might want to live on the farm someday. That's what he told Ashley. He still had a family that lived in the main house taking care of the farm and overseeing the help. My living back on the farm was a great idea to Dad and he worked hard putting the place together.

We rolled down the pebbled, clay road to our farm house. It looked clean. The fields were covered with snow. The Angus was out in the pastures and the hay was bailed and covered. I could see the tractors had just finished plowing around the farmhouse and they were lining up for the next snowstorm that was due soon.

Then I spotted it. A big addition adjoining the old farm house came into view. It was completely finished. What was this?

"Dad, when did you have time for this big project?"

"Well son, there is a lot of people out of work right now. So Tom and I decided to gather some of the men from town and share the work. We kept them at the farms all week, fed them, paid them, and brought them back on weekends. There are some fine older workers here and they worked hard."

As we drove up to the door some of the farm hands came over to greet us. Dad introduced me to the new ones I didn't know. I told them how pleased I was that everything looked great. I thanked them.

Dad just smiled.

"Let's go take a look. I had this designed for you and Ashley if you want to live here after you get married. There's a second apartment in case I want to move back here some day. Meanwhile use it for your friends, when they first come to Greenfield."

As we walked through, it felt very warm and cozy. The kitchen had a big fireplace. The ceilings had wooden beams and the walls were barn board with wallpaper on the top half. The floors were wooden and had scatter rugs here and there. There was a big pine kitchen table with wooden chairs all around it. On the side of the table, against the wall, were two Captains' chairs. The counter tops all around the kitchen, and the cabinets, you could tell were hand crafted one of a kind. There was a hutch built into the corner. Since we all spent most of our time in our kitchens this was a dream come true.

We moved on to the living room greeted by another beautiful stone fireplace this time. A living room set with a smoking area to the side, large windows draped with dark green and gold curtains and a large braided rug that made the whole room comfortable.

On the right side of the hallway was the master bedroom with a queen size bed with four posts, two dressers and a small table with two comfy chairs. The furniture was all handmade and beautifully finished. In the corner was a small vanity area. A good size closet in another corner and a big full size bathroom completed this room. It was on the sunny side of the house in the daytime. This was perfect.

The other side of the hall had almost the same thing, except there was a small office to the side of the room instead of the vanity. Both rooms had hardwood floors and large thick rugs.

Both of these rooms adjoined with doors to another room. As we went through the door of one room, it looked like it could be a children's room. Right now it had a large bed and a set of dressers, a desk and chair, and a lounge with a couch and a table and lamp. There were small bathrooms with closets, and this was great if someone were to sleep over.

At the end of the hall was a den with another big old stone fireplace. Some big leatherback chairs were spread around the room with a couch in front of the fireplace, a pool table, a dart board on the wall, beautiful hardwood floors, and a teakwood coffee table right in the center of all the chairs. Where did Dad ever find something so unique? It was a topic of conversation for sure. To one side of the room was an office, complete with a good size entertainment bar. Large windows with green and gold drapes and a large soft rug over a hardwood floor, made this one of the most comfortable rooms I had ever seen. I loved this place from one end to the other. Now I really had some things to think about. I just turned and looked at Dad.

"I love it, love it, love it, this is the best." I gave him a hug as we walked back to the kitchen again.

"The other side isn't fully finished but it's pretty close to the same layout. We can check that out later. Let's go back to the house. I have some calls to make. I'm sure you have some things to do and you haven't seen your own room yet. Now that everyone is gone we can get back to a little normalcy again. Janice needs a rest."

We got in the car. It looked like more snow coming and the wind had picked up some. The sky was getting dark with big billowy winter clouds. Something was brewing.

We drove all the way back talking about the war and the fighting. I went over what a day schedule was like over in England and all about the Hitler mission and how it got started. He wanted to know about our planes, where they were, and what kind of training we received and how many men were there on the base. We went on like that all the way home.

It was around supper time now. I swear you could smell Janice's cooking all the way down the driveway. It was just starting to sprinkle snow as we put the car away and headed in the house. We knew something was coming. I was glad to be home safe and warm.

Leave . . .

We made our way into the kitchen and had some of Janice's good food to warm the heart.

After dinner I went upstairs to see what Dad had wanted me to see in my room. He had bought me a Crosley, Lancaster radio, wood and wood veneers with an oak finish cabinet. It was a classic radio and turntable with a bronze faceplate. This I had never seen before, it was a masterpiece. I turned it on and the sound was so clear. I sat down on the bed and listened to the talk station that was warning us of the coming snow storm. It sounded bad.

I went downstairs to thank my Dad for the radio and asked what I could do to prepare for the storm coming in.

Dad was on the phone to our farm giving some ideas to ready the farm help. There was a good possibility we would be snowed in a few days. When he finished on the phone he handed me the phone and said it would be a good idea to call Ashley. The phones could be out for a while if the snow gets heavy.

I gave him a big hug, thanked him for the radio, and went over to sit down and make that call. I had mixed emotions about this call. I was upset that she didn't tell me anything about her mother. What else didn't I know?

Her father answered the phone. When I asked to speak to Ashley he told me she was still out somewhere, maybe she was at the apartment. I wasn't sure of the number so I asked.

There was no answer at the apartment.

I saw Dad putting on his old boots, heavy coat, hood and gloves. I got into my gear and followed out behind him. We put the shovels near the inside garage doors with the bag of salt. We hung the tire chains over the bar so we could put them on the truck later if needed. This was definitely going to be one of the first big snow storms of the winter. The fact that he was away all last week in Washington, and having people stay at the house a few days, set him back a little getting things ready.

Janice had taken care of the food and there was plenty of wood for the fireplaces. His offices were notified what had to be taken care of if the offices were closed a few days. The planes were in storage. Marion was going to stay in town in case she was needed at the hospital. She could walk to her office in two minutes.

"Did you get a hold of Ashley, Dad asked?"

"No Dad, there was no answer at either place"

"She's got a lot going on Billy, try calling her again later."

"Dad, did you know about her mother having problems?"

"No son, I just knew she had picked up another job besides going to college and working at the bank and part-timing at the library. I guess someone in town has asked her to do some Historical accountings for the paper. I didn't know her mother was sick. She didn't talk to me about it. Let's go in. It's getting colder and the snow is coming down pretty heavy."

We put the old horse blanket that we kept in the garage, down around the front door to keep our boots on.

Janice had just finished cleaning up the kitchen so we all went into the living room. I started the fireplace and listened to the news on the new radio.

The temperature had dropped to about 10 degrees. The wind was blowing through the trees and shaking the Christmas lights and old crusted snow off the branches.

I called Ashley again at the apartment and still no answer, where was she? I called Joey. He answered.

"Hey Billy are you ready for this big storm coming our way?" He sounded excited.

"Yeah Joey, were okay here, how's it going there?"

"Were all set and I'm spending a lot of time with my mother and sisters. I'm feeling a lot better now that the infections are under control. I knew something was wrong on the way home in the plane. Have you heard anything from the service yet?"

"Not yet. I'm trying to get hold of Ashley. I've tried both the apartment and the house. No one seems to know where she is. Did you hear anything from Lette Mae?"

"No, she's busy helping her mother get some extra cooking done for the holidays. She will probably stay at her folk's house tonight with this storm coming in. I'll call her for you. If she knows anything I'll call you back. Stay in touch Billy," and the phone went dead.

I went back over to the couch and sat down for a while. I was really upset not being able to make contact with my girl. Where could she be? It was almost eleven o'clock and the storm was howling all around us. I sat and stewed over my problem for a while. I made another call to the apartment and still no answer.

Around midnight Janice had gone to bed. Dad and I had listened to the radio and fallen asleep off and on for the last hour. This time, Dad woke up and got dressed and went out the front door. He always liked to get right out and start shoveling, before it built up. I knew he wanted to stay ahead of the snow piling up. He was going to shovel the walk and out to the garage. I dressed and followed behind him. I put the front lights on first.

The snow was wet and heavy. As soon as I started shoveling, my shoulder pained from my injuries I had overseas. The fact that the snow was so heavy, or it was so cold out, or it was so late at night, didn't helped me any.

Dad had started working his way down the driveway. I started at the garage. He was moving a little slower now, this stuff was heavy.

I thought I heard him call my name. I looked his way as he slowly fell into the snow in front of him. I ran over to him and tried to pick him up as he grabbed my arm and slowly pulled himself up to his feet.

"I guess I fell, this stuff is slippery."

I looked to see if he was alright and I helped him walk back to the house. My heart was in my mouth. That was no fall from slipping, I knew that.

"The snow will be there in the morning Dad; you have people to do your plowing. Let's go inside. It's late!"

He made no comment just held my arm and we went inside. I helped him get his heavy clothes and boots off. Then I sat him in the living room in his big chair by the fireplace. He moved slowly.

"What's going on Dad?" I asked. "Are you in any pain, does your chest hurt, are you dizzy?"

"No, no son, don't worry. The snow was heavy that's all. I might have lost my balance. Don't worry. I'll just sit here for a while and warm up."

It was late now. I put a heavy blanket from the couch over him. I didn't leave his side until he fell asleep. I went upstairs and changed into my robe and slippers. I took the quilt off the bottom of my bed and hurried back downstairs. I played with the fireplace for a while bringing it back to life, and making sure it was going to last until morning. I slept in the big chair with one eye open just in case Dad needed something.

He woke up around six-thirty to the smell of fresh coffee. Bacon and eggs were frying on the stove. Janice was up.

I helped him out to the kitchen and he sat down at the table.

"Good Lord, what's wrong with you. Did you have another spell Sir?"

"Another spell, what do you mean Janice?" I asked.

"No, now don't get my boy all excited. I just slipped on the snow last night."

"Okay Sir, but you better get yourself to a doctor. You're playing games with the devil! Tell him Billy."

"This is the first time I have heard anything about this Janice."

"Talk to Marion, Billy. She has been trying to get him to see a doctor for some time now and he won't go."

Dad tried to change the subject. "Alright now, let's have breakfast I'm starving. Everything smells good as usual Janice, a fine job."

After breakfast I went and looked out the window but couldn't see a thing. I went to the front door and opened it. Boy, what a mistake. We had at least three feet of snow and drifts up to six feet along the house and garage. When I opened the door, snow came drifting in and covered me going down my neck and all over me. It fell in the hallway and all over the floor. I quickly brushed it off me and shoveled it outside as I shut the door. It was still snowing hard and it was in the single numbers below zero. I grabbed a towel and tried to dry myself off a little, and then I went and listened to the radio for some weather reports. Omaha had about six feet of snow and it was just beginning to slow up a little. Drifts were ten feet high and the winds were still blowing quite hard. The lines were all down and the snow was very heavy with the branches bending and falling everywhere. The small number of plows we had in our city were not able to do much with all the branches down. So the prognosis was grim and I thought I'd better try our phone in case I needed it for Dad. Just as we thought, the line was dead. Oh great now what. I still had not heard from Ashley and Joey never called back. My anxiety level was rising. I could feel it and I was worried and concerned about Dad. This was going to be a long day.

Dad didn't try to shovel snow after breakfast. He moved into the living room and listened to the radio for most of the day. I took care of the fireplace keeping the house warm. He changed and put on his warm robe and slippers as he caught up on his papers he brought home from the office. It was a very quiet day, except for the occasional wind blowing through the trees. You couldn't see out the windows because the drifts were too high.

We waited the storm out and in the afternoon it began to slow up a little. I went out the back door this time by the garage. Opening the door I was ready. The snow came in again all over me but I had my shovel ready. I managed to shovel out a path to the front door from the garage. I cleaned a few windows so we could see and some of the driveway before I had to quit. My shoulder was killing me.

I went inside and Janice had the cure. "Drink this, it's hot and it will do the trick."

I sat down in my chair near Dad, and fell asleep. When I woke up I heard noises outside. Dad was standing by the window. Some of Dad's crew that plowed out his businesses were taking care of our driveway. What a relief. I went outside to see what they knew about the roads and conditions in the city. One driver said the roads in the city were bad. You needed chains to get anywhere and the towns around us were non-existent. Plowing was going to take a few hours before anyone could get around. This was heavy snow and it had to be pushed or trucked away. There were only a few people plowing.

It was winter in Iowa.

A few days later, things were coming back to normal again. Dad was back to his office working. We had high snow piles along the roads to the city and towns but people were getting around.

I was on my way to find Ashley hoping she would be at her house in the city. The drive over was slow and tedious. It was one lane with snow still falling lightly, and sometimes slippery, as I plugged along. The winds were still blowing and causing drifts to build up. I had my chains on the pickup and it held the road pretty good.

Coming up the driveway I stopped and thought about what I was going to say. I had been very angry about not knowing about Ashley's mother being so sick. I wanted to try to control myself before I went in. I could see her car was still covered in snow. I made my way up to the front door. Nothing had been shoveled around the house. I knocked on the door and her father came to the door. "Mr. Thomas, is Ashley here?"

"Oh hi Billy, come on in. Ashley's upstairs with her mother. I'll call her for you." I nodded. I took off my coat, hat and boots and sat at the table.

I heard her call down that she would be right there. A few minutes later she came down the stairs. It was like everything was fine. I hadn't heard from her for a few days and it wasn't okay? I was even more upset now that I saw her. I came apart as my voice rose.

"Ashley, what is going on? I couldn't get you on the phone and nobody knew where you were. I've been worrying myself sick that something might have happened to you out in this storm."

She came over and kissed me on the forehead. She could tell I was upset. She sat down beside me and held my hand.

"Billy my mother has been very sick the past few months. She has a disease that's taken over her mind and she has become someone else. She sees things that are not there and she cannot remember much anymore. We can't let her out of our sight. Dad and I take turns with her and we have someone during the day come in, so we can keep working our jobs. School is regular hours for me. My other jobs are part time so I can make my own hours. I'm sorry Billy, I didn't want to trouble you while you were overseas, and we had such a good time in Washington. I didn't want to spoil it. We don't have the phone upstairs. When it rings it sets her off to hear it. I don't hear it downstairs. The doctor can't tell us much because these things take their own course. She's not eating much and that's not a good sign. She is very weak. It could be weeks or days we have no way of knowing. But I do know I will be here with her until the end. I'm sorry Billy. Only Lette Mae knew how bad she was getting. She helps us out from time to time."

I sat still and thought before I spoke. I felt bad for her but I was so worried. I had no way of knowing about any of this and she knew I was upset.

When I opened my mouth some things came out that I didn't mean to say. I raised my voice and found myself yelling.

I'm sorry for you and your mother but I was so worried not hearing from you. I don't like being left out of things especially from you. You should have told me about your mother. Everyone else knew she was ill, that's not right. I thought we had something good going on with us. Now I don't know." I caught myself and lowered my head as a flash back of my Dad yelling at me came back from the farm. I shook my head. "I'm going back home, my Dad's not doing to good. I'll be there with him if you need me." I got up, put my boots and coat on, and moved to the door. "I'll have your place cleared out as soon as I can get a plow over here. The roads are still bad out there. If you have to go out be careful."

I opened the door and left not hearing any response from her. I was still mad. I was upset she didn't let me know about her mother, and I was mad at myself for spouting off like that. She didn't need that. I couldn't help myself. What was it about this yelling and acting out? I tried to control it.

I got in the truck and took off to see Joey. A usual hour drive took me just over two hours on the snowy roads. I had time to calm down a little.

Greenfield was still in need of a lot of plowing but I wasn't having any trouble with my chains on. I was so mad I probably could have driven through a blizzard.

I drove over and found Joey outside in the barn with his horses. His sister Anna was with him and they were feeding the new baby colt. Joey loved his horses and I could see he was sharing that feeling with his sister. I sat down on a bale of hay and just watched them for a while. Anna went inside and Joey came over and sat down.

"What's going on?" That's all he said.

I went on and on about what was happening and what I just did. He sat back and listened not bothering to stop me. He knew I wasn't finished yet. I finished with Ashley and went right on about Dad and his snow shoveling. After a while I did slow down. I looked over at Joey and he had a little smile on his face. Again I opened my mouth without thinking. "What's so funny?"

He reached his foot over and kicked my bale of hay over shaking me off onto the floor. I climbed back on.

"Things were easier in the service Billy. We knew what to do and when. Here it's all messed up and we have been away too long. We are not in control here. That's all that's going on. I have stuff going on here too. I tried your phone several times yesterday and today. Service is out. I'm glad you're here. He kicked the bale of hay again and I fell over again. We both laughed. We talked in the barn for over an hour hashing everything over and over.

Tom came out and saw my truck outside by the barn and came in to say hi. I told him about my Dad and his fall, shoveling.

He said the same thing as Janice. "Take him to the doctors." He said Judy had just made some hot corn bread and coffee if we were hungry.

We put the big old blanket over the new colt and secured him in the pen. We went in the house, throwing a few snow balls on the way.

It was good to spend some time with Joey and his parents. We talked over our life in the service and what coming home has been like. I felt left out here because of what Ashley had done to me. Tom and Judy talked things over with me and let me talk. I left just before dark feeling better about my problems. Talking things over with some different points of view always helped.

The next day when the mail came I received a registered letter from the Army Air Force. I panned down to the bottom of the letter, to see where I was going to be stationed. It was Foster Air Field in Texas. That was in Victoria, where we had graduated and got our wings. I had about six days left before I had to report in at the base. We could fly down this time because we had special treatment now, being Colonels.

I went inside and tried the phone. It was working so I called Joey and asked if he got his papers yet?

"I haven't been out for the mail Billy, what does it say?"

"We are going back to Foster Air Field, that's where we graduated, remember?"

"Yeah Billy, that's not bad and we can probably fly in. When do we have to report in?"

"They gave us six more days before we have to return. I don't know about you, but I'm ready to go back today."

"Take at easy Billy, things will work out. I'll call you later."

I went in the kitchen and talked to Janice a while. Dad came in early and looked very tired. I told him the good news, he seemed glad for me. He suggested we go into Greenfield tomorrow night and look at the tree and lights. Marion wanted to go with us and get some pictures of us, you in your uniform. And I want to show you off, what do you say?"

"That sounds good, Dad." He reached over and gave me one of his big hugs. Then he took his papers and went in the living room to listen to the news. He sank into his big chair and ten minutes later I went to check on him. He was fast asleep with the papers on the floor all around him.

I went upstairs to pack some of my things and think about what I wanted to do about my problem with Ashley. I put on the radio and made a list of things I wanted to take care of here before I left for Texas. Number one was to get Dad to the doctor's office. First thing tomorrow I'd make that call. I heard Dad go by the door on his way to bed. I went downstairs and checked the fireplace. After picking up my cat I turned in myself. That night I had a hard time sleeping. I could feel myself thrashing around in bed. I was dreaming of German planes coming at me. That image never left me and I often woke up shaking in the middle of the night. I left the radio on low and eventually I must have fallen back to sleep.

I got up early in the morning, put my light on, and read through some of my manuals for flying. It kept my mind occupied and soon the light of day was coming through the bedroom window.

I got dressed and went downstairs. Dad was already down and having his coffee with Janice.

"Bad night Billy, I saw the light on in your room early this morning? Do you want to go to work with me this morning? I could use some help with some papers I'm trying to catch up on?"

"Sure Dad, whatever I can do. I have a checkup with the doctor this morning around eleven. Will you come with me? I need to get some records for the service."

"Sure son."

"Dad I need to get you checked out before I leave. I want a doctor to look at you. Marion set us up an appointment for eleven. I waited expecting some excuse from him to get out of it.

"Wow. I feel like you guys are ganging up on me but I'll go. I haven't been feeling that good lately. Let's eat and get to work."

At the office I found myself doing paper work and really enjoying it. I was doing something useful probably the first time since I've been back home. The phone rang. It was Joey.

"How did you know I was here Joey?"

"Janice was only too happy to tell me you went to work with your Dad. I got my orders, same as yours. She also said you two are going into town tonight with Marion. Maybe I'll take Lette Mae and meet you guys there. Around six sound about right?"

"Sure, let's have some fun tonight. I've got to go now and get some work done. I have an appointment set up for Dad at eleven this morning. I'll call you later."

About ten thirty we left work for the doctor's office. Marion met us at the doctor's office and we all went in. Marion introduced us to Doctor Fine and I got to go in first to speak with him. I explained about my injuries in the service, and the injuries I had on my back and head as a child. To my surprise, he had my records from my doctor back in Greenfield. Hum. I think Marion had this visit planned for both of us for some time now. He checked me out, took some tests and said I looked to be in pretty good shape for what I had been through. Not having any problems that the service couldn't take care of when I returned, I was able to go. Next he took Dad in the office while I sat outside with Marion.

"Yes I brought your records here for you and I hope that you don't mind," said Marion.

I reached over and gave her a hug. "You know I think you are the greatest." We waited for the door to open. What would be taking so long, I wondered? I was anxious but glad I got him here.

About an hour later, Dr. Fine came to the door and asked us both to come in. We sat near the desk. Dr. Fine asked if Dad wanted to tell us or should he? Dad gestured for him to proceed, but he seemed uncomfortable.

"Your Dad needs to take some time off. Since that is a pipe dream, I have to tell you the stress he puts on himself is literally killing him. His heart is trying to tell him something, he is not listening. Now I can give him some medication to help the heart, but he has to make some changes in his life style and his eating and drinking habits. His blood pressure is too high and shoveling snow could kill him. Other than that he's fine." We left the office with a new pill for him to take and a list of things to change in his diet. Doctor Fine was going to check up on him monthly. I liked that idea. Marion thanked the doctor for the appointment and we left.

We went to Marion's office. I don't think Dad really wanted to think about himself having anything wrong. We talked of everything but his health. Twenty minutes later Dad and I left to go back to the office. On the way back he said he was going to be more careful and take better care of himself. I think he tried to make me feel better because I was leaving soon.

We worked for a few hours. I could tell he was stewing about his doctor's results. The next thing I knew he was by my desk and ready to go home.

Marion came by the house around five and we ate and got ready to go to Greenfield. I dressed in my uniform and heavy overcoat. We left together.

We spent the evening in Greenfield. The town always decorated the tree with lights and ornaments made by the people in town. It was a special time of the year and this town made the most of it.

It was a clear cold night and the stars were all coming out. As we approached the Court House and tree, there was the biggest crowd I'd seen in a long time gathered there. Marion turned around from the front seat and said, "This is a special celebration for you and Joey, from the town. Congratulations to our new Colonels."

I got out of the car and looked around as people started coming over to us taking pictures. All I could think of was, did Joey know about this? I spotted him a few cars away. We walked over to him. Tom and Judy, Lette Mae and her parents were making their way to us. Most of the important people in town had been seated by the tree, and the High School Band was playing Christmas music.

We were asked to stand by the tree for pictures while some people gave us recognition for a job well done overseas. More pictures, more music and sincere handshakes from all, we enjoyed the evening. Our two families stayed together and we took some pictures of our own.

The Greenfield Boys

There were tables set up with hot chocolate, coffee and cake, cookies for the kids, and other goodies people made from home. The band played on. People danced where ever they could find a spot, and we found a table to sit and be together. About 9:30 Joey stood up and asked for our attention. Lette Mae came to his side and they announced they had set a date of June 15th for their wedding. Everyone cheered and clapped as they kissed each other. I was surprised and very happy for Joey, as he looked to me for support. They walked around the tables with their news and Lette Mae showed off her beautiful ring.

While I sat at the table, someone tapped me on the shoulder. I turned around to see two young boys standing there. One asked if it was all right to talk to me while I had my coffee. I turned around and faced them. They seemed about eleven or twelve years old. The tallest one introduced himself as Matt and the other was Ben. They took turns talking and told me they were twelve, and twelve and a half. That seemed to be important that one was a little older. Matt told me they were best friends, just like me and Colonel Calhoun. They both wanted to fly someday like us, when they were old enough to join the Air Force. As they took turns talking, I could see they were impressed with the medals and ribbons on my uniform so I asked if they wanted to know what some meant. They came closer as I went through the display of colors and pins and wings. I could tell they wanted to hear it all. I asked how long they had been best friends. Ben said he had been adopted last summer, so only about a year. He lived about a mile from Colonel Calhoun's farm and knew the family and all about him being adopted.

Then he said, "I want to be just like him."

Matt said he only had one parent and his father died two years ago. This really hit me in the heart. My mind instantly shot back to my past as I looked these two young boys in the eyes. Matt went on telling me how they go to the new airport that is being built. They sit on the hill and make believe their flying some of the planes. We walked away from the table talking. They were real nice kids, polite and well spoken and seemed to have a direction and a good imagination for twelve year olds. As we walked along I told them how I got started flying with my Dad and they were never too young. I told them to go see Mr. Phil Jones next week and I'd see if I could get them up in a plane going around the airport. I knew my Dad could work something out.

"Get permission from your parent's first." I handed them a paper with my name on it to bring with them. It was like the best Christmas gift they ever received. They both tried to hold the paper at the same time. A 'thank you Colonel Stevens', and a handshake from their two very small hands and they were off running. My heart skipped a beat when Ben hit Matt on the arm, and Matt hit Ben back as they put their arms around each other smiling. That was me and Joey, not so long ago. I took a few deep breaths and I went back to the table and told my Dad.

Ashley was not here and I wondered if she knew about this news with Joey and Lette Mae.

We all sang songs and the night went on. It got late and people started to leave saying their goodbyes. They knew we were leaving for Texas this week.

As we walked to the car, I saw a car coming our way and it stopped right next to us.

Ashley poked her head out of the window and yelled out, "I'm sorry Billy. I couldn't get anyone to stay with mother. I only have a few minutes and I didn't want to miss this surprise for you and Joey. I love you Billy." She was crying.

We were all around the car now, I felt like a chump. I went to the window and we looked each other in the eyes.

"Ashley I'm sorry, I've been a jerk, and I'll call you tomorrow." I kissed her on the forehead, and we pulled away from the car.

She pulled away and left for home. Everyone looked at me. I just stood there dazed.

"Let's go home," Dad said. We all moved to our cars and left for home. It was a quiet ride home. I said goodnight and I went to my room. Marion stayed overnight.

I had another bad night of dreaming about the war. I had to do something about this because I need my sleep.

Next morning I went downstairs and checked the fireplace, put in some new wood, and went to the kitchen to find Janice and Marion talking at the table. Dad was on the phone.

Janice asked in her usual way, "What's bothering you boy, you look like you were running a race all night?"

I sat down and proceeded to tell her how I wasn't sleeping very well and having bad dreams again. Marion spoke up and said, "Stress must be running in the family these days. You have a lot of stress going on with Ashley, leaving for Texas soon, and not knowing how your Dad's going to be. Just take things one day at a time Billy. We are here to help you out."

"Thanks Marion and Janice, what would I do without you two."

Just then Dad called me to the phone. "Someone wants to say hi," as he handed me the phone.

It was the Vice President on the line. "Billy I'm sorry I missed your surprise last night. I just got back from Washington on business. There were a few things I had to take care of. I'll see you at Foster's Air Field in a few days. I just wanted to say hi. I only have a few minutes so put your Dad back on. Take care."

I worked with Dad at the office all day. During lunch I made a call to Ashley and made plans to see her at her house after work.

That seemed the only way we could spend time together. Dad heard my plans.

Around three thirty Marion came by the office with a bouquet of red roses and put them on my desk. As I looked up, she smiled and patted me on the shoulder and said, "Good luck tonight kid. These might help," as she went into Dad's office. I thought good news travels fast in this office.

After work Dad and I drove back home. I changed and was out the door.

It was snowing again and it was getting real cold now that the sun was going down. I headed to Ashley's house.

When I came up the driveway Ashley's car was home. She was waiting at the door when I came up. I handed over the dozen roses as she leaned over and kissed me. We went inside. I took off my boots and heavy coat, and we sat down at the kitchen table. The house was warm and there must have been a cake in the oven because it smelled good.

She started talking this time and I just listened. It was all about her mother and how she had taken a turn for the worse. Her father was upstairs with her while we talked.

When she stopped, I started by telling her how sorry I felt about her mother, and how sorry I was that I got so upset. I tried to explain how I felt left out and I felt I should have been told what was going on. She listened. I kept talking. Eventually I ran out of things to say.

We sat back in our chairs and just looked at each other. Finally I asked if she knew about Joey and Lette Mae setting their wedding date.

She said, "Lette Mae had the feeling he might be going to do that but she didn't know when." Then she asked, "How did it go?"

"Pretty good I guess. Both parents seem happy."

I could hear her mother screaming out some loud words but couldn't understand any of it. Immediately, Ashley jumped up out of the chair with panic written across her face. I was scared and didn't know what to do.

"I've got to go. I'm sorry Billy. I think father might need me. She kissed me on the forehead. Do you want to stay and wait or what?"

"No I'll go; you have enough going on here." I was confused.

"Thank you for the roses, I love you Billy." She left to go upstairs.

I put on my coat and left. On the way out I wondered what I could have done if I had stayed. I really didn't know her mother very well and I probably would have made things worse. I thought her father was a very quiet man and I didn't know him very well either.

Still upset over this visit, and while I was just out riding around to cool down, I went over to the Hotel to see who was working there now. I used to know all the guys serving tables and doing dishes. I sat at the bar and had a beer. There were a few familiar faces at the table. I'd been away for a couple of years now and things had changed. Some people looked at me because of the publicity in the newspapers. A few guys from school remembered me and came over to talk. One guy from school was married and had a two month old baby boy. I saw the pictures. Another guy worked as an auto mechanic and said his father remembered my father working as a mechanic in town. He talked about what he had heard about me, and what a great mechanic his father told him my father was. Just by chance another guy came over and hugged me and started talking about the service. He couldn't believe I was a Colonel, or a pilot. We talked for over an hour about what it was like to be in the Air Force and go overseas. I told him how we never knew if we would be returning from our mission or not. It was always a challenge with death. Mission after mission, each day it was rough and men didn't come back. It was hard to make friends. They might be gone next mission. You might be the one watching him go down. Most guys didn't want to talk after a flight. Some took a long time to settle down. I knew how many hours I had flown and I knew how many planes I had shot down. Someone always kept track of that stuff for you. I could feel myself sinking away to that feeling again. I had another beer and we talked a while longer. After going on for a while I started to get a little mellow and quieted down.

One of them asked, "How do you sleep at night?"

My reply shocked them. "Not too good I'm afraid. Pilot memories are not always something you want to talk about."

We changed the subject to the weather and soon I realized it was time to head for home.

I made one more stop on the way home. I went to see Dr. Deering. He was outside clearing the large window that had iced up from the last storm. I jumped in and helped him and moved the gutter away from the window. It looked like it had been pulled down and was draining on his window. I think he was surprised to see me at first, but he said he knew I was back for a while. He asked how I was feeling. He had heard about me being shot in the shoulder. I told him of my troubles shoveling, then I put his broom and shovel away in the garage, and we walked toward the house.

"You got a few minutes Billy, I was going to try and find you tomorrow. This is so much better. Would you like some coffee, I put it on just a few minutes ago?"

"I'd like that. I've been over at the Hotel with some of the guys and had a little more than I planned." I helped him set the table and he put out some homemade apple pie from the oven.

"Hey, I didn't know you were such a good cook." We laughed.

"Do you mind if I light my pipe?" he asked, as he reached up over the stove for a light.

"No I really enjoy your pipe. Be my guest. It brings back memories of us sitting on the porch with Mom, when I was little. How old were Mom and Dad when they got married, do you know Doctor?"

"Yes. I think Sara was 23 and John was 29. Sara's parents never liked the idea of John marrying Sara. They thought he was a poor farm boy. John was a hard worker and was never a poor farm boy." He poured the coffee and we sat down and continued our conversation.

"Doctor you delivered all the babies in town, did you deliver both my Dad's?"

"Yes I did Billy. What is it you want to know?"

"Why were they so different, and why did my Dad John hate me so?"

"Billy you have to let that go now. It had nothing to do with you and that hate was not your fault. John missed Sara so much he took out his anger on you. You were there. It took a while. None of us saw it coming or we would have taken you out of that situation sooner. Sara kept him grounded. He loved her so much he was lost without her. You're a lucky boy and you have your real father to take care of you now. You both have a second chance for happiness. We all have a second chance at life again."

I left after giving him a big hug and making sure he was comfortable for the night. He asked me to keep in touch.

It was late when I got in and the house was quiet. Dad was in his room upstairs. I tapped on his door on my way by and said goodnight.

I heard, "Hey, how did things go son?"

I pushed the door open and said, "She loved the roses. We're okay. Her mother was bad today. I stopped by and saw Doctor Deering. See you in the morning."

Today I knew I had one day left before going to Texas. Dad said he called and made arrangements for things to be done at the office.

We left for the airport after breakfast to check out the plane we would be flying to Texas. Dad had made plans to land his plane at Foster's Air Field, with Colonel Stevens and Colonel Calhoun on board.

When we arrived at the airport to check out the plane there was snow on the ground. Not much, but it was messy on the runway. We thought it would probably be alright for takeoff tomorrow. When we approached the land crew they didn't seem too concerned. We were scheduled for an eleven o'clock takeoff.

We left and went to Greenfield. Dad had an appointment to make and he wanted some company. I wondered what he was up to now. We drove up to a good size building with a "For Sale" sign in the front window.

"What's this Dad," I asked.

"This is our new office. When you're ready it's yours. What do you think? Plenty of parking, good location, right in the center of town, I'll have it up and ready, when you're ready. Do whatever you want with it, what do you think?"

"You never stop amazing me Dad. Are you not busy enough without taking more on? You are supposed to be taking it easy Dad, remember?"

"Billy I have the guys lined up to do the work and I have plenty of work around here to keep this office going full time. I'm giving people jobs that really need to work. It's all paper work to me. I'm not doing anything physical. Don't worry, it will all work out. So what do you think?"

"This is a big surprise. I love you Dad." I just looked around and couldn't believe he did this.

"Anything you want to do before we go back son?"

"Do you think they plowed out the Greenfield Cemetery yet? I'd like to go there for a minute, Dad."

I found the gravestone and paid my respects to Mom and Dad. Again tears came to my eyes as I looked down on my Dad's stone. We both stood there for a while.

It was around noon when we got back to the office in the city. I dropped Dad off and I went to Marion's office at the hospital. After a lengthy visit, I went back to the office and worked a while cleaning up some of the paper work on the desk. I looked over and Dad looked real tired today. I thought he was working too hard, but of course you couldn't convince him to take some time off. I asked him if he wanted to go home early today where it was our last day together for a while.

"You know son that sounds good. Things here are under control, let's go home. I'll call Marion in case she stops by here, and tell her we are leaving early." He took some papers from the desk, and I said my goodbyes to the office staff. We got home around 3:30 and Janice was quite surprised.

"What can I do for you two, are you hungry? Do you want time to yourself, let me know." She put our boots near the door to dry and took our big coats to hang them on the door. She had a big pot of soup on the stove, and was just ready to put in the dumplings when we arrived. I sat and watched her work as I used to when I was younger. Janice was like the Grandmother that I never had. She ran this house like her own and we loved it.

Dad put his papers on the desk in the living room and came out to join us. "Something sure smells good Janice. I don't think either one of us had lunch." He looked my way. I nodded, he was right I never even thought about it until now.

"I'll have something ready in just a few minutes for you boys just hold on now." She set out the bowls and we laughed about all the great meals she made us all these years. Janice was loved here, very much. After a delicious meal, Dad left to take care of some paper work and read the rest of the papers. I sat with Janice while she cleaned up. Cleo sat in my lap. I told her what Dad had showed me this afternoon. I kind of had the feeling she knew something of the new building but she never said a thing. I told her about visiting Dr. Deering and some of my problems I was having with Ashley. She was a great listener and always had some great ideas. I listened.

Later Joey called and we talked for a while. We planned to meet at the airport tomorrow around ten o'clock, ready to go. That was our plan.

I thought about what the doctor said and what Janice had to say about my problem with Ashley. I called her and we talked for a while. She sounded tired and sad that I was leaving without spending much time with her. She promised to write and call me. I did too.

Upstairs I finished packing and brought my bags down by the front door. When I opened the front door to see the weather outside it was very cold and spitting snow again. I went back to the kitchen and gave Janice a telephone number to call if the snow started to get heavy when I was away. Dad's crew could start here at the house and then go do the offices. I had talked to one of the drivers and he said he would take care of it.

"Now you sound like your Dad, Billy." She put the number in her apron pocket and gave me a big hug.

I went in the living room and sat by the radio with my cat, and listened to some music and a few weather reports for tomorrow. I think I dozed off a while. When I woke up Dad was sleeping in his chair and I was ready for bed. I woke him and helped him up the stairs.

It was dark when I woke up early in the morning and my cat was playing with my boots. I guess it was the leather he liked to scratch on. Moving the curtains I could see it was icy out there, everything was shiny, and long icicles were hanging off the trees. Oh boy.

I dressed and got my room cleaned I grabbed my little warm furry friend and went downstairs. Janice was cooking up a storm, and I wanted to keep that great smell in my nose forever. She knew I'd be leaving soon. She had tears in her eyes.

Dad came down and went right to the phone. I stood by his side only to hear that the airport was taking care of the ice problems. He tried to look confident that things were going to be ready when we got there. All I could think was, more stress, just what he needs.

"Go eat Dad. We still have a few hours and maybe the sun will come out."

The three of us sat together and I told them both I loved them and enjoyed my time at home with them. I promised to call often and write. They both smiled.

A little later we put our bags in the truck and headed for the airport. The roads were icy. It was slow going and it took longer than we expected to get there. We drove up near the plane. What I saw wasn't pretty. On both wings, the ground crew was chipping away at the ice.

Joey drove in with Tom and Judy. The plane was loaded as we all stood outside and watched. The runway was being plowed at the same time. The crew started the plane, it rumbled quite a bit, but it started. We waited about ten minutes warming it up, and then we said our goodbyes.

We got in the plane and Dad took control as we taxied down the runway. We knew the runway was slick, but Dad knew his plane. The engine was skipping and sputtering along. Dad played with the dials and gears and the rudder, he made it as smooth as he could while picking up speed. Eventually the engine cleared and we started lifting. The plane rumbled a bit, chips of ice fell off flying by the window. We were up about 500 feet so he leveled off to see the conditions on the outside. Everything looked fine, the engine was warmed up, no rumbling, and Dad had a smile. He loved this plane and he knew we were golden.

We sat back and settled in for the long ride to Texas.

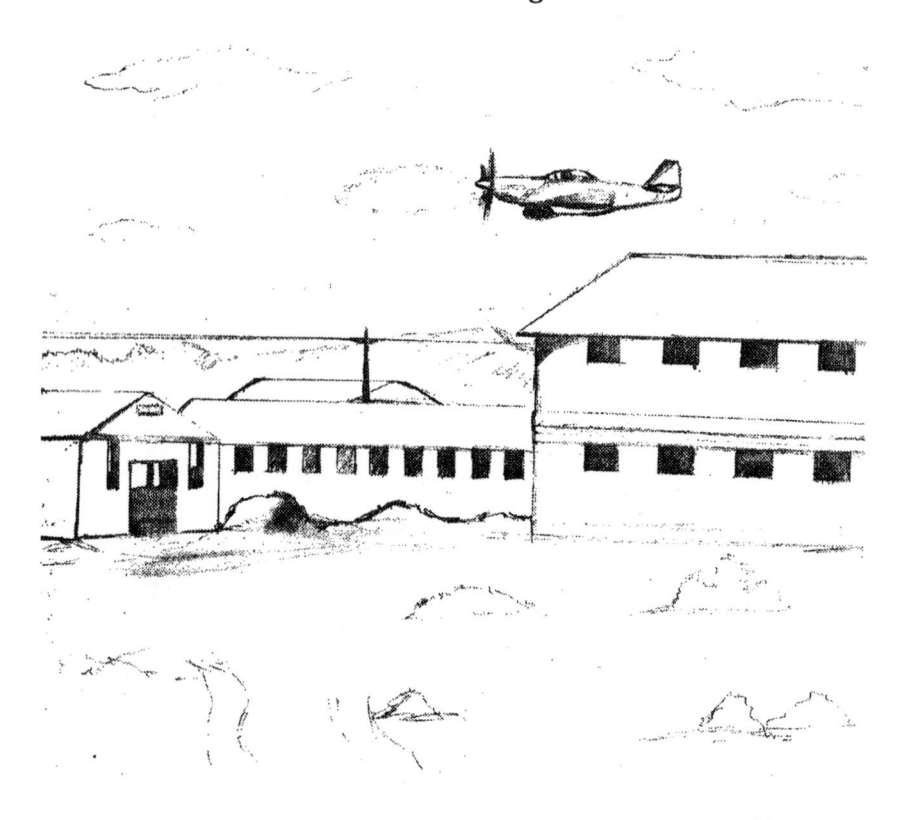

Foster Air Field

Chapter 23

Foster Air Field

We arrived at Foster Air Field and were greeted by Lieutenant Madison who was assigned to taking us to our quarters. Our bags were put in the staff car, and Dad had to shuttle his plane to another place. Something was arranged for him and we would see him later. The Lieutenant took us to the Officer's Quarters where we had our bags dropped off.

Looking around, the base seemed to have changed for the better since we were here last. Many more buildings had been constructed on the site for housing and training facilities, for instructors, and for incoming equipment and newer aircraft trainer planes. The cadets used the North American AT-6 advanced trainer, the Curtis P-40 trainers, and PT13s and PT17s, for drill and aerial gunnery. New planes were coming in all the time. The story was the buildings were all filled to capacity as fast as they were put up. Many buildings used for schools, were being expanded even while they were being constructed.

Many pilots returning from overseas service were taught to become air combat instructors at Foster Field. The classes were being redesigned and responsibility was assumed by both flying and technical training instructors. Just before we arrived on base, there had been a terrible accident with two planes colliding on the runway. Drastic changes had to be made. The two training commands had undergone a rapid expansion to keep up with the needs of the Army Air Forces. The Army Air Force had gone through a period of refining and adapting the protocol. The basic training and technical schools were full. The pilot training center was putting out the largest class of graduates since the base opened. The Air Force was in need of instructors who could take on the challenge. That's what we were here for. We had the expertise for flying these planes and the experience firsthand.

While the war continued in the Pacific and in Europe, the demand for pilots began to catch up.

We went to a new building that had just been finished. Lieutenant Madison told us this was where we would be teaching and the program was set in place. We would be in charge of several hundred trainees. I looked at Joey; he looked back at me with those raised eyebrows I expected. We walked around and took notes of what we actually had to work with. It was a large room, about 200 chairs and desks, benches all along the sides of the room, plenty of good overhead lighting, large windows, a large coal stove over to the right hand corner, and blackboards around the front walls. It seemed sufficient. I didn't plan to be in the classroom very long, I wanted to be out in the planes. After the look around we headed for the mess hall to meet some of the officers and instructors we would be working with. We had dinner. The men seemed glad to have us on board. They spent most of their time talking and asking us questions about our time in England. We soon found out none of the current instructors had ever been overseas. Most of them stayed in the States working on other bases. That surprised me. We learned that once a pilot came back from overseas, you were either injured, or you stayed for leave and was sent back. No one retired during this time, they were all needed.

The course was going to last for two months. During that time some men would be shipped to another area for eight days for specific training skills, then return a week before graduation. The program sounded organized and ready to start.

Some of the instructors showed us around. They had heard we were like brothers. Our publicity had arrived here before us and they all had questions to ask. We both found the men to be friendly and eager to help us any way they could.

Later I asked if my Dad had taken off in his plane yet. A call was made and we were taken by car to another part of the field.

I looked out the window and Dad and some other men were checking out his plane on the tarmac. He looked ready to go. I didn't like the idea of him going back in his plane all alone. We got out of the car and I heard some commotion going on behind us. As I turned I caught a glimpse of the Vice President coming our way. He came over to us and asked how we were doing. We just looked at him in surprise.

"We have something here for you boys but they waited for me to arrive before they showed you. I'm late returning from a meeting, Oh, I'm going back with your Dad Billy, that's why we asked him to wait. Follow me." That was a great relief to hear that.

We followed along a large new hangar. When the crew opened the doors there were two P-51s right in front of us. My plane 'The Farmer', and Joey's plane 'The Storyteller', were just sitting there. How did they ever manage to do this? Again we just looked at each other. They were in England the last time we saw them. We both went over to our planes and looked them over. I noticed the back seat had been put in both planes. We had talked to Marty about making that change if he could ever get the parts for it. What a great surprise.

Dad spoke up. "We figured you might like to have your cadets see the actual planes while you're teaching. You might want to fly them, being the fact they are now yours. We're making space and doing the paper work for these planes, at our new airport in Iowa."

"Dad when did you have time to do all this?" I asked.

I could see Joey had tears in his eyes, he couldn't believe it either. He just stood by his plane and rubbed the sides as he made his way around it. A big hug was given on his way by Dad, he couldn't speak. This was an emotional moment for both of us.

"I had a little help boys," looking at the Vice President and smiling. "We had something else going on for today to, but planes are running slow because of all the bad weather. We are going to head back now. Let us know how things are going here."

Dad gave me and Joey a big hug, and they left to get in his plane for home.

We stayed in the hangar for a while. We had a lot to talk over and we wanted to look at the inside of our planes. Marty had made some other changes we liked too. What a day.

Our classes would start tomorrow.

We woke to the sound of the bugle boy, right on time.

The instructors working along with us knew we had about 200 students broken down to 25 cadets in four classes. We had instructors, squadron commanders, flight commanders, and assistant flight commanders. We had a few dispatchers. You had to have at least 220 hours of flying time, then you were put through a training course and had to pass a check ride with the military. A lot of the instructors here had been tow plane pilots and from the glider program. Some did their own logbook signing, known as Shaefer time, some were young and some were older. Flight time was not a top priority. The instructors got paid twice a month. Classes lasted about eight weeks, six days on, Sundays off, then two weeks off at another base towards the end. Depending on the need for pilots, we were told to rush them through, eliminate the weak. If the student was slow, let him go. A normal solo took between 7 to 8 hours of flight time. If you ran 12 hours before solo, you were a washout. Cadets flew mornings one day, afternoons the next. This gave them a mix of the weather conditions. We flew with about 45 trainer planes a day. With that many flying all day, it was important to have traffic checks constantly.

Something we insisted on with the planes was a fixed rearview mirror, below the fuel tank, in the center section. We could see the student's facial expressions. A lap belt held them in, and we had seat pack parachutes. There was no electrical system and no starter in the trainers. It was an inertia starter that had to be cranked by hand outside the plane. The first few days, the planes were started by the instructors until the students got the hang of it. The planes were very noisy. Most of the classes went from the Stearman to the AT-6s.

By the time Joey and I got the students, they already knew they wanted to become pilots. Up about 1000 feet, you knew if this was for you or not. Students flew in the front seat. There was a bucket of water, and towel, sitting on the flight line, for anyone who needed to clean up after his flight.

The instructors made out grade slips and commented who might be good or bad as a pilot. Green slips were good, pink slips were bad. Three pink meant you had to have a check ride; that was not good.

Early in the morning our new routine started. After breakfast and sign-ins we got our assignments for the day. Joey got classroom training. He was still not signed off by the medical doctor to fly yet. We could change schedules when he was ready. I got the trainer AT-6 for a while. My job was checking out the new pilots that claimed they had flown before somewhere else. Oh happy day.

The very day we started training classes, twelve new P-51s came on the base. This raised a lot of commotion as to where to store them. Some room was made and the planes were ready to fly the next day. We all shook our heads wondering where this order came from.

Most of these pilots had been flying for a while on their own. Then they came here and I had to test them to see just what they could do. I say that because, I really took it easy on them their first day. After my first day I wondered what they really knew. I decided to get out my manuals and check things out here.

Joey experienced much the same issues during his classes. We talked about it at dinner and realized we had to make some serious changes, if we were going to prepare these guys for combat fighting in the P-51s. For the next few days we found time to work out a program that was more to our liking. We had some good ideas and had free reign on what we did. These planes did far more than what was being taught. I was sure I was the one to teach them. We put the new program in effect.

Knowing that our first test flight in England was really a combat mission these boys were not ready. Did they know about the Merlin engine in this Mustang and that it could fly higher and carry more fuel and had an outstanding rate of climb? Did they know they had a three hundred mile radius for travel? Or that they were made for bomber escort work? They were the best in the air. These cadets acted like it was a jaunt in the sky and back down again. I guess it was time to separate the pilots from the rest. If they were going to fly for me, they were going to be the best.

Joey changed some of the reading materials we were working from. They were out dated already. I changed the style of flying they were doing. To be ready for combat you had to picture yourself in the seat by yourself facing the enemy. We could both put that fear we felt into words and feelings as we taught the newbie's. Knowing every inch of the plane and how it handled was crucial when you were all alone up in the wild blue yonder. You had to know how to react every second. That's all you had sometimes. This was life or death and you might not come back. You make choices and they better be the right ones.

We had a good program set in place and we worked it to the limits every day. This was a job and serious business. We sat together at night over dinner in the Officer's Club and talked of what we wanted to try next. I had heard of the link trainer course for instructors that were offered and Joey and I signed up.

So we taught pilots to fly. We were told we had a unique way of teaching that had been noticed about us all the way through the Service. Now we had been given the opportunity to teach our methods to others. We let it all out at times.

Joey was first to tell of his first flight return story about heaving his guts out overseas, and feeling queasy for a couple of hours after. He would be sure to teach that method. We laughed about that one a lot.

I thought I was so cool my first flight. I was flying high in the sky in my own plane until I met my first German fighter plane coming right at me. My stomach did giant flip-flops. I could see him sitting in his plane and my window got shot at, Oh yeah! We could give a few lessons on the feelings of being a real pilot. Could we teach them your plane is your life, your mechanic, your God! Let's hope so.

We did our jobs and did them well. In the evenings we got to work on our own planes. We both signed up for classes. I took some law classes and Joey got started in business management.

The beginning of the third week we were both taken off the job and replaced with substitutes. We were taken to a hangar and someone was standing back to us, talking to the Lieutenant at the desk. The man turned around and we both had our mouths open. It was our friend Marty. Our friend and mechanic from Boxted, was now a Major. What was he doing here? He came to us and we all hugged, and connected like friends do.

"What are you doing here?" I asked.

"It's so good to see you guys again." Marty hugged us again. "Special orders came from the Vice President and a promotion to Major for me. I was sent home with my family for a few weeks, and then relocated to this base. I'm late arriving because of the weather. I came over after your planes were shipped to the States. I'm stationed here now and I'm going to be head of Mechanics here on the base. You know I'm the best. I missed you guys. How are you doing Joey?"

The rest of the day Marty hung out with us and we talked our way through our past couple of weeks and our trip to Washington. We went with him to some of the hangars and he looked over his territory here on the base. I couldn't help but ask Marty, "So how are you going to keep your jacket on as Major, while you're under the planes in the grease, Marty?"

"You know me guys. I'll just have to work late at night with my flashlight on."

We just raised our arms up in the air.

We talked about our families and about Joey's new family. Then we started on Joey about setting a wedding date. We had a lot to catch up on. Marty started in on his family and we talked our way through the night.

Later we found out where the special orders came from. Dad was at it again.

It was good to have Marty back with us.

Here we were and all together working at what we liked to do best. The next morning I called Dad and we all talked to him showing our appreciation. His comment was, "It's all in a day's work." He made sure to ask Marty to visit as soon as he could.

During the week on the base our new improved courses were working. I would take the cadets one on one, and test each one in the air. We had several instructors and many of the cadets were training and turning out just fine. We had a few that still thought this was fun and games. I planned to take care of a few of them this week. This morning I had a cadet named Jim Ware, who caught my attention last week. I waited for the opportunity. He dressed up and waited his turn by the plane. As I walked over to the trainer I yelled out, "Let's go, let's see what you can do Ware."

We climbed up and taxied down the runway. "Okay, whenever you're ready Ware."

He moved down the runway cautiously at first then lifted up circling the runway.

"Level off at 1000 feet and then check out your readings."

He was quick to respond and he knew he was good! That was okay. I remember how I felt in the beginning.

"Let's go up to maximum." He proceeded to lift. Then I heard "How high do you want me to go Colonel?" came quietly from the seat. "You should know Ware." I could tell by his voice he was a little nervous. I let him climb and this was higher than he had been before. So I waited and said nothing. He tried to look over at me. He was anxious and looking side to side squirming a bit. The plane started to sputter. Now I had him right where I wanted him. The smirk was gone now and he straightened up and was not fidgeting. He looked serious now and that's the look I wanted.

"Okay Ware, let's do some loops." He pulled off to the right and began to dive down and circle into some fine loops just a bit slow. I took the stick and dropped down while looping. A couple of quick flips and he was hanging on for dear life. "Okay Ware, your turn. Pick up the speed this time and quicker on the flips. Imagine yourself being chased by the enemy and they have zeroed in on you. You have only seconds. This is your last chance to get out of the line of fire; now show me how to handle that. Get free and show me how to do it. You're running for your life."

Over he rolled and into a great dive and a loop. I had him do this three times. He was scared but he reacted well for a beginner. I had him go in for a landing. His landing was shaky but I knew that wasn't a problem for him. When we climbed out of the plane I noticed the smirk was gone. He went inside a little queasy and didn't show up the rest of the afternoon.

I had another cadet I wanted to see this afternoon too. He needed some work on his landings. I took notes on him last week and didn't like what I saw. It was hard to believe how bad he was. I got him settled in and he took off. He was real shaky. He said nothing. So off we went climbing higher and higher, until I knew we had some space for sizing up the runway.

"This is the way we're going to practice your landings. I want them smooth and slow, so you can see what you're doing. I took the stick and down we went for the landing. That's what I figured he needed work on. I sailed down fast, when I heard a loud banging on the seat. My partner was freaking out on me. He was holding his hand over his mouth and he was beet red in the face. It was then I realized he was sick as a dog and turning green. This cadet was scared and in big trouble. How did he ever make it this far flying? The landing scared him to death. I soft peddled it coming in on the landing. I tried to talk him down so he wouldn't do anything stupid.

When we landed I opened the hatch and got him on the ground. He had thrown up all over the inside of the plane, his clothes and the ground where he stood. I took him over by the hangar and we talked. He was done in the air and he knew it. I sent him to the showers. Later I met with him, checked him out, and we went to the office to decide what other plan of action he would be fit for. I had in my mind, maybe Marty. He might be good with his hands on the ground. He seemed like a good kid.

The next day I had another cadet who really had things together. He kind of reminded me of myself at his age, like I'm real old now! Joey asked me to take him on my flight that afternoon. He could fly and had no fear while he talked his way through most of the flying time. I was impressed. Nice smooth take offs and landings, he was good. I checked out his book work and he had it made there too.

In the afternoon I had another one that could fly like a bird. His dives and loops were just like mine. I was impressed. Joey had picked them both out from school work and he sent them up to be tested. He couldn't wait to talk about them to me.

"What did you think of the two I sent you Billy?"

"So far they are the best I've ever seen except for us." We both smiled.

Some days were challenging. We tried new ways to handle these cadets. They knew we were serious and we were there for them. They could talk to us. I guess it was because we were younger and had some real experience to pass on to them. Sometimes when the classes were over, and before Joey and I had to go off to our classes at night, some of the cadets would gather around outside our door on the steps. They just seemed anxious to learn all they could about what they were going into, and as much about us as they could.

Joey had more time to talk during the day in classes. The questions were coming in about the changes in the classes. The cadets seemed to be doing better, and were in a better frame of mind for learning. No one was late for classes or flying. Joey said sometimes the black boards were full of questions. Some were educational and some were even personal. He was amazed when he walked in the room each morning, just what they wanted to know.

We both had a hard core speech we had made up for our cadets. Today was my day. It went something like this:

"Ok, sit down and listen. Look to your left, look to your right, in a class of 20 cadets, 10 of you will not come back if you were in combat. Pay attention to us. This is your life, we are your lifeline. Yes you will be scared, yes you will feel lost, afraid to make friends; you will watch your friends die. Sometimes you will not even be able to eat. It's tough over there, but you can do it. You have it inside of you. Your biggest advantage is you are an American. You have something special to come back home to, and a country to protect. You have the best Air Force training in the world and the best planes in the sky. God Bless America. Do your best and come home safely. We look and act like heroes but were darn glad we're here alive. If the truth were known, I wouldn't send any of you overseas, because I know some of you won't come back. Go with God. End of speech."

We left the class together, Joey asking me again if I thought the two cadets today were pretty good. I looked at him and just said, "Better than us when we went over. If they listen to us they might have a chance of returning."

Marty was waiting at the door and he just shook his head. "You scare me to death," He said. "I don't know about them, I hope they listen," looking over at the young cadets.

We took our classes at night right on the base. We studied until around eleven most nights.

One night we came out of the classroom and the sky was lit-up with color. The background sky was a soft gray. The bottom of the sky was a creamy vanilla background. The sky danced with pink and gray swirls, shaped like tall ballerinas, dancing and floating across the sky. You had to stop and look up at the sight. It was cold and the ground was covered with snow, but the sky was dancing. We talked all the way back to our quarters.

During the day our classes were over about two o'clock. Marty worked longer hours. His time was spent keeping all the planes in the air. He told us he had found time to get all his training in, and was now able to teach if he were needed. Some weekends we would fly with Marty, teaching him some of our techniques. Marty had no fear and learned fast. We think he had his eye on a plane he wanted to own someday.

When the mail came in Marty received most of it. He had the biggest family. Joey's sisters would write and Judy wrote once a week. Marion would send me cards for the holidays. Dad never wrote. I'd get a call from him every week on Sunday mornings.

This afternoon I got a letter from Ashley. I quickly took it inside and ripped the envelope open. A lovely picture of Ashley fell to the desk. I noticed it was one that I had taken in Washington in our room. She was so beautiful. I held it in my hand as I started to read the letter. I kind of knew what she was going to say. She felt guilty she couldn't spend more time with me and sorry her mother was so sick and needed constant attention. She talked about her classes in school and the time she spent in the bank after classes. She had special projects going on at the library and she was involved in setting up a Historical Group. People could check out their ancestry and how Greenfield came together with some of the first families that actually moved in. And people wanted to know what they did for a living when they got here. These subjects sounded like a great idea but it required a lot of time and work. She had no help. Just papers being dropped off all the time. To her surprise, most people would write out the things for her if she gave them some forms to follow. Her desk at the library was full of papers and pictures to file. Last week she said Joey's mother Martha asked her to do a family ancestry on her family for Joey. She had some papers she wanted him to have, before she passed away. She also agreed to help Ashley out if she could. That proved to be a big help to her. She was very good at filing and giving out the forms from the library. So you see Billy, I am keeping busy most of the time but I miss you really bad and I love you. I want to spend my life with you. Please call me or write me as soon as you can. I think of Washington every night. The letter ended with I love you, Ashley. The paper was perfumed and lipstick kisses were all around.

I held the picture to my heart. I'd call her tonight.

Hiatus . . .

It was Saturday night when I got a chance to call Ashley. It was a good time for her. It was quiet and her mother was sedated for the night. I told her how much her letter meant to me and I promised to be home in about two weeks. I had planned a quick trip to Florida and then home for about six days. We would spend as much time as we could together. She sounded pleased and couldn't wait to make some plans for us together.

I asked how her mother was doing and she said the outlook was poor but she was sleeping more now. That made it easier for her and her father.

I told her I loved her and we ended the call. Just hearing her voice I knew she was doing better.

The next morning was Sunday. We took Marty to the Officer's Club for breakfast. We built up that meal all week. We really played it up. He would get all his favorite things to eat. As we walked in we were greeted by many of the Officers that came for Sunday breakfast.

We sat Marty down among many of our friends and parents that were visiting. Marty was intrigued. On his own he would never come here for breakfast. He never ate out anywhere.

So they brought out the coffee. I looked at Joey, he had his eyebrows already lifted, and a slight smirk on his face. It was so strong, I swear, the spoon could stand up alone. As you drank the coffee, the cup was stained black inside. They passed out big donuts with it to kill the bitter taste. The donuts were so hard you could bounce them off the floor. The main plate consisted of greasy fatty bacon, and 'SOS', tasting like wall paper paste. A little pile of scrambled eggs, were off to the side of the bacon, lying in grease. Joey started the conversation with, "Boy this makes it all worthwhile, working so hard all week, huh Marty?" I almost choked as I looked at his expression, trying to be sincere.

Marty had the last laugh. "It's just like home boys, thanks." He ate everything on his plate and went for seconds on the coffee.

Some of the people at our table wanted us to tell some stories of our training experiences so far. One set of parents went out of their way to tell us, their son thought we were the best trainers he could have had. Their son talked of us in his letters home. They wanted to meet us. They were surprised how young we were.

After breakfast we left and went to the hangar with Marty. We had our laughs over breakfast but I think Marty had a good time with us. We set up some plans for the coming weeks ahead. This was going to be our first time off for about eight days. Joey planned to fly home. I had plans to go to Dale Mabry Field in Florida, then come back and pick up Marty. We were going to bring him home with us to Iowa for a few days. Joey and I planned to show him around and he was looking forward to it.

That night Dad called with a story about two new friends he made this week. He said, "While I was walking around the airport checking out some things being done, two young boys, approximately eleven or twelve years old, called out my name. I stopped and turned as they approached. They were dressed in Army fatigues, cap and black boots. But on their backs they had Air Force jackets. They carried a special paper that seemed very important to give to me. For two young men they had a strong handshake. They introduced themselves as Ben and Matt. It didn't take too long for me to realize, these were the boys you had talked about. They handed me a paper signed by their parents, that you had given them. They told me all about Colonel Stevens and Colonel Calhoun and said they wanted to be just like them. I asked if they had ever been in a plane before, and neither had been. I knew they were anxious, so I took them for a walk around in the hangars and explained what they were looking at. There were a lot of planes being worked on. This was a good time to see everything. Matt asked if Colonel Stevens or Colonel Calhoun's planes were anywhere that they could see them. I said, 'Let's see,' as I walked them around to another hangar, and opened the doors. They were by my side in a flash. Mouths wide open, they didn't dare move. I called out and my mechanic came over. I asked if he could ready the two boys for a quick ride around the airport. There were some clothes over in the corner that might fit them for a ride. I went and made our time for our flight. It was not busy and most of the planes were in for the day. I gave notebooks and a pen for taking notes, just like I did with you and Joey on your first ride. They were so excited I had a hard time making them listen to the rules while I readied them in the plane. In they went, and we taxied down the runway. Ben was in front leaning out the window to see everything, and Matt in the back. We pulled him up so he could see better, he got real still. Lift off was real smooth and we circled the airport as we lifted higher. I took it easy on them. Matt was scared I could tell. We leveled off about 1000 feet and I let Ben take the stick and get the feel for it. I let him give the numbers on the radio, he was elated. I started to make a turn and Ben sat back tight in his seat. Matt was looking out the window but held on tight to the door. Ben thought the noise was loud, and Matt thought the plane was real bumpy. They both sat tight in the seats until I landed. They enjoyed seeing the lights coming up on the runway and they really wanted to see all they could. We landed and got out of the plane. Matt was okay, but I knew if I made a big deal out of landing he would probably have been sick. Ben was fine. I told them they did a great job for the first time in the air and I said they had the makings of great pilots. A nice thank you and they left smiling, after putting everything away for my mechanic. That was enough excitement for one day. They couldn't wait to get home and tell their story. 'Drop by again boys and we'll talk,' I called out as they left.

"Nice boys Billy, maybe they will come back again. Well I just wanted you to know and I'm waiting for you and Marty to spend some time here soon. I love you son."

The end of February came and we got our time off. The cadets went over to the Gulf for special training.

Joey took his plane and flew home. He had been checked out by the base doctor and was okay to fly now. He had plans to get his wedding bands and get fitted for his clothes for the wedding. Final plans had to be made. Lette Mae had his time planned. He also had his extended family to deal with.

His older sister Mary was dating a man she met in town. She put herself back in school and still worked part time in the hair dressing shop. She told Joey the first night he was home, that she met her new boyfriend while out with her friends from the shop. They always went to the Hotel for a drink after work and talk. She said one evening a tall handsome man came to the table and asked her for a dance. Since the music was soft and low, the girls could watch and talk as she floated around the small dance floor with this handsome man. We talked softly and smiled our way through several dances. When we sat down at the table, he introduced himself to my friends. His name is Walter Jordan. The girls just stared as they looked in his deep brown eyes. He had dark brown hair, a gray suit and tie, nice black shoes, and he pulled out the chair for me. So I asked him, "Who told him to look me up?"

"Walter said it was someone at the hospital. She said you were the best hair dresser in town."

"So I asked him what he did for a living. I thought maybe he worked at the hospital.

"Walter said, No, I was visiting with a friend. He said he was in politics and running for the Senate. My whole family has been involved in politics all their lives. So I figured why not. I liked being out and traveling to different places. I'm an Attorney for the State, I can work in any field, but I'm kind of leaning towards the Military Arms Committee. They are designing a new airport here and I'd like to be part of it. Let's have a drink Mary, I have to leave soon.'

"He brought a fresh bottle of wine to the table, and a toast was made to 'new friends.' Walter left, paying our bill, leaving me a card, and said he'd call me. My friends teased me all the way back to the car that night.

"Joey you're not going to believe who he turns out to be. He is related to Billy's Dad somehow. And guess what? Marion told him about me. You have to meet him."

My sister was much too happy.

Joey called me in Florida the first night we were away. It sounded like he was going to be busy for a while.

I took my plane over to Florida to Dale Mabry Field. Some of the guys were still there, but not many, they had moved on. I talked about our change in scheduling with their instructors. We really had some good ideas we were working with that seemed to help the cadets keep their interest. The instructors were impressed and I made some contacts for later, to find out if they see any difference when the next class comes in.

Everyone asked about Joey. We were kind of famous here being in the papers and the story about the Bunker. The guys even wanted to know how to play our famous game, BUH. We made the magazines and radio talk shows even down here.

Most men wanted to know how rough it was overseas. Many of them were on their way over in a few weeks. We sat around talking about the conditions overseas right now, as I rolled over some of the adventures I had, and of course the injuries I received. Sometimes I would drift off talking about my flying. The guys' faces would go blank. I think I went a little too deep into my feelings and scared them. I certainly had their attention. I felt it was really important to stress how well you should know your plane. Some small fact could save your life. Business was over now and it was time for a little fun at the club. The next morning I flew back to the base, picked up Marty, and left for Iowa.

I met Marty Riley in Florida on the base and we became good friends. When we were sent to England, Marty was assigned to our ground crew carefully picked to go over with us. When he took care of your plane it was not unusual to see him working late at night with a flashlight and his bucket of tools. He could always fix the problem and not always the conventional way. Marty was a pilots' dream. Any problems with the engines had top priority. Marty worked diligently all hours to get things ready for the next flight. Things like flak shell rips and tears, broken sheet metal on the wings, glass damage, fuselage problems, hoses and tires, he was the best. As the story goes, when we were in the air, he was praying for the safe return of the planes, then the guys. He often talked of buying some of these planes after the war.

In his spare time Marty talked of nothing but his little town in Spring Hill, Maine. Spring Hill is just outside Berwick. This was the strawberry festival capital of the world according to him, and his big family. This was his whole life.

Marty was the third boy out of five, to go off to the Service. He was 27 years old when he signed up.

His oldest brother Michael was married and had two boys and owned a sand and gravel company in Spring Hill. He did his four years in the Navy and returned home, taking over where he left off.

His second brother Bud ran a tree cutting and logging business in Spring Hill. Bud did four years in the Navy and was stationed at

Pearl Harbor. He was wounded in the leg in the service and came back home and went back to his business. His business did well.

Marty was newly married when he signed up in the Army. He trained as a ground mechanic but he also got his pilot's license. Marty owned a farm equipment business in Spring Hill and was franchised with a large company, one of the biggest companies around. He did work on engines, cars and trucks, anything that ran he could fix it. He ate and slept in the garage. It was a good business and everyone came to Marty.

The garage had an old pot belly, wood burning stove in the corner, and a bunch of old metal chairs from the junk yard, circled around with old cleaning towels draped over the seats for padding. Most nights after work, his friends would gather around the stove and tell stories late into the night while having some homemade brew.

His forth brother Nick was not married. He had a car and truck business out on the highway in town. He did well buying and selling vehicles. Nick owned a seven acre farm and had several breeding horses and a riding school on the back three acres. He built a small farm house with a large stone fireplace. He enjoyed his 'farmer's porch' on the front of the house. He was a 'connoisseur' of the grapes and made his own wines for selling.

Nick was in the Army stationed in Camp Kilmer, New Jersey, and never went overseas.

The last brother Hank sold fruits and vegetables to all the local stores in the area. His wife ran a seven day a week farm stand out on the highway in town. Hank went off to the Army like Marty but was injured in some flying maneuvers over the Gulf of Mexico. The service discharged him and sent him home.

Marty told these stories about his family so many times, we all felt like we knew the brothers. Spring Hill was a busy little town with the Riley's running things. He was a great story teller, and he made sure we all promised to go to the Strawberry festival when we returned to the States after the war.

Marty and Iowa . . .

Marty and I landed in Des Moines at the airport, and were greeted by Dad. The car was ready for the trip home. After meeting Marty we made our way home. The plan was to take turns showing Marty the city and our small town of Greenfield. I especially wanted him to see my farm and Joey's farm. We had hopes of having him come to Greenfield with us and have his own place.

Janice had a nice meal waiting for us. She was pleased to have another mouth to feed, especially when he was such a good eater. She also liked the fact Marty had been so good to me and Joey while overseas.

After unpacking our bags upstairs, we came down and sat and talked to Dad about what we wanted to do.

Dad asked if we wanted to go see the airport. A lot had happened since we left around Christmas. We went in the pickup, and of course on the way, Marty asked how long it had been since Dad had the oil changed and the front end lined up. The rest of the way was about fixing up the truck. Marty felt at home with Dad.

Coming into the airport, I could see there was a lot of construction going on. Dad motioned to the activity over on the right hand side of the airport as we drove in. We felt like we were on a special tour from here on in.

"That is going to be a major highway, route 35 coming through. That will bring opportunity for business to the airport. The freight trains already came along side of the airport, and that will supply food and equipment, and take out stock and products from our area. The major part of the airport will be a business center for the military. We just got a military contract from the government. This month we will begin to see more people and more jobs available here. That excites me. It will be important for our future, and a section will be for a Military Installation Center and a section for Army and Air Force. I plan to keep a small air craft section and a personal travel center for civilians. We also want a medical transport center for helicopters to transport medical emergencies. This will be good for our big hospitals in Des Moines. We plan to expand our medical facilities, make it Statewide, and convenient access to all. The highways and trains will act as a commuter service to get people to and from jobs from all around the State, and the planes will be available for business travelers. I can see a transport and Military Center for the center of the country right here." Dad stopped the truck and just looked at the grounds before him. He was completely wrapped up in his thoughts.

"I guess I know where you get some of your ideas now Billy. Looks like you have your work cut out for you right here," said Marty.

"I am going to need all the help I can muster up Marty, how about you and your brothers coming out here and being part of this with us," asked Dad.

I know Marty could see the potential for a great business opportunity, but I knew he was committed to his family and his small town of Spring Hill.

His comeback was quite a surprise.

"Give me some time to think about this Sir, It looks like there is plenty of work for all of us. I'd like to look around and see what kind of property is available. Farm land and animals are a big part of our family; I'll get back to you on this."

We took Marty back to the house and I called Joey. An hour later he was sitting at the table having pie and ice cream with us as Marty told him about the airport.

Janice had a nice dinner for us when the girls came by after work. It was good to see Ashley again. We spent some time in the other room talking before dinner. Her father was taking care of her mother tonight and everything was under control.

The girls were so happy to meet Marty as they fussed with him through the meal. Ashley, Lette Mae and Marion told stories about their lives and how they met us. We talked our way through the night until it was time for them to go. The girls left for their apartment. Joey stayed and took the other spare room. Marion went back to town to her place. We made plans for tomorrow and spend whatever time we could together. Our plans were to take Marty around the city, and then go see my farm. Later we would go to Joey's place. Marty would probably stay there tomorrow night.

After dinner Marty, Joey, Dad and I, sat around the fireplace for a while talking about all the things going on with us right now, and how bad things were getting in the Service.

The next morning we went into the city and showed Marty some of the work Dad was involved in. After a while, we dropped Dad off at the office. We left to go to Joey's place in Greenfield, but first we showed Marty where we went to school, where we went swimming and some of our hangouts as kids.

Marty met Tom and Judy first. Joey was very specific about introducing them as his parents. After meeting them and talking for a while, we went next door and met his mother Martha, and his two sisters. We spent the morning talking with them. Marty was impressed with the size of the farm Joey lived on. He got the tour including the barns and Joey's prize possessions, the horses.

Tom had some large green houses built alongside the barns. This was for Joey's new project he was creating in his spare time. Talking to the Vice President, he happened to mention he was working on a hybrid seed that could withstand the insects, and a fertilizer that would not hurt the soil. Much interest was put on these subjects through the mail to Joey, from the Vice President. This was one of his interests and he wanted to keep in touch with Joey, if there was anything he could do to help. Many people in the West wanted to find something good for the soil. And a stronger seed would be of some value to the farmers especially during the drought and the heat. Joey had some good ideas, and had been working on some experiments for some time now. Again Marty was surprised and quite impressed. Marty knew something about the soil and he was a great farmer on his land back in Maine. We talked for a while about all the possibilities of farming in Iowa.

Later the three of us left for my farm and we toured the many acres with the foreman. I showed them the apartments Dad had built and what he had planned.

We left for the diner. Marty met with Lette Mae's parents as they made us the 'workman's special' for lunch. They were delighted we stopped by, and they came out and sat down with us while we ate. We hung around until it started to get busy again around three-thirty. I dropped them off at Joey's and left to go back home. Joey had plans to take Marty into town with his family tonight and show him around, maybe go bowling and have a drink or two.

I went to the office. I had something I wanted to talk to Dad about and no sense waiting any longer. When I arrived, some of the people had left for the day. I went in and sat down beside him.

"What can I do for you Son? Where's Marty?"

"He's staying with Joey tonight. Are you busy right now?"

"Not for you Son, talk to me. What's on your mind?" He sat back in his large chair and wanted to light up a cigarette, but he hesitated. He was trying to change his habits.

"Dad, I know how busy you are and you never stop with your law office. You get people jobs and set things up for me for my future.

I appreciate that, but I want to ask you something. You know I am going to school for my law degree, I'm hoping to become a General in the Air Force before I'm through. I want to keep flying and help get this airport set up, but I have to be in the Service for a while yet. I want you to think about something. What about asking Marion to become a partner with us in the firm? She is certainly qualified and she has her Law degree and has been your right hand man for some time now. She knows the business and has a great business mind. I like Marion and I feel real good about this idea. Can we make some kind of a deal with her? I can't be here with you as much as I want to be, we could both profit from her being here with us. I worry about your doing too much and I know you like to be busy. But you're not getting any younger. Your heart is telling you to slow down and take it easy. I want to ask her, if it's okay with you. What do you say?"

"You know, it's funny you should hit me with this today Son. I was looking at all the things you have going on, and the things you are planning for the future. You are going to be busy for a while, and I don't want you worrying about me and my little problems. Maybe you have a good idea. I'm so pleased you feel that strongly about Marion. She always talks about you like she's your mother. Go ahead and ask her, see what she says."

We got up and he walked me to the door. I told him I'd be back to pick him up. As I headed for the truck, I felt light snow flakes coming down and landing on my face. They quickly melted, but the icy cold flakes felt good. I swished the driver's side window with my glove and got in. The sky was playing with the wind. Clouds were rolling fast above the land. My first thought was we might get some serious snowfall before the evening was through. I hurried to the hospital.

Marion was walking down the hall near her office when I opened the door from the stairs. She went into her office. I knocked and followed her in. She was glad to see me and came over and gave me a big hug. "Come sit down. What are you doing here this time of the day, Billy?"

"I have something special to talk to you about. Dad and I have just put this idea together. First of all, I am worried that he is doing too much and I'm not there to help him. My time is with the Service for a while. We want to know if you would consider being a partner in the business with us. You certainly are qualified and know every inch of the business and what we want to achieve in the coming years. Maybe you could organize his meetings, and make better use of his time for him. You could still run your work at the hospital. You said you wanted to cut back here a little. I'm asking you because I feel you are so right for my Dad, and I love you. I would feel better if you were right here in my place while I am away. What do you say?"

"I am so surprised you would ask me Billy, I never want to get between you and your Dad. He loves you very much and has set everything in his life, for you for later. I would never step in the middle of that. I'm just so happy you would ask me. I would be pleased to help out as a partner. I am worried about him too. I'll talk with him about the paper work and get back to you. Thank you for the vote of confidence. I love your Dad very much and you probably realized that by now."

"Billy there is something I want to talk to you about too. I'm in the process of running for Senator of the State. It's a challenge for a woman, but I'm qualified. I have been asked by the Governor to take a temporary position which I'm taking, starting next week. It's an opportunity to be active in politics and I really want the position. Official elections will be in November and by then I will have proved myself for the position. Wish me luck Billy."

"You've got it Marion. Wow! Anything I can do for you just let me know."

I gave her another hug as I left to go back and pick up Dad. This had worked out fine so far. She's amazing.

This time it was snowing hard as I came out into the parking lot. It was really coming down and the wind was howling.

When I pulled into the law office parking lot I could see Dad was on the phone. I went in and waited for about twenty minutes, a little jumpy about the weather getting worse. Finally he got his things together, and we left for home. Dad talked all the way home and never asking how I made out with Marion. Then he said, "So what do you think of her running for Senator of our State? That's my girl." He grinned, and I knew that he was on the phone to Marion before I had come back for him at the office. I couldn't imagine why he didn't ask me as soon as I got in the office. Those two were a pair, married or not. They worked so well together. I found myself falling right in with them and I liked that idea. We got back home just before dark. It was really snowing.

Good Times . . .

We had a good time showing Marty the lifestyle we had in Iowa. He liked the area and wanted to talk to his family about it.

We went back to Foster Air Field and continued to teach the pilots for a few more months.

One morning we received a strange request to come to the office. The General had called a special meeting.

Joey and I showed up on time, to be greeted by an entourage of uniforms and Military fan fare. The Governor and Vice President were there and we wondered what they had planned for us this time. This was a private meeting. We were applauded for the work we were doing and what we had achieved here at the base. Now they had something else for us to do. This was an assignment to work with ten ace pilots on a special class that we would be running for ten weeks. These men would be flown in, have their own quarters, and after their special training they would be sent overseas to bases waiting for them. I mentioned we were running special training classes now, and asked, "Why just these ten men?"

The answer surprised me, and as usual Joey's eyebrows went up. "These men are a special force of young Negro pilots, [term used in this era], most of them ace pilots, who have been picked to go through our course for special fighter pilot training. We would be allowed to set up our own training course and we were told we had the best pilots coming in to train. These men would become pilots, navigators or bombardiers overseas on special missions. These men came from Alabama to learn our techniques and distinctive training skills." The Governor said we were more than qualified, and we had the confidence of the Vice President behind us.

Our base was starting something different. We had heard about these pilots and their records preceded them. They were not the first Negro flying pilots, but we had the chance to make them some of the best. It was an honor. The P51-D mustang was the plane they were going to train in. Joey and I got excited. We felt that was the best plane in the force right now. We got new planes for this assignment. These men had been using P-40s. I couldn't wait for them to be in a real plane and all its specialties. These men were part of a large Air Force Unit, just never recognized. When the U.S. Army Air Corps employed the Negros, a special training base was set up. Some of their best pilots were coming to Foster Air Base to train with us. That was an honor.

And as we sat there taking it all in, we were being given special compensation for this assignment straight from the Vice President. When we finished, we would be promoted to Brigadier Generals. Our friend Marty, who was in charge of maintenance of the planes, would also be included in this assignment. He was not able to make this meeting, but he would become a Lieutenant Colonel in special training when he was finished. Good mechanics were highly valued now. We accepted this assignment. We had no idea this was coming to Foster Air Field. This was challenging and exciting, and one of the best kept secrets of our time.

Chapter 24

Changes All Around Us

The war news was coming in regularly now. How reliable it was, we had to find out for ourselves. From the beginning of our training and teaching at the Foster Air Field, we knew serious fighting was going on. We knew all our trainees were going directly overseas. Top pilots, bombardiers, right down to the map readers and mechanics, were in dire need overseas. Transport planes were loaded with men and supplies all week long. Soldiers, sailors, air men and marines were being rushed over. The forces were fighting in Europe, Japan, the Philippines and all the islands that could be reached by carrier-based planes.

Some of the events hit home. We knew some of our men that we trained were there.

On January 11, 1945 we were told the air raids began on the Japanese bases in Indochina. It seemed like every few days we would get more news. I was lucky because the editor I had met when I was young, decided to send me local newspapers and keep me and Joey updated here. By the end of the day, our papers had been sent all around the base. So we knew that February 19th the U.S. Marines invaded Iwo Jima, a war that was only going to take 5 to 10 days. It took 74 days. One of the most important pieces of equipment used was the LCVP (Land, Craft, Vehicle, Personnel) which made it possible for the troops, equipment, and supplies to land any place there was an open beach. Vital in the Mediterranean and Pacific, and Normandy's beaches, this LCVP was an important weapon. More than 20,000 LCVPs were made right out of New Orleans. The men were not trained for this type of battle. The Japanese had been settled in for months in the trees and in caves. They were all around and well hidden and camouflaged. Thousands of Marines died and graphic pictures were taken and sent home. The President released the vivid war scenes stating, "This will never happen again." When the flag went up in Iwo Jima it was good for the morale and helped sell war bonds back home.

On March 2nd, the U.S. Airborne troops recaptured Corregidor in the Philippines, and then we read on March 9th and 10th, 15 square miles of Tokyo erupted into flames, after it was hit by our B-29s.

On April 7th, our B-29s flew their first fighter escorted mission against Japan. The P-51 Mustangs were based on Iwo Jima.

The next big news on the front pages of the papers was April 12th, when President Roosevelt died. Harry S. Truman took over as President.

On April 16th the banners went up over the city of Berlin.

Newspapers came in April 28th with the Mussolini execution and hanging in public, and April 30th Adolf Hitler's suicide in his bunker with his girlfriend. We got all the news and it began to look like the War in Europe was coming to an end.

On May 8th, Europe rejoiced in celebrations. V-E Day (Victory in Europe Day). The WWII Allies formally accepted the unconditional surrender. The Americans woke up to the news and it became V-E Day. U.S. President Harry Truman turned 61 that day and he dedicated the victory in memory of Franklin D. Roosevelt, who had died almost a month earlier.

On July 10th, it was estimated 1,000 bomber raids against Japan began.

On July 16th, the first atomic bomb was tested in the United States. On July 14th Joey and I were sent a letter from President Truman, to be at the testing grounds in Socorro, New Mexico on the White Sands Proving Grounds. We were escorted to the base and updated as to what was going on. This was going to be the first testing done, code name *Trinity*. We were told the dangers of being here and this was a highly dangerous experiment.

We were sworn to secrecy about the location, while dozens of cameras were set in place. We were put in the base camp bunker southwest of the test tower ten miles away. At 5:29:45 local time it exploded. We felt the heat of an oven and the sky lit up like the sun, only brighter! It only took 40 seconds to reach us, but the explosion was felt 200 miles away. We were there to give our opinion on the type of planes they were using to carry the bomb. The fastest plane would be the P-51, but the B-29 had a bomb site in the plane and the P-51 didn't. The bomb was going to be a plutonium device, code named, *The Gadget*. Our opinions were noted. After the bombing was done, we were flown to Washington to speak to the President. There we were given top secret information about the prospects of the war. The President had the war plans set and we were introduced to many of the top officials and military figures in Washington. Our title of Colonel meant something here. We were high priority and felt the pressure placed on us, for the privilege of a private meeting with the President. On our way back to the base we realized things around us were happening fast now. A full alert was in force from here on in. At the base, transport planes were carrying men and supplies out daily now. You could feel the pressure building.

On one of my Sunday calls from Dad, he was all excited about a new Government contract being proposed to him. The Government wanted him to design an area at his airport for the new jets coming in. These planes would take over the Air Force. There were plans for a great number of them to be shipped overseas. What an opportunity, he already had the transport carriers ready. Mass production was going on at the plant. Dad went on and on about this project and he was involved already. This meant his airport would become the central regional transporting center and just what he had wanted all along.

Later I talked to Marion and I got another side of the story. Yes Dad was excited, a little bit too excited and had to see the doctor for chest pains and uneven heart rhythms. Now he had another pill for anxiety. Marion had a friend who was a semi-retired doctor, who was also very interested in the expansion of the airport. She asked me if she could send some information about him to me, so I could see what she had in mind. A quick synopsis was she wanted him to help her and Phil with the airport affairs. Government contracts took a long time to prepare and understand, and she simply didn't have that kind of time. This man was familiar with this area of expertise, and was a good friend to her, and now Phil.

After hearing about Dad's health, I was eager to get her some help.

Joey and I had heard about the new jet planes coming out in the Air Force. We were told in Washington that we would be notified when and where the training programs would be. Our training time would be set up, as soon as possible. We looked forward to this with excitement. It was another chance to fly with the newest planes available.

On our base there were no leaves being granted, not even for a weekend pass. Not even Joey could get home to have his wedding. Everyone was on full alert now; our country was feeling the desperate times. No one felt secure.

Our Sunday calls were a touch of home I really needed to continue. I could feel the connection to the people I loved. I think Dad felt that way too.

On Aug. 6th the first Atomic Bomb hit Hiroshima dropped from a B-29 bomber. The news of the bombing, and the pictures that were released by the press, were devastating; but were held from the public until the second bomb was set.

Then on Aug. 9th, the second Atomic Bomb was dropped on Nagasaki from another B-29 plane. The Emperor and Prime Minister decided to seek peace with the Allies. Many thousands of people were killed, and the bombing area completely destroyed; radiation covered the land.

On Aug. 14th the Japanese accepted unconditional surrender. President Harry Truman announced it from the White House in Washington that the Japanese had surrendered.

On Sept. 2nd the Japanese signed a surrender agreement; making this date known as V-J (Victory over Japan) Day.

We all woke up to a new era in front of us. The War was over!

This meant the bases would be starting to close down some of their training programs. The first to go would be the basic and primary training classes. Some of the trainers had gone to work for the commercial airlines. Many of the good pilots had jobs set already. Another thing happening was some of the bases were going back to public air transportation. I took some of the names of the guys we worked with, and had talked to them about working with us after the War at our airport in Iowa. Jets were the new planes of the Service, and public transportation; we were getting our training in now so we could train and teach for conflicts in the future. We planned to stay in the Service, there were many job offers. Military contracts hired a lot of the pilots from the Air Force; great jobs, and good money. And some of the guys that had endured enough of the War simply went back to crop dusting.

We had just finished our last group of pilots going through the training program. We could see the Air Force was re-grouping; this was a good time for us to take care of our personal affairs back home. We packed our bags. Marty went one way to Maine, and we went on our way to Iowa. We had a marriage to attend.

Chapter 25

The War is over!

This time we flew our own planes home to Iowa. Dad had made space for my plane and Joey's to be stored at the new airport. When we reached the airport it didn't look anything like we remembered. So much of the land was developed, and so many new buildings were erected. It looked like a large metropolis, with planes, trains, buses, lots of activity going on all around. One big change was the name of the airport. A large sign had been erected. It read, Stevens Aviation Center. We followed the runway in and taxied to the area we were directed to park the planes. I thought I could hear music playing. I quickly looked down the runway, to see my Dad coming down the runway in a large, red fire engine, followed by the High School marching band. The town people had come to cheer us on as we got out of our planes. People rushed to our planes all excited to see our famous, well talked about, P-51 planes complete with body art, and in need of a good paint job. I felt we had found a home in our state for these planes that meant so much to us. We were home.

I hugged my Dad, and asked him about the new name at the airport. "Do you like it?" he asked, donning a great big smile.

I liked it.

This was a celebration of our return and people had taken the day off for this. Joey and I were pleased and somewhat embarrassed. We were not the only people in town coming home from the War. Dad showed us around all the new buildings as some people followed along. We toured some new offices. He was in his glory. I once heard a comment that he was called the champion of women, which was probably true. Dad was well liked by everyone. No one could seem to do enough for him. We did meet some new people working in the offices, as if I was going to remember them the next time I saw them. When we came out of the last building, Marion was just driving up in her car with Ashley and Lette Mae. What a great surprise for us.

Lette Mae came running over to Joey, hugging and kissing him. Tears of joy ran down their smiling faces. Ashley looked great. She came over to me and we hugged and kissed, but I think she felt a little embarrassed at the same time. There were a lot of people there. Marion got her kisses from both her boys too. We walked and talked our way through the smiling crowds. Another vehicle came up to the area and it was Joey's parents. As they got out of their truck, Joey was there to greet them with hugs and kisses, as we stood by the planes and watched the people admire them. The band had finished playing and the kids put all their instruments back in their cases. Then they headed for the conference center. As we walked in there was a large cake with our names on it, setting on the table. Balloons and flags were everywhere. Lette Mae's parents had put together a wonderful table of food for all to enjoy. Fried chicken was my favorite, with finger sandwiches, homemade pickles, cookies and candies. There was coffee and lemonade. It was a luscious chocolate cake, with butter cream frosting and all compliments of the diner. Joey was on the phone to the parents, and we thanked them for the wonderful spread they put out for us. We sat around enjoying the food and coffee, while listening to Joey tell some of his stories, as we laughed our way through the afternoon. Later when things quieted down and some of the people had left, Dad announced he had made plans for all of us to have dinner at the golf club near our house tonight. This was something new I thought. I walked around enjoying all the people who had come by to see us.

I still couldn't believe the War was over. I had a 30 day leave and had no plans except to get Joey married.

I heard Dad and Tom talking over in the corner of the room as I passed by.

Dad had heard of a housing project of two hundred or more homes to be built, just outside of our town. Dad and Tom talked of all the changes that were going on in our town and city. Jobs had started picking up and the pay was better. All the service men and women were returning to their homes and businesses. More people coming in, more supplies needed, and more activity for the airport, everyone would be happy. The prediction was now the families would start having babies, because they felt secure about the future again. The young service people would get married and buy a house, get a good job and have a family. Across the front page of most papers you could find the phrase, America was coming alive again.

While the men talked of the future, the women at the table only wanted to talk about the wedding. The way it sounded the wedding was set for next weekend.

Joey and I had a few plans of our own we had hoped to check out on this visit. Maybe tonight would be a good time to talk over our ideas with the family. I hadn't discussed when he was going to tell them. This was his project.

We all went back to our house to clean up for dinner. As I came through the front door, Janice was there with a big hug. I asked if she was coming to dinner with us and she answered, no. She was going to listen to her favorite radio program with a hot tea, and her feet up. That was a good evening for her and we all laughed.

The golf club was very sophisticated and very fancy. People came over to park your cars while you were taken to your table. Piano music was playing in the background near the red velvet drapes along the wall. This was nice. Dad knew everyone there. I'm sure most of them were his clients. As usual, everyone fussed with him and he liked it. We had superb service. I got a chance to ask

Joey if he wanted to speak of his project tonight or not. It was a go.

While we were waiting for the table to be cleared for dessert, Joey asked for our attention for a few minutes. Everyone looked at me. I just put my hands out saying, "Don't look at me."

He started by telling them he wanted to open an orphanage near his home. He wanted to run it and build a place for kids to live and work. He had strong feeling about this and wanted to put his time and money into this project. I had already told him I was behind him 100% and would help all I could. Tom and Phil looked at each other and nodded in recognition. The girls all looked at each other in awe. Judy thought it was a great idea and asked what she could do to help. He continued to put out his ideas. Then he told them the Vice President, retired, was looking for some land he could use for the orphanage to be built on. There were government grants and loans available for projects like these, he thought there would be no problem setting something up, and there was nothing around here like that. He was more than willing to help Joey. He told him to get things ready, because he would be going out of office with the next elections. He would have more power now than later.

We certainly had plenty to talk about the rest of the evening. We left the club around eleven o'clock and we all returned home.

I drove Ashley home and we went inside and had coffee. Her father joined us for a little while and seemed glad to see me. He asked me to call him Paul, Paul Thomas. I felt good about that, I hadn't spent much time with him and I felt a little strange about that. Later when he left, Ashley talked about what we were going to do the next couple of days. She was almost finished with school and had a job offer at the Court House as a secretary. Her father had been waiting for her to take over the Greenfield Bank for him. She had the idea that she could do both. I told her that Joey and I had paperwork we had to do while home on leave. We were finishing up our schooling from the base and this could be done by mail. We were lucky to have had the opportunity to take these courses while working on the base.

We talked about Joey's wedding and what she was wearing. I was easy with the black tux and a ruffled shirt. Judy and Tom had a big wedding set up for Saturday afternoon. Lette Mae's parents were taking care of the food, the cake, and tables and chairs.

We sat in the living room for a while. I realized how much I missed her this time while away. It was good to have some time alone with her again.

Two days later I got to meet Marion's friend and retired doctor, Dr. Henry Potter. He was in his late fifties, a tall thin man with grey hair and horn rimmed glasses. He was dressed in a grey business suit and tie. He had a pocket watch chained to his front pocket. For some reason, the watch had me mesmerized. I couldn't take my eyes off it, until I realized I was staring. He had a great speaking voice and a firm handshake. I was instantly impressed with him, and the watch. We talked about the airport and some of the other projects he was involved in. Then he asked me if I liked the name of the airport?

"Yes I do," I answered, "Very much. Whose idea was it?"

Dr. Potter said Marion and Phil worked on that project together. Then he added, "I like it too."

I returned home during the morning and got a call from Marty. He told me he had been sent to Lynn, Massachusetts for a training class on jet engines. He was all excited.

"Billy, this is where they make the engines, and I can learn how to take them apart, and put them back together. Of course, you know I jumped at that chance. It came from the higher ups again, so I figured you and Joey knew about it, Did you?" he asked. Before I could answer he said, "Oh, and by the way, now I am in charge of special Training, and again in the right place at the right time. How about that Billy? All I have to do is stay in the service, learn and teach about jets, and my outstanding service, time and grade, warrants my promotions. There are four of our crew members from the base here with me and this is a really big deal."

I told him to study hard because we needed him to be the best as always. He laughed. I really liked that guy, he was a good friend.

Later when I met with Joey I told him what Marty had said. We didn't know anything about his schooling. We climbed in our truck and went to see the building Dad had shown me last year when I was home. We thought this might be a good place to have the office for a while, so we could get things going with the orphanage. We went in and a girl was making coffee in the corner of the room with a plug in warmer. She turned and smiled, and introduced herself as Susie. We introduced ourselves. She smiled and pointed to a picture on the wall. It was the two of us in uniforms. She told us she was just a file clerk and she paid the bills for all the offices. She kept a record of all the checks that were made out. She worked for Dad. She was organized and neat. We figured she was probably about twenty five years old. She had sandy blonde hair, wore a business suit, and high heels, but the pleasant smile captured us both. We told her of our plans for this building and we took measure-ments for what we would need later.

"Okay, now we have an office for you to get your business started, what's next Joey?" I asked.

"My wedding is and I'm a nervous wreck." was his reply.

"What's left to do? Do you know where you're going on your honeymoon?" I asked.

"Yeah, were going to Niagara Falls for four days, you want to come?" He sat back in the truck and laughed.

"Think of it this way Joey. When you get back you'll have another story to tell. My advice to you, is just take notes." He reached over and pummeled my arm in jest.

I dropped him off at the farm and hollered out the window as I left, "don't forget to do your schooling and get it in the mail." He threw his hands up in the air, like he always did, just what he needed, more things to do.

I took a ride over to see Doctor Deering. The car was gone, but the lights were on inside and the back door was unlocked. I called out his name as I went in.

"Come on in Billy, I'm in the living room."

There he was on the couch. I went over and sat down beside him, while checking out the room. I instantly knew something wasn't right.

"Doctor, where is your car and what's going on here?"

"Don't worry Billy; I'm just having a little trouble getting around these days. My sister has the car over at her place; she doesn't want me driving. I guess she's right. My eyesight is slipping a little. Tell me how you're doing. How's Ashley and what's your Dad up to lately?"

"Ashley is doing fine. Her mother is in poor health these days. I spent some time with her and her father. I'm getting Joey ready for his big wedding this weekend. He is a nervous wreck these days. Dad is trying to eat better, and he has stopped smoking and gets to bed early now. Can I get you anything, how about something to eat?"

"No son, I'm just fine. I'm so glad you stopped by. Ask your Dad to drop by when you get a chance will you?"

"You got it. Are you sure I can't do anything for you while I am here?"

"No I'm fine. I'm really glad you came by. I am just going to rest for a while now."

"I hope you do." I leaned over and kissed him on the forehead as I pulled the light blanket up over him. "I'll stop by again after Joey's wedding and tell you all about it."

He raised his hand a goodbye and I left taking note of all the pictures all around his kitchen table. I saw one of me and Dad, a picture of two little boys a long time ago, my Mom and me, and one of a woman I didn't know. It could have been his sister when she was young. I don't remember seeing all these pictures on the table before. I thought about reminding Dad to stop by, while the pictures stayed on my mind. I mentioned it to Dad that night and he seemed curious too.

During the days I got my schooling done, and then I'd go down the office and get involved with some of the projects going on. There were all new people working at the office now.

Another day I went to the airport and checked out our planes. A commercial airline had taken the hangar next to ours so I asked who painted some of their planes. I was able to get someone to come and look at our P-51s, but I was told the government takes care of all the maintenance of their planes. I felt more at home at the airport than I did at the office these days. I snooped around looking in all the buildings wondering what they planned to do with them all. Another runway was being constructed and this was going to be just commercial jets coming in. I talked with a lot of the pilots and asked what kind of training they had. Most of them knew me, and started asking me about my time overseas. Some even asked what kind of training I was offering that they could sign up for. That surprised me. Most of them had seen my plane and had commented about its current condition.

Joey spent his time setting up the new greenhouse on the farm, and helping out with the irrigation system that was being put in on the new acres his father had just bought. This was hot and heavy work this time of the year. Most evenings before he was done for the day, he would take out one of his horses for a ride through the fields. When we talked on the phone at night we both seemed to feel a little lost right now. We knew we had to return to the base and our service life was top priority for a while.

One night after work I picked up Ashley and we headed over to see Joey. He sounded tense and we figured if we talked a while, we could be of some help. Lette Mae and his parents were there. Joey's father disappeared a few minutes. He came back carrying a shiny steel saw. He sat down in his chair, and squeezed the handle between his legs, and held the other end in his hand. The teeth were facing his body, as he ran the bow gently back and forth across the back edge of the saw. The sound was something like a woman's high pitched singing voice. The sound varied as he wobbled his hand or shook his leg. The sound lasted a few seconds. What a surprise and he sounded real good. You could tell he really enjoyed playing for us. I thought to myself, you had to have a strong left hand to play that instrument. I never knew he had this talent. We all enjoyed the music and it seemed to take the pressure off what was going on there. Each one had approached me separately and thanked me for stopping by.

Well this was the big day. This morning I woke up, got dressed, and took my dress bag and black shoes downstairs. Today was the day my best friend was going to marry the girl of his dreams. I have to admit, I was a little anxious for him. I ate and went out the door on my way to Joey's place. Dad and Marion would be by later. Driving down the pebbled clay driveway, I could feel the excitement as the tent was being put up, and the table and chairs were being unloaded from the truck. Joey came out of the barn on one of his horses and another trailing behind him.

"Come on Billy, let's take a ride."

I parked the truck by the barn and jumped up on the horse. We were off through the fields and I felt the wind in my hair, as I bounced up and down on the saddle. Joey had a pretty good speed going on and I was lagging behind a little. We rode a while and he pulled up to the old wooden bridge near the creek. He pulled back until his horse came to a stop. I caught up, as we got down and tied the horses.

"What's up Joey?" I asked.

"Aw, I don't know. This wedding is such a big deal. Why can't we just go to the church, get married, come home and live happily ever after? All this big deal stuff makes me nervous."

"Hey, I'll be right there with you. And—you better be there for me when I tie the noose around my neck." I knew I was going to get a punch for that one, so I moved quickly. I was right, he missed me. He spun around and laughed. Then he asked me if I thought this was a good idea?

Out of my mouth came, "To late now pal," I was sorry I said it before it was all out of my big mouth. I tried to cover it up. "Of course it is. You love Lette Mae and we all know she loves you. You have a place to live, and she can come to the base after your married. You have a great job, she can work at the hospital nearby, and you two got it made. What's the problem?"

"Billy I always thought you had it made. You just go along and everything seems to be taken care of for you. Am I right? Have you made a commitment or set a wedding date yet?" He looked right at me waiting for an answer.

"Sad to say, no I haven't. I guess Ashley is kind of busy with school and her mother dying, and her father expecting her to work for him. We just haven't set a wedding date yet. Don't worry, I'll wait until you two get back from your honeymoon."

He just smiled and kicked a little dirt with his boot. A case of anxiety, I thought.

"We've been through a lot Billy and I wouldn't be here today if it weren't for you, my best friend."

We hugged and I knew he'd be okay. We climbed back up on our horses and rode the plains for a while. When we came in later we got dressed for the wedding.

I could hear the commotion when Lette Mae and her family and friends drove up the driveway. Joey's mother and two sisters quickly rushed her into their apartment next door.

Marion and Judy had been outside checking out the tables and chairs and getting the food warmers set up. It was a big deal, Joey was right.

The next thing we knew, we were placed in our prospective places under the rose arbor in the garden and the music began to play. The girls came down the walkway, followed by Lette Mae. The color of the day was peach and the dresses were long and flowing. The slight warm breeze caught the ruffles on the dresses and the girl's soft, flowing hair. It was a perfect day for a wedding. The bride was happy and looked like a princess out of a story book. Joey just stared as she made her way towards him.

Everything went as planned. They became Colonel and Mrs. Joey Calhoun.

There were lots of pictures taken. I made a toast to my best friend and his new wife. The food was great, and the yard was full of happy people. Joey had reached another plateau in his life. Things would be different now and this time I was left behind. Maybe that is what he was feeling all week long.

Ashley and I spent the afternoon together with the newlyweds and they opened their gifts and laughed and kissed their way through their day.

As the couple went to change clothes, everyone started cleaning up and we waited for the chance to mess with the car. The parents had done a great job on the wedding. The couple came out the front door to a Military Saber Archway Salute. This was a very special moment and the parents cried. The newlyweds proceeded to the car, ready to go to New York. Everyone said their goodbyes as they left. They were dragging cans and balloons down the driveway behind them, and a few firecrackers went off along the way.

Ashley, Marion, Judy, the mother and two sisters were all crying. I was feeling something too. After all, jokingly he did ask me to come with him. I had that little laugh to myself as I watched the tin cans bouncing along on the pebbled driveway. I turned to Dad and he was staring right at me like in a daze. I could almost read his mind.

"He'll be back and your life will be a little different. Let's go home son," was all he said, as he put his big arm around me.

"Did you stop by the doctors yet Dad?"

"I'm going over tomorrow. Do you want to go with me?"

"Sure Dad, I'll go with you."

Later that night at home he asked, "Have you and Ashley made any plans yet, son?"

"No not yet," was my answer.

Dad went to bed and I sat up and read for a while. I must have been asked that question sixteen times today, if I was going to be next. Was I?

They drove down the highway to New York for many hours. They were both tired, and they decided the next motel on the side of the road they were going to stop for the night. Just then one came up, all lit up in white stars and lavender colored lights. 'Evening in Paris' was across the marquee. Joey got their room and opened the door, holding their bags. After peeking inside to make sure it was clean, Joey picked up his bride and carried her to the over sized stuffed bed. Then he ran to the bathroom. How romantic Lette Mae thought.

She picked up the bags by the door and quickly got a few things ready for her first night with her husband. She was excited as she looked around the room in hopes of finding a radio for some soft music. She was in luck. The bright lamp by the bed had to go. She had a silk scarf just perfect for putting over the lamp, and dimming the room in a rose colored tone. She hurried getting things ready; turning down the bed, getting his pajamas, not that he would need them, and spraying the room with her scented perfume. He finally came out of the bathroom. She thought he looked tired but she didn't care. This was the night she wanted him to remember the rest of his and her life. As he came to her, looking around the room, she gently kissed him and held him close to her, as she whispered in his ear that she would be right back, and she picked up her ditty bag. He flopped on the bed, probably half asleep already.

A few minutes later the bathroom door opened and she stood in the doorway. Joey's head was turned to the side so he could see her out of one eye. What was she doing he thought, he was so tired. She was breathtaking. He turned over and smiled. He knew what the new Mrs. Calhoun had on her mind.

With the rose colored room, the soft scent of her perfume, and the beautiful woman coming toward him, he wasn't tired anymore. She was beautiful and she moved like a soft breeze, floating across the room. She stood by the bed with her blonde, curly hair resting on her white shoulders. She wore a lovely blue silk negligee cut low in the front exposing her very round breasts.

The gown was very revealing; and every curve was plainly in view. She knew all the right things to say. She gently opened the shoulder ribbons and let the gown fall to the floor.

He was out of his clothes in a second. He pulled her down to the bed and kissed her like never before. As he moved over her body, he was afraid he was going to crush her. She squealed and he loved it. He knew what he wanted and took no time pushing inside her soft, tight body. She put her hands gently over his hairy chest, and pulled him to her. She could feel the excitement building inside of him as she kissed him again. He was on fire; they were moaning with desire and anticipation of the final moment. He came with such pleasure and exhaustion; they knew the moment was good for both of them. They fell apart, as she quickly moved to his side and kissed him over and over. They held each other as they said all the things they wanted to hear. He kissed her tenderly on the lips and worked his way down her body. She squealed with pleasure as he smiled. He was pleased with himself, she could tell. They lay in each other's arms knowing this was just the beginning of their 'Evening in Paris'. To them the night was young. They fell asleep telling each other this was the way they always wanted to end their nights. Together in each other's arms, feeling the love they had tonight. Joey could smell the scent of her hair as she cradled herself up against him and fell asleep. This was a wonderful feeling he thought, maybe marriage wasn't going to be so bad after all. Colonel Calhoun fell asleep a happy man.

Niagara Falls was lovely this time of the year. A lot of newlyweds made this trip from all over the country. Now that the War was over in Europe and the soldiers were all returning home, marriages were on the rise. There was plenty to do and see, as they spent their time talking and planning their future together.

Joey was gone for a week. During that week our P-51 planes were painted at the base and the windows were replaced. Marty called and updated me about his schooling. He was in building 30, known as Fort Knox. The General Electric plant in Lynn,

Massachusetts specialized in aircraft, electrical systems, and components during WWII. Massachusetts Institute of Technology did the research resulting in the improvements of the jet engine power. This was the best kept secret for a long time. Marty knew how lucky the crew was to be training there and learning the new engines, from the inside out.

Chapter 26

Back to Work

With the wedding over and Marty back with his crew, things went back to normal. One morning the three of us were asked to report to the General's Office on the base. When we arrived the President was sitting with the General, waiting. Good thing we were dressed for the occasion. Reorganizing the training command was what we thought was going to be top priority. It wasn't. We were. We all sat down at the table after being introduced and the President stood up and started the conversation.

"Good to see you boys again. You have created quite a stir around here and I'm here to thank you for all the hard work you have put in at this base. First of all you have all been promoted. You two ace pilots are now 1st Brigadier Generals. You have shown strength, you've made good decisions and given outstanding service, with all the pilots going through your training programs. I tell everyone about you, I only wish I had more like you. There is no one here on this base that puts in the time and energy to these programs like you men do. I appreciate you and want the entire base to learn from you. Marty you are now a Colonel. I'm so pleased you have taken on the jet planes with such enthusiasm."

The President looked over to the General. "We want to ask you if you will set up the Air Force Reserves program at this base and stay on and run it. This base is special. We want the three of you to work out a plan that one of you will be here one weekend a month. This will give you time at home while we have the base covered. Special conditions will be given to you as long as you take over the responsibility. The classes are in your control and I can't say enough about your training programs."

"Marty, how did you make out with the jet training?" the President asked.

"There were five of us Sir, we are ready to take on the teaching and training that is required. Thank you for the promotion Sir." Marty was in his glory.

"Special pilots do the job right and you boys are the best we have in this part of the country, and your training programs are being duplicated on all our bases now. So let's get things going here, I'm very confident you will have things in order quickly. Anything you need I want you to ask the General here, or call me. I mean that." He sat down as the General took over.

We just sat there in awe. We had a lot to think about. The promotion itself was overwhelming. New planes would be coming in soon for training purposes. We were also asked to set up a hold over plan, for the service men passing through our base on their way home. The training space would be available for 50 to 100 men during the week. It was a place to stay, eat and rest, while waiting for the trains and planes to carry them home.

I stepped in and asked if they knew our airport was up and running in Iowa. The General answered, "Yes we're looking into it. I think it's being checked out as we speak."

I continued, "We have trains and transport planes, and a commercial airline flying in and out all day long." Notes were taken down.

The meeting was over and we were sent on our way. Marty couldn't believe what just happened. I felt there was a lot more going on here, than we knew about. Joey was excited about the fact we could set our own time for the programs.

The three of us went to the officer's club and had a cup of coffee. Marty cleared his throat. We both looked at him, he got our attention. "Well boys my wife has decided to give Greenfield a try. Billy your Dad found us a big farm we really like. He sent pictures to my wife and she's already packing. After we set things up, two of my brothers are coming over to be with us. There is plenty of land and we can all do our own thing. What do you think?"

Joey and I just looked at each other. Joey said, "We're wondering how you're going to work in your fancy uniform and keep your fingernails clean." We just laughed. Then Joey gave Marty the usual punch to the shoulder he was famous for. I myself, was feeling blessed to have him and his family move close by. This was the start of a great day for all of us.

Early the next day I was out on the field when a man in his thirties approached me. He saluted. Then he said, "Permission to speak, Sir." He stood in front of me, holding a piece of paper.

"Yes Lieutenant, what can I do for you?"

"I have something from my Mother I would like you to sign Sir, and I was told not to go home without it signed, Sir."

I looked down. It was a newspaper announcing the news about the war, and a picture of Joey and me across the bottom as big as life, receiving our special medals.

"And you are," I asked as I looked up. He was a heavy set man, a 1st Lieutenant in the Air Force. He was dark haired, taller than me, blue eyes and a nice friendly smile.

"I am the son of Martha Harris, the bus driver who took you and General Calhoun to boot camp, Sir. Mom remembers you two. She has kept all the pictures and files that have been dated on you both. This picture she especially likes of you receiving the Special Medals. I have to get it autographed. I'm on my way home later today." He passed me a pen.

"I remember her well. She scared us to death. She certainly had control of her bus." We both laughed. "Tell her I said hello," as I signed the bottom of the paper. "What did you say your name was again?" He stood at attention and said, "1st Lieutenant Joe Harris, Sir."

"We will be living in Greenfield, Iowa if you're ever in the area. General Calhoun plans to set up an orphanage and facility for hybrid plants there. I'll be running the new airport and flight training center were developing. If you're looking for a job later, come see us."

"Yes Sir, maybe I will." He turned and left, as my mind traveled back to the days of the famous bus ride.

Later that afternoon, I got a call from Dad. I figured he wanted to tell me about the airport. Someone must have been talking to him and he always got the news before me. I was wrong. I told him about the promotion and the special terms, and told him about Marty. I think he knew about Marty moving, but the promotion was a nice surprise to him.

"Son, I called for another reason. Ashley's Mother died. Marion wants to talk to you." He gave the phone to Marion.

"Hi Billy, I mean General Stevens, I'm so proud of you. Ashley's Mother died this morning at the hospital. We think the heart just gave out. She was so weak. Can you get away maybe for two days or so? I know you just left here, but I think Ashley really needs you Billy."

"Is she alright?" I asked.

"She's holding up. Lette Mae and Judy and the sisters are by her side. Her father Paul is a mess. He is not responding to anyone so she is really alone."

"Marion, I will call and see what I can do, and thank you for calling me." She passed the phone back to Dad.

"Let us know what you are going to do Son. We are going back to Ashley's place. I'm so proud of you, congratulations on your promotion. I love you, Son." The phone went dead.

Well the way I looked at it, nothing was set in place yet, so the special privileges would probably hold up here. All they could say to me, was no.

I was on my way home the next morning. Dad met me at the airport and we went to see Ashley. Marion was there and came to me, as I walked in the door. "Ashley's in the kitchen with her father. He is not doing well at all. He won't talk to anyone. We need to get the plans going. Can you try, Billy? Maybe you can get through to him. Ashley is very worried. He is not responding to her." Marion led me to the kitchen.

Ashley came running to my side crying and shaking. I held her close and we walked to the other room together. "Billy I'm so glad you're here. How did you get away so soon? You just got there." She hugged me so close I almost couldn't breathe.

"It's a long story but I'm here. What can I do?" We sat in the parlor for a few minutes and came up with a plan. Now we had to see if it would work. After a few kisses and a comforting hug in my arms, we both went back to the kitchen.

I went over to her father at the table and sat in front of him. He looked dazed and far away. I put my hand across the table and held his arm. I called his name, as he had told me to call him Paul, just a few days ago. "Paul, I'm so sorry your wife died. Paul, are you listening to me, please look at me." He slowly moved his arm away and took both my hands in his. "Paul, I want to take care of things that have to be done right now, will you let me?"

Tears were rolling down his face, and I could feel his pain and how shaky he was. He finally looked up at me and whispered, "Yes Billy, I need help and I can't do this myself. Please help me and Ashley to get through this." I took both his hands and told him I would take care of everything. "Thank you" was all he could manage. He got up and went upstairs to his room. Dad went up with him. Paul was very shaky on the stairs.

"Thank God for you Billy, he wouldn't listen to anyone before you got here," Marion said.

We all thought he must be in some sort of shock right now. I'm glad he listened to me. We had permission to get the things done now. Judy and the girls came back into the room. They had been moving things around in the house in preparation of the funeral to be in the home. Ashley got busy letting the family know of the plans we just made. Marion and Judy took care of the rest. Dad and I checked out the cemetery arrangements.

Early the next day, Joey and Marty came in dressed in their uniforms, for the funeral.

Everything went smoothly. The showing was held in the parlor. From there they went to the church and then a burial at the cemetery. Paul cried all the way through the church and cemetery services. He really seemed depressed and out of control. A sister to Paul, came to stay with him for a few days. We all felt much better about leaving him alone, while Ashley was working. She seemed to be handling the death, but was concerned about her father. Ashley was always a quiet person and kept her feelings to herself.

After all the rooms were cleaned up and the personal things put away, Ashley and I spent some time together out by the lake for a while. She knew I had to go back to Texas but I didn't want to leave her. We talked about what had to be done for her father, and I told her how to get in touch with me if she needed to talk. I promised to call this time, and I would. Things were going to be different now that we had a better schedule. I explained the new program at the base to her. She was elated. "That means you will be home more." She gave me a big hug and kiss. I held her for a while and we looked out at the lake from inside the truck. We spent the rest of the day together.

I returned home to find Dad and Marion just finishing up their glass of wine and saying their goodbyes for the evening. Marion gave me a kiss on the cheek as she left by the front door. Dad and I sat in the living room. "So Dad, why haven't you married Marion?" I asked.

"It's a long story Son. I was not there for Sara. I wasn't there for my first wife, and I feel I wouldn't be any better with anyone else. I will carry this to my grave, the feelings I have in me. I am only concerned about taking care of you, my Son, my blood, and my life. Marion is a good friend and we enjoy each other's company, and that's enough for both of us. That's all I can say about it Billy, she is a good woman."

I gave Dad a big hug and went upstairs to my room. There was some noise in the corner of my room. I turned the light on, only to see Cleo climbing out of one of my old boots. Up he came to the bed, as I sat and rubbed his belly. I'd call Joey and Marty in the morning to set up our flight back to the base.

The next morning Dad and I went to visit the doctor. Dad said Doctor Deering had been ill and not doing well these last few days. As we pulled up to the house, Dad warned me that his sister had been looking after him the past few weeks.

We went inside to find him in bed upstairs this time. I went to him and sat down beside him on the bed. I was upset looking at him. I didn't know what to ask him. I was glad Dad was here with me. He went over and checked his temperature. "Tell us what we can do, where here to help. Where's the nurse I sent over to take care of you?"

His voice was soft and low and he tried to sit up a little so he could see us. We both lifted him up and put some pillows behind his head. He seemed to be breathing better sitting up.

"I'm glad you came together. Sit down for a few minutes; I have something to tell you. Billy you know I was a good friend to your Mom. She had some hard times after her parents died in that awful fire at the store. She was not a well girl. I dropped by often to talk and help her try to find some peace. She told me one day that she had something to tell me. One day while cleaning out a closet in the spare room, she found a box of pictures. She found a picture of two boys, one looked like John, and the other one maybe a brother. When John came home she showed him the pictures and he told her about his brother William. He showed her the last picture he had of him he carried in his wallet. Sara took one look and knew those eyes immediately. This was Phil Jones from Des Moines. She said nothing. A few days later, Sara took you Billy, on the train to Des Moines. She had intended to find Phil and have him meet his son. She took a cab and went around to all the favorite places looking. Around noontime she was stopped at a light, near a café when four people got out of a car and went to get an outside table. She spotted him. She asked the driver to go a little closer and stop. She looked through the window but couldn't bring herself to get out. Billy you started fussing and crying. Her stomach was churning and she got all sweaty. The anxiety of getting out or not getting out, telling him about you Billy or not telling him, she was torn up inside. Would he even accept you Billy, and what if he did? She couldn't think of what to do now that Phil was right in front of her. John loved her and you, could she break his heart? She sat back in the seat, her heart pounding in her chest. She thought about her marriage. What should she do? She had her hand on the door; tears were rolling down her face. She cleared the steamed up window and took one last look at the man who fathered her child. Billy you were crying as she asked the driver to take her to the train station.

She hugged you tight and tried to stop the tears, but inside her heart was broken and she felt the pain.

When she came back to the farm she called me and I came over. She was still upset telling me this story. I told her she did the right thing, as I struggled with myself at this unbelievable story. I comforted her as best I could, then I went to my sister's house to tell her what I just found out.

He looked at my Dad. "You see William, I lost my son when you moved to Des Moines at a young age. I watched over you and your brother John for many reasons. The biggest reason was Jessie and I had conceived you out of loneliness and deep love that we had for each other. James, your father never knew about this. You are my son William, and I have loved you all my life. I have always been by your side. I'm surprised our crystal blue eyes never made you wonder. When you showed up at court for Billy, I was elated. And the bonus is my grandson, a boy I always loved as my son. That makes me your grandfather Billy. I promised your Mom I would always watch over you Billy. You will never want for anything. Everything Sara put away and everything I own belongs to you. My sister has all the papers. I couldn't go off and die without telling you both the story I promised Sara I would tell.

I'm sorry if I have hurt you in any way by not telling you before this, I just couldn't see any reason to spoil what you two have together now. Having a brother, while you were young was a good thing William. Was I wrong?"

He put his head back and closed his eyes before we could answer him. It took a lot out of him to tell us what he just did. He went fast asleep. I helped Dad put his head back down on the bed and we covered him and went down to the kitchen.

Dad had tears in his eyes. I had not seen him so upset. I didn't know what to say. I waited a few minutes then I smiled and said, "Dad, now I have a grandfather."

He looked at me and smiled. "You have been a joy in my life from the minute I met you. I tried to take all your unhappiness away. Now I find I had another father who tried to keep me happy. What a strange bunch of circumstances we have lived through Billy."

"Dad I always thought of Doctor Deering as my grandfather, did you know that?"

"It's funny; I always looked after him from our day in court with you. I felt something but never knew he was my father. I had a father in Greenfield. Strange how things work out." He shook his head and stared out the window.

I got up and checked out the stove. He needed wood so I went outside and brought some in. The nurse was coming in when I came back. She went up and checked him out. I worked on the fireplace and stove. Dad talked to the nurse in the kitchen for a while. I checked on the doctor again, this time realizing he was my grandfather now. I kissed him on the forehead, took his hand in mine and smiled. His eyes were open, such blue eyes, why didn't I ever think about how few people have such blue eyes? "I love you grandfather, very much." Now he smiled. He fell asleep.

When I came down Dad was ready to go. We left our number with the nurse if she needed anything. Dad went upstairs to say goodbye and I waited outside. When he came out he was crying and shaking. I drove home. Our heads were spinning with thoughts, but the car was quiet.

Dad called Marion and I called Joey after we settled down. Janice had a full table for dinner that night, as we told our story to our friends.

We arrived back at the base three days later. Some changes were very noticeable. Many Soldiers, Sailors and Marines were on the base, carrying their bags and boarding our aircraft transport planes. I took some time to talk to some of them. Many had travelled a long distance on their way home. The excitement was there, but most of them were exhausted. We supplied food and showers and a place to rest while they waited. They enjoyed the chance to tell their stories as they waited with others. I kept that idea in mind for our airport back home.

One morning while working outside, Joey was called in for a phone call. "Hello."

"Well Joey, I should say Brigadier General Calhoun, I'm so proud of you boys. This is the Vice President, retired. Joey I hear you got yourself an office in Greenfield for your project, the orphanage. I found a nice piece of land just outside town, perfect for all the ideas you talked to me about. The home, a farm area, place for animals, and there is even a stream flowing through, it's just awesome. I've got a Government loan and some financial advisors, and donors, ready to step in and help. I can send a construction company that works for me, out tomorrow. I want to be involved in this project. We will set up your office, get the plans in and start the construction as soon as you say go. My advice is, don't wait too long. Construction is picking up."

"I'm overwhelmed Sir. Please by all means, start as soon as you can. I'll let my parents know, and the office. I've made a few changes on the plans that I'll get right to you. I'm so excited. I can hardly believe it's true. I've got to call my wife. Thank you Sir. I am so blessed to have you as a friend. You don't know what this orphanage means to me." I could hear my voice cracking, as I went silent. "Thank you Sir."

"You're more than welcome Son. I know this will be a great adventure for us and our State. Say hi to the missus, I'll be in touch." The phone went dead.

Joey came back in his jeep skidding to a stop. He jumped out and ran to my side. "Billy, you'll never guess who I just talked to?"

A day later I got a call while at my desk in the office. "Billy, Brigadier General Stevens, this is the Vice President, retired. How are you?" I felt butterflies in my stomach.

"I'm fine Sir. What can I do for you?" I asked.

"No, no Son, I have some news for you. Yesterday I spent the afternoon at your airport in Iowa. I like the name. Things are moving along there, but I think I can help out with some of my guys, who are looking for work. You need that extension runway completed and you need a big welcome center for the people passing through. We're not done fighting yet. I'll update you later. I have the interest, and the means to get this work done now. Let me help. What do you say? I didn't see your Dad there. I guess he had spent the day at the law office."

It took a few seconds for this to sink in. I jumped at the opportunity to get the work done. I know Dad was pushing every button to find the money and the help, to get things done. "Sir, I would be so happy to be able to get things moving there. I know I'll have more time to get home in a few weeks, but Dad is killing himself to get things done. We didn't even want to think about the Welcome Center, we just couldn't afford it right now. I would be so grateful for any help you can give us Sir."

"Okay, Billy. Will set things up, see your Dad and we will get things moving in a few days. I'm so proud of you boys, your both giving back of yourself; we can't do enough for you. We will talk soon." The phone went dead.

I went out and found Joey. "You'll never guess who I just talked to?"

We thought these calls were the surprise of the century, but I guess the retired Vice President wasn't through yet.

That afternoon, Marty got a call out in the maintenance center. "Hello."

"Marty, this is the Vice President, retired. How are you son?"

"I'm fine Sir." He couldn't believe who it was; his mouth was frozen in as open position.

"Marty I want to ask you about your plans to move out here to our part of the country. How many of your brothers are coming out here?"

"Well Sir, we found some land to build our farm, it has plenty of room for a garden, animals, a place for the kids to ride horses, and maybe two of my brothers will come over here with me, Sir."

"I understand you have some brothers in construction; removing trees, clearing land, putting in cement foundations, bring them along with you Marty. We have some government contracts coming in for housing, and land to be cleared for roads and highways. See if they can all come out here. We would like to have them here. There will be plenty of work for them in Greenfield and neighboring towns."

Marty sat and listened with such surprise. "I will ask them Sir, I'll call them tonight. Thank you Sir. Thank you so much."

"Okay Marty, let's get things rolling. I'll check out your plans for the farm and get you some help. Talk to you again soon." The phone went dead. Marty made a bee-line out the door to find his friends. "Guess who just called me?" Marty was smiling ear to ear.

Later that night we celebrated at dinner on the base. We sure had a lot to talk about. I left first, around 8:30. I called Dad to see if he knew what was about to happen. Marion answered the phone.

"Hi Billy, I'm glad you called, I was just going to call you."

I jumped in all excited to tell her my news. "The retired Vice President was at the airport yesterday and must have missed Dad. Does he know what's going on out there, Marion?"

"No, I'm afraid not Billy. He has been in the hospital again, this time it was a big heart attack. He is stable and driving everyone crazy, and wants to go home tomorrow. You know him. I'm getting his clothes and some things he wants. I think he will come home tomorrow, no one can say no to him. He has to quit working for a while, that's no problem, we have plenty of help. But he is concerned about the work at the airport. He never stops. I'm here for him and he's okay, he is just slowing down some. The prognosis wasn't good this time. He has damaged his arteries and heart with all the stress. I'm sorry I have to tell you this Billy."

"Marion I have good news. Don't worry about the airport. The retired Vice President is taking over the construction and a few other things. He just called me about it. Tell Dad not to worry anymore. I'm in charge of that now. Have him rest. I'll be home again soon. I love you Marion, let him know everything will be fine. We have the workers now and their ready to start."

"Okay Billy, I'll tell him tonight. How in the world did you manage this?"

"Tell Dad, right time, right place, and I'm doing my best. Just like he taught me, it works. Bye Marion."

The last two days were almost too hard to believe. Things were coming together for all of us. I called Ashley to see how she was doing. She sounded tired, but glad I called. She said she missed me, in almost every other sentence. I found myself missing her too. I guess it was time to make another big change in my life. Once again words came rushing out of my mouth just like before. "Ashley, this isn't the time or the place," I hesitated. I felt myself biting my lip. Then I said, "Ashley I want to marry you when I get back home this time. Will you marry me?"

I heard nothing. Then I heard her blowing her nose, as if she were crying.

"Yes Billy, I've been waiting and hoping for you to ask me. I want to be with you always. It's time."

"Ashley, let's do it. Can you set up the plans?" I listened to see if she was going to change her mind.

"Yes I will get everything ready. I know I will have plenty of help around here. I love you so much Billy."

"I love you to Ashley." I caught my breath and then I asked, "How is your father doing?"

"This will make him feel a lot better Billy, he really likes you."

"That's good. Ashley my Dad had a very serious heart attack yesterday. Can you stop by tomorrow and check him out for me?"

"I'll be there Billy, school is out, and the finals are over. I'll call you tomorrow night and let you know how he is doing."

"Okay, tell him about us. He loves you and this will make him real happy."

"I love you Billy, I'll start making plans, tonight. Bye, and see you soon."

About four weeks later, was our first weekend away. I asked Joey to stand up for me at my wedding. We both had some special reasons to go home to our small town of Greenfield.

The wedding was nothing short of spectacular. The fact that I was a Brigadier General in the Army Air Force, a new member of the Chamber of Commerce, part owner of the new Government and Commercial Airport, a lawyer, and marrying the daughter of a prestigious banker in the city, her working in the Court House and now the town Historian, Phil and Marion and Paul invited everyone to the wedding. Ashley wanted her wedding to be at her home in Des Moines. The President sent large flower baskets that were placed at the entrance of the two large doors coming into the foyer. This home was designed for parties but I think this was the first one they ever hosted. With both families' importance in town, came all the workers and helpers you could ever need. They were quickly put to work and they made the home beautiful. Ashley had managed to take care of her wedding dresses for the bridesmaids, Joey's sisters, and her matron of honor, Lette Mae. Joey was the best man. Ashley had her wedding gown made for her in the city. It was tight fitting to the floor, with sequins and pearls at the wrist of her long sleeves, and around her low cut neck line. Her veil flowed down to the floor with sequins and pearls scattered about. It was on a comb and put into her hair done up in a bun, with spindles of hair hanging down the sides. She looked elegant. She wanted to be married in front of the winding staircase in the large foyer. This was always her dream.

Marion and Judy worked on the decorations and food, while Paul and Tom handled the car service for guests, the preacher and other details of the day.

Photographers from the newspapers, and the White House, and some magazines were all there. As the retired Vice President and family arrived the morning of the wedding, followed by some Air Force personnel and friends of me and Joey, extra police were put on duty for the traffic problems.

Colonel Jamerson from England flew in as a surprise to us all. I managed to speak with him a few minutes during all the wedding excitement going on. We went into the parlor and I had the chance to ask him if he would consider working with me and Joey and Marty at the Air Base. I told him how we were setting up a Reserve Program and we could use a fourth person to handle the base on weekends. I also asked him if he would work with us at the base in Iowa. He wanted to hear all about it, but I didn't have time to go into details. However, I did have a firm yes on him helping us at both airports. That was the best wedding gift I could have ever dreamed of.

Martha, the bus driver, and her two boys were there, and Theresa Walsh the Ferrier pilot drove over. This was the wedding of the year in Des Moines.

As the time drew near, Phil brought in Dr. Deering and placed him in a special chair just by the staircase. He was to be the guest of honor at his grandson's wedding.

The music started and Joey and I came over to the bottom of the stairs and waited. Ashley stood there at the top of the stairs, and we looked at her, the elegant beautiful woman she had become. She floated down the staircase as all eyes were upon her.

The ceremony ran smoothly and the party began.

That evening as the bride and groom said their goodbyes and appreciation to everyone who put this lovely wedding reception together, they left through the front doors. A Military Saber Archway Salute stood ready to pass them into another life as Brigadier General Billy Stevens and his lovely wife Ashley.

I said goodbye to my best friend Joey and gave him a handshake of friendship. We knew we would be best friends forever, and we would always be known as *The Greenfield Boys*.

Epilogue

Joey did complete his orphanage naming it "Joey's Place," and filled it with many children needing a place to stay. Paul Thomas sold his big home in Des Moines and moved to Greenfield to become Joey's financial advisor. Joey also set up a hybrid facility for plants and vegetables and later introduced his own brand of animal food products, made from soy.

Lette Mae became the head nurse at the Greenfield Hospital. She had three children and took care of her parents, while running the farm and businesses with Joey.

Billy built one of the busiest airports in the country. The Army and Air Force Reserves moved in on the base. Billy ran a commercial and private flying center. Most traffic going across the country, made their stop in Iowa. Ashley and Billy moved to the farm with his Dad and Marion. Billy and Marion ran the law offices together.

Ashley worked in the Court House in town, and became the town Historian and advisor for the town. She had three children, one set of twins. She took care of her father and lived on the farm.

Marty's whole family moved to Iowa. They made more money than he had ever seen in Maine. The Riley name was everywhere. He also managed to have three more boys. He was a happy man.

Phil and Marion sat quietly on the porch swing at the farm, watching their grandchildren play with the new cat they called Eli. Life was good for them, at least today.

Joey's Place

The Greenfield Boys

This book has been written by author, Ruthanne Lyons, and has been certified and copy written by the Federal Government on July 2, 2010 in the State of Massachusetts.

Certification # 70093410000130709037

Ruthanne Lyons

Other work published by Ruthanne Lyons

International Library of Photography—"Faded Impressions"

International Library of Poetry Editors Choice Series—"Collected Whispers"

The Writer's Café, Parkland Library, Fla. Volume 39

Eber & Wein Publishing Library of Congress—Eternal Heartland Highway 80

I make this Promise to you!

If you follow with me through a few years in the lives of *The Greenfield Boys* I will pull every emotion out of you. You will feel anger and love, happiness and surprise. You will cry and feel pain as the tears roll down your face, coming from within you. Your emotions will soar as you grow with these young boys and the relationship that forms through pain and heartache. You will go through the perils of two fighter pilots in the middle of WWII, fighting in the skies over Germany. The bond these boys form tears at your heart. Young love and joy, friendship and conflicts, challenges and real life drama, are all rolled into one small town story that will leave you feeling good. Some events are real. The characters are pure fiction and from my mind. One thing is for sure, you will remember Billy and Joey, *The Greenfield Boys* from Iowa.

I have lived in Danvers, Massachusetts all my life and always enjoyed writing in school. After graduation I wrote and published poems and many short stories. I felt inspired by Oprah when she said, Find your passion. *The Greenfield Boys* became my passion and opportunity to put my dreams on paper. Feel the emotions and meet the characters. You will love them.